Flora

By the Same Author

Novels

Unfinished Desires (2009)
Queen of the Underworld (2006)
Evenings at Five (2003)
Evensong (1999)
The Good Husband (1994)
Father Melancholy's Daughter (1991)
A Southern Family (1987)
The Finishing School (1984)
A Mother and Two Daughters (1982)
Violet Clay (1978)
The Odd Woman (1974)
Glass People (1972)
The Perfectionists (1970)

Story Collections

Mr. Bedford and the Muses (1983)
Dream Children (1976)

Nonfiction

Heart: A Personal Journey Through Its Myths and Meanings (2001)
The Making of a Writer: Journals, 1961–1963 (2006)
The Making of a Writer, Volume Two: Journals, 1963–1969 (2011)

Flora

GAIL GODWIN

B L O O M S B U R Y
LONDON • NEW DELHI • NEW YORK • SYDNEY

First published in Great Britain 2013

Bloomsbury Publishing Plc
50 Bedford Square
London
WC1B 3DP

www.bloomsbury.com

Bloomsbury Publishing, London, New Delhi, New York and Sydney

A CIP catalogue record for this book is available from the British Library

Hardback ISBN 978 1 4088 4086 3
Trade paperback ISBN 978 1 4088 4087 0

10 9 8 7 6 5 4 3 2 1

Typeset by Westchester Book Group
Printed and bound in Great Britain by CPI Group (UK) Ltd, Croydon CR0 4YY

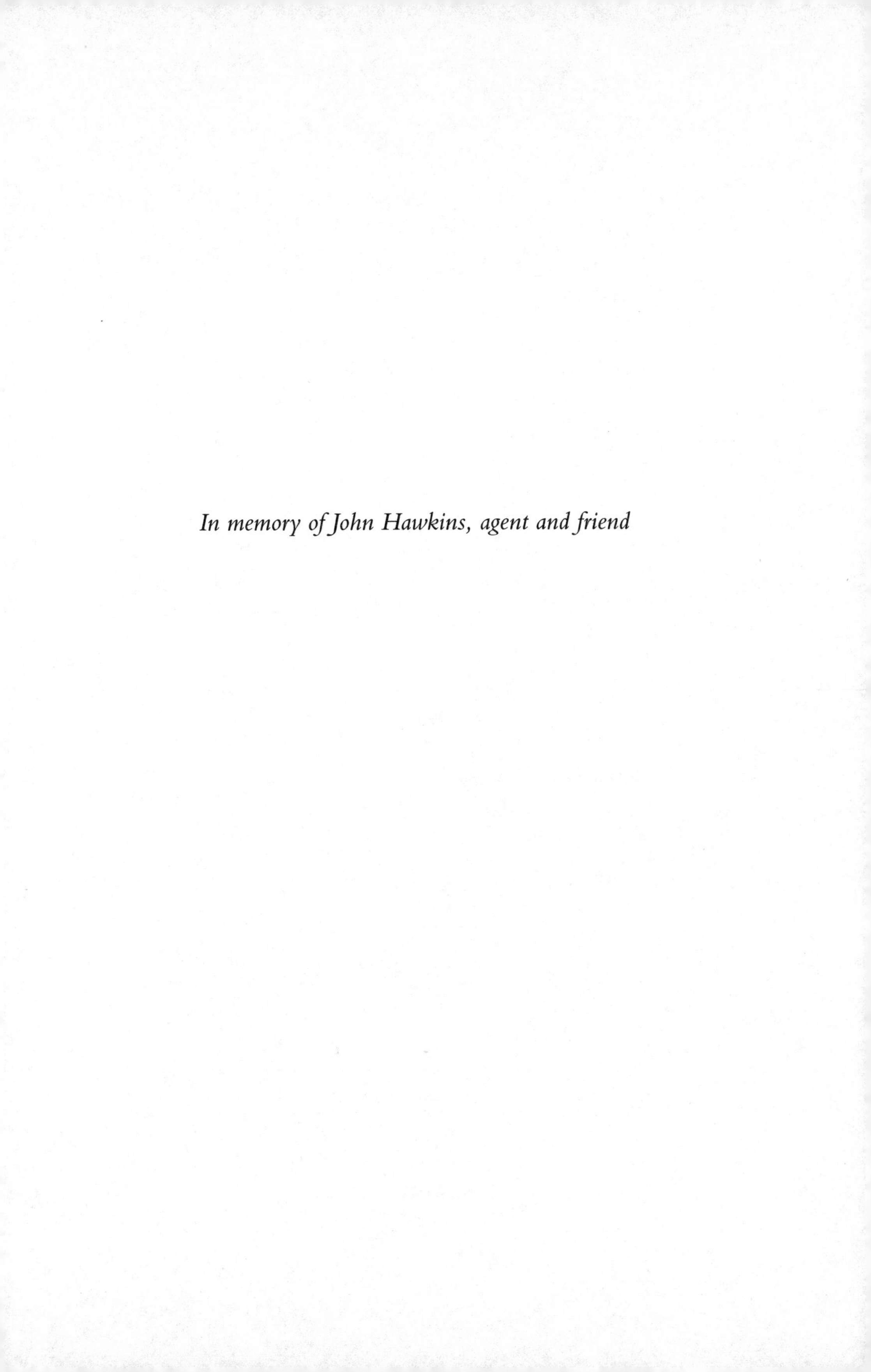

In memory of John Hawkins, agent and friend

I.

There are things we can't undo, but perhaps there is a kind of constructive remorse that could transform regrettable acts into something of service to life.

That summer, Flora and I were together every day and night for three weeks in June, all of July, and the first six days of August. I was ten, going on eleven, and she was twenty-two. I thought I knew her intimately, I thought I knew everything there was to know about her, but she has since become a profound study for me, more intensely so in recent years. Styles have come and gone in storytelling, psychologizing, theologizing, but Flora keeps providing me with something as enigmatic as it is basic to life, as timeless as it is fresh.

At the beginning of that summer with her, I seesawed between bored complacency and serious misgivings. She was an easy companion, quick to praise me and willing to do what I liked. My father had asked her to stay with me so he could cross over the mountain from North Carolina into Tennessee while the public schools were not in session and do more secret work for World War II. This would be his second year at Oak Ridge.

The summer before, my grandmother had still been alive to stay with me.

Flora had just finished her training to become a teacher like my late mother. She was my mother's first cousin. Embarrassingly ready to spill her shortcomings, she was the first older person I felt superior to. This had its gratifying moments but also its worrisome side. She was less restrained in her emotions than some children I knew. She was an instant crier. My grandmother Nonie, that mistress of layered language, had often remarked that Flora possessed "the gift of tears." As far as I could tell, layers had been left out of Flora. All of her seemed to be on the same level, for anyone to see.

Nonie, who had died suddenly just before Easter, had been a completely different kind of grown-up. Nonie had a surface, but it was a surface created by her, then checked from all angles in her three-way mirror before she presented it to others. Below that surface I knew her love for me resided, but below that were seams and shelves of private knowledge, portions of which would be doled out like playing cards, each in its turn, if and when she deemed the time was ripe.

My father, who was principal of Mountain City High School, was described as "exacting" or "particular" when people wanted to say something nice about him. If they were being politely critical, they might say, "Harry Anstruther can be very acerbic and he doesn't suffer fools gladly." His social mode was a laconic reserve, but at home, after a couple of drinks, he stripped down to his comfortable mordant sarcasm. His usually controlled limp, from a bout with polio in his teens, became more like a bad actor's exaggeration of a limp.

He married my mother when he was in his early thirties. He was assistant principal of the high school at the time and also taught the shop classes for the boys. He had learned carpentry when he was convalescing from polio. My mother-to-be, a new teacher in her early twenties, came to his office to protest her new assignment. She had been hired to teach English, and after she got there they had added Home Economics, which she felt she had to swallow, she said, because new teachers couldn't be picky. But now the public school curriculum had introduced something called Girls' Hygiene into the Home Economics hour. "I cannot stand up in front of a class and teach this," she told my father. She held the little booklet apart from her body like a piece of garbage. Her disdain along with the "cannot" impressed my father. Though she was from Alabama, she spoke like someone trained for the theater. "The girls would be shocked and disgusted," she told him. "Or they would laugh me out of the room."

My father took the booklet home, and after dinner he and Nonie took turns reading aloud from "Social Hygiene for Girls." As I got older, Nonie would recall hilarious examples from this booklet. It became her way of imparting the facts of life to me without the hush-hush solemnity. ("I'll tell you one thing, darling. It made me glad I was brought up on a farm and saw animals go about their natural business without all the clumsy language.")

My grandmother asked if the well-spoken new teacher was "the kind of person we'd like to invite to dinner." She probably wouldn't come, my father said, because she was a chilly sort and hadn't seemed to like him very much. But Nonie insisted on asking her and she came. Her name was Elizabeth Waring, but by the end of the evening she had asked them to call her Lisbeth. She had been orphaned at eight and raised by two uncles and a live-in maid. The first thing she said when she walked into our house was how wonderful it must be to live in such a house. "I fell in love with her first," Nonie liked to recall. "And then, one night, when the three of us were playing cards, Harry finally looked across the table and realized what he could have."

FLORA CAME WITH her father, Fritz Waring, to my mother's funeral. They rode on passes because he worked for the railroad. My mother had caught pneumonia during a stay in the hospital. "There was a lot of it that year—if only they could have gotten sulfa in time they might have saved her." When I was older Nonie explained that it had started with a miscarriage. "They'd been trying to get you a little brother or sister, but I guess you were meant to be one of a kind, Helen."

I was three when my mother died and have no recollection of the funeral, or of fifteen-year-old Flora, though Nonie told me Flora would sit me on her lap at meals and try to feed me little morsels from her plate, which I refused. "One time she cried into your hair. She had been telling us how, since she was a small child, she and your mother slept in the same bed. She confided to us she had always slept with one leg over Lisbeth to keep her from going away. At this point your father rolled his eyes and left the table.

"It was a very strange week for us. This was the first time we had met any of your mother's people. This little man with shaggy eyebrows and a bulldog face steps down from the train with his arm around a sobbing young girl in a black coat way too old for her. 'She feels things' were Fritz Waring's first words to us. Immediately after the funeral, he apologized for having to ask us to drive him back to the train station. He had to be on duty next day. 'But we've hardly even spoken to the two of you,' I said. 'Oh, Flora can stay on with you awhile,' he said, 'if she won't be any trouble.'

"I was pretty surprised but I tried to hide it. I told him we would love to have her stay on *for a little while.* After all, this was your mother's own first cousin. Shouldn't we want to know her better? And, as a student of human nature, I have to say I found Flora's visit eye-opening. It was interesting to observe how very different two girls could be who had grown up in the same house. Though of course there was the big age difference: Lisbeth was twelve when the infant Flora came to live with them. Even their speech! Whereas Lisbeth spoke like a stage actress and held herself back in speech and person, Flora's southern accent was so thick you could cut it with a knife and she burbled and spilled herself out like an overflowing brook. She asked us the most intimate questions and offered disconcerting tidbits about her people in Alabama. She wanted to know why your mother was in the hospital in the first place and where everyone slept, and she would stand in the open door of the wardrobe where your mother kept her clothes and snuffle into her dresses. She told us proudly that the black coat she wore had been borrowed from the Negro woman who lived with them. One time when she was retelling how she had slept with her leg over your mother 'so she wouldn't abandon her,' she went on to explain that her own mother had left town as soon as she was born. Your poor father found more and more excuses to go out on errands, and by the end of Flora's visit he was taking his cocktails up to his room."

The year after my mother's funeral, Fritz Waring was shot during a high-stakes poker game and Flora and Nonie's great correspondence began. The sixteen-year-old Flora had written Nonie a long, emotional letter with the gory details (he had been shot between the eyes) and Nonie had answered back. Immediately came a second letter and Nonie felt it was her duty to reply, and this went on until her death. Flora always started her letters "Dear Mrs. Anstruther," and signed them, "Your Friend, Flora Waring."

"The poor child thinks I am her diary," Nonie would remark, reading Flora's latest letter. Sometimes she would shake her head and murmur, "Gracious!" The letters disappeared before anyone else could read them. "Young people shouldn't write down personal things they might regret later," Nonie said.

FLORA RODE THE train to Nonie's funeral in the spring of 1945. She was in her last year of teachers' college in Birmingham and hoped to begin teaching in the fall.

"Flora's turned into a looker," said my father, making it sound like something short of a compliment. "Though not in your mother's style."

When friends came back to our house after the funeral, Flora greeted them and passed platters and refilled glasses like she was part of the family, which I suppose she felt she was. After the crowd had thinned, we noticed that a cluster of people had gathered around Nonie's wing chair and then we saw that Flora was sitting in it—the first person to do so since Nonie's death. She appeared to be telling a story. Everyone was rapt, even Father McFall, the circumspect rector of Our Lady's, though he was careful to register a degree of separateness by the quizzical twist of his brow. Flora, softly weeping, was reading from something in her lap. When my father and I edged closer we saw that she was reading aloud from Nonie's letters.

I can still see Flora, the way her large, moonlike face floated out at you from the frame of the wing chair. She wore her dark hair swept back from a middle parting, then falling in soft waves over the ears and pinned up loosely at the nape of the neck, a style you often see in movies and television dramas being faithful to the late 1930s and early '40s. Her forehead was spacious, though not high, and her wide-apart brown eyes, when they were not silky with tears, conveyed an ardent eagerness to be impressed.

What she was reading from my grandmother's letters seemed to be snippets of the kind of soldierly counsel Nonie loved to dispense to everyone. About taking control of your life and making something of yourself. But after listening for a minute, my father sent me over to tell Flora he wanted to speak with her in the kitchen and that was the end of the performance.

I have often wondered if that was when he broached the idea of her staying with me while he went back for his second summer to the construction job in Oak Ridge, where they were making something highly secret for the war effort. This would have been in character. My father loathed displays of emotion and he may have decided to offer me up, since he needed someone anyway, rather than to reprimand Flora about the letters and evoke her gift of tears.

II.

My grandmother died while choosing her Easter hat. She was downtown in Blum's department store and had just pinned on a Stetson trilby with a dashing black plume that had tiny seed pearls sewn into it like random raindrops. "You're coming home with me, handsome," she addressed the hat in the mirror. Her last words were "Mrs. Grimes, could I trouble you for a glass of water?" When the saleslady returned with the water, Nonie was pitched forward, her hand deep in her purse. She had been reaching for her vial of nitroglycerin tablets. Mr. Blum insisted we were under no obligation when my father said he wanted to buy the hat. "But my daughter wants it, you see," my father explained. "It was Helen's idea." "In that case, allow me to make a gift of it to her," said Mr. Blum. "It's a becoming hat that will never go out of style. She can wear it herself someday."

This exchange was reported to me by my father. Just as Nonie's last moments were reported by others to him. Yet I saw both scenes as though I had been there. I was also achingly present at an alternative scene in which I had been standing right behind her, watching her try on the hats in the three-way mirror.

"This one suits me, doesn't it, Helen?"

"Oh, it really does."

Whereupon she would have addressed the handsome hat. And then: a sudden widening of the eyes, a hand slapped to her chest: "Quick, darling, go in my purse and fetch me . . ." She trusted my nimble fingers to do the rest: root in the bag, twist open the familiar vial, hand over the doll's-size pill.

("And if I should have already fainted, Helen, you know what to do." "Open your mouth and slip it under your tongue." "That's right, darling, like a baby bird feeding the mama bird.")

We had rehearsed it.

Later, when I had attained an age she never reached, there was a television commercial that never failed to choke me up. A man and his son are walking in the country when suddenly the father clutches his chest, the landscape turns a sickly sepia, and the father falls. But the son whips out a Bayer aspirin, the father rises to his feet, embraces the son, and Technicolor is restored to their lives.

"Don't worry, I have every intention of sticking around till I've finished raising you," Nonie always assured me after one of her episodes, and I could hear her saying it again that day—the day we never had. If only she had waited till my school was out so I could have been there to whip out the little vial in Blum's and save the day.

The day after Nonie's funeral, my father and I drove Flora to the train station. She had to return to her teachers' college and finish the semester. "For the rest of my life, whenever I see or hear a locomotive, I'll miss Daddy," she said, starting to weep as the Birmingham train pulled in. My father rolled his eyes and handed over his handkerchief. "Keep it," he said. "We'll see you in June."

"Why did you say that about June?" I demanded as soon as we were alone.

"I've asked Flora to stay with you this summer while I'm at Oak Ridge. I can't pay her a whole lot, but she'll be saving on her expenses, and she wants to do it."

I was stung. All the more so because this had been decided between them behind my back. "You mean, like a babysitter?"

"Ten is not old enough to stay alone, Helen."

"I'll be eleven in August."

"Even if you were going to be sixteen in August, that still wouldn't be old enough. I thought you and Flora got on."

We were driving across the bridge that arched above the railroad yards. The "put-upon" voice that my father always employed with Nonie when she was backing him into a corner was now being directed at me. Did Flora and I get on? It was more like Flora praised and deferred to me and I tolerated her because she was my mother's first cousin and showed up at family funerals. Until now, I had assumed both my father and I considered her somewhat awkward and childlike. Yet here he was putting her in charge for the summer.

"This is such a strange time for me," he said in the same keep-clear-of-me voice he'd used when he picked me up at school on the day of Nonie's death. "Mother is gone," he had said. "Just like that, in Blum's. Don't ask me what we're going to do next because I don't know."

EASTER THAT YEAR fell on April first, only a few days after Nonie's funeral. I felt self-conscious in church. I had gone everywhere with Nonie, and I could hear people silently wondering how I was ever going to manage without her. Those who hadn't known us well enough to come to the house for the funeral reception gathered round after church to offer condolences. My father and I were worn out by the time we got home. He made us grilled pimento cheese sandwiches in the skillet, letting them get too dark, and washed his down with Jack Daniel's in an iced tea glass. Then we sat side by side at the dining room table and answered more sympathy letters. He wrote the messages and I addressed the envelopes and licked the flaps and put on the stamps. When I pointed out that the recipients would notice our different handwritings, he said, "Fine. They'll be all the more charmed and touched." His voice had edged over into sarcasm by then.

Then came a letter that made him swear.

"Who's it from?"

"That old mongrel we saw crying at the funeral home."

"What does *he* want?" I knew my father was referring to the old man who had shown up at Swann's funeral home demanding to "see" Honora and had broken down and cried when we told him she had stipulated that her casket remain closed. It was Nonie's hated stepbrother, brought to her father's farm by the housekeeper who would become her father's second wife. His name was Earl Quarles and he had inherited all the property that should have gone to Nonie.

"He says he wants to keep in touch," my father sneered. "Get to know us better before he meets his Maker. Swann told me he came back to the funeral home after we left and tried to bribe him to open the casket."

"Fat chance," I said.

"Most people have their price," said my father.

"But if Mr. Swann had taken the bribe he wouldn't have told you about it, would he?"

"I probably shouldn't say this, Helen, but I look forward to the day when you can spot the unsavory truths about human nature for yourself." He crumpled the letter in his fist and to my disappointment shoved the whole wad, envelope included, into his jacket pocket. No chance now of my fishing it out of the wastebasket. Without bothering to put in fresh ice, he sloshed more Jack Daniel's into his iced tea glass and lurched upstairs.

I wandered into Nonie's room, which was on the ground floor, next to mine, and climbed up on her bed. I turned down the spread and buried my face in her pillows. Her smell was markedly fainter than yesterday. The insidious Sunday afternoon light pushed at me through the drawn curtains. Nonie, who could bend time to her purposes, was no longer here to protect me from emptiness. Even when she had closed her door to lie on her three pillows and take her appointed afternoon rest, the connection between us had been maintained. It always felt like she was in there refueling for us all.

Desperate to burrow back to that connection, I ground my face and body into her bedclothes. This time last Sunday she would have been lying here. The sheets had not yet been changed. She had died on Monday, and Mrs. Jones, whose day was Tuesday, had been postponed for a week. Nonie's black satchel purse presided aloofly from the top of the dresser. Inside was the little vial of nitroglycerin, useless now. "Handsome" languished, unseen on Easter Day, in its hatbox on her closet shelf.

How could she be so here and not here? I tried to make myself cry into her pillows before the smell of her cold cream vanished altogether. If she was gone, what parts of me had she taken with her? The parts she talked to, taught things to, told her stories to, would never again be addressed by her. And yet her way of saying things was all around me, they were inside of me.

All around me was our house, which pulsed with her stories of it. Old One Thousand she called it, because that was its number; it was the last house at the top of Sunset Drive. She and my grandfather and their young son had shared its rooms and porches with the Recoverers, back in the days when it catered to a few well-paying convalescent tuberculars or inebriates, and occasional souls whose nerves weren't yet up to going back to ordinary life.

If Nonie were still here, lying on her raised pillows on this Sunday afternoon, I would likely be upstairs on the Recoverers' south porch, reading or daydreaming on the faded horsehair cushions of a chaise longue. Back when Old One Thousand had also been Dr. Anstruther's Lodge, there was a view of the town below and the ranges of mountains encircling it, but now the view was blocked by a hectic tangle of branches just beginning to leaf out. The Recoverers would sit on this porch playing cards and sharing the news of their latest clean X-rays or sobriety day-counts or sessions with the local psychiatrist until the sun had moved over the roof; then they would gather their things and move over to the west porch. They were all just figments now, the real people departed long before I was born, but Nonie had told me about them and also about the grandfather I hadn't known, Doctor Cam, a man thirty years older than herself. How she as an eighteen-year-old girl had been walking to town carrying her valise, running away from the farm and her greedy new stepmother and menacing stepbrother, when this man had reined in his horse and called down in a low-country accent from his cabriolet: "Young lady, can I carry you somewhere?"

"It was a turn of phrase South Carolinians used, but I'd never heard it before. A cabriolet? It was a small, two-wheeled buggy with a retractable hood. The hood was down, so I could get a good look at him before I decided whether to get in. He more than passed inspection—he had a neat gray mustache and nice clothes and was old enough to be my father, if I had been lucky enough to have such an elegant one—so I climbed aboard. While we were settling my valise in the little space in front of my feet, he asked where I was wanting to go and I said, 'Today I'm only traveling as far as the Battery Hill Hotel, so anywhere you let me off in town will be fine.' I had prepared this answer in case I was offered a ride. The Battery Hill was the best hotel, and I was hoping to get work there as a maid or laundress, but I wanted to convey the impression I was staying there as a guest waiting for a train the next morning. He said it would be no trouble to take me to the hotel, and then started right in giving information about himself, the way thoughtful people do when they want to put you at your ease. He was a physician and a widower from Columbia, South Carolina. His wife had died of TB in a sanitorium here, and he had fallen in love with the pure air of the mountains and decided to stay on and establish a home for convalescents who were out of danger but still needed rest and care. This morning he had gone to an estate auction in the country and had been lucky enough to acquire some useful items, including a twelve-gallon ice cream freezer, which he was having delivered. It was the same estate sale my father and stepmother and odious stepbrother had gone off to that morning, which had given me my opportunity to escape. I remember sitting in that cabriolet taking me further and further away from the farm and recalling Elise telling my father that very morning she was going to come home with that ice cream freezer if it was the last thing she did. It made me smile, and the doctor noticed it and looked at me so kindly that I almost told him the truth right then. But I thought better of it. It's best to keep yourself to yourself—especially when you are running away. So I just smiled and kept silent. Oh, I can still see that horse's sleek rump rotating in the sunshine, and I can smell the leather from the reins in the doctor's hands and the masculine scent of the toiletry he wore. It was a beautiful May morning and everything was starting to bloom. Before he let me off at the Battery Hill Hotel he gave me his card and said he sincerely hoped I'd get in touch if he could be of further assistance. The card had his Columbia address scored through and he'd written below in a fine copperplate hand: Anstruther's Lodge, Cameron Anstruther, M.D., Director, and the local address.

"That was the first Anstruther's Lodge; it was right in town. We bought this house on Sunset Mountain when Harry was going on ten and people had cars. I'll take you past the old lodge if you like, but do keep in mind it was in a better part of town in those days and looked a lot nicer than it does now.

"I got a job as a laundress at the hotel until they found out I could cook and promoted me to the kitchen. But then my father tracked me down and sent my stepbrother, Earl Quarles, to bring me home. Earl made a scene at the hotel. But I had things to hold over him, and I told him if I was forced to go back to the farm I would see that my father was informed of those things and Earl would be out on his ear.

"What things? Oh, darling, Earl had so many bad traits it would be hard to single one out for you. Let's just say he was sneaky and bullying and thought nothing of taking what wasn't his. He had his eye on that farm from the beginning. I don't know what lies he told them when he returned without me, but Father didn't send him back again."

"Didn't you and your father ever make up?"

"No, darling, we never did. Fate was unkind in that regard.

After I had Harry, I was planning to go out and see Father and show him his grandson. And then I opened the paper one morning and saw his obituary. He was only fifty-two but had died of a massive heart attack. The obituary was in the paper from several days back so I couldn't even go to his funeral. But I'm getting way ahead of myself.

"Earl's scene at the hotel had cost me my job. It was not the kind of hotel where visitors of employees were allowed to threaten and scream. It was then that I remembered the doctor and called on him at his lodge. It was only a few minutes' walk from the hotel. I started cooking for his convalescents and ran the household for him. Until one day he asked me if he was too old for me to love, and I gave him a good long look and said, 'No, you are exactly right.' "

NONIE WAS A born storyteller. It is not so remarkable that I have made a life and a living from storytelling. But there were dangers and drawbacks in her ways of telling and her ways of not telling. Gradually I have come to wonder how deeply her methods have infiltrated mine.

III.

Flora had three interviews for primary school teaching jobs in Alabama and couldn't come to us until the second week in June, but my father was to report for work on June first. He had his gas coupons and four new tires from the Ration Board for his second summer at Oak Ridge, where he was being promoted to paymaster for a big new complex under construction, and made no secret about his impatience to leave. He'd much rather be outdoors supervising an important project for the war effort, he said, than kowtowing to small-town faculty egos. He had been the principal of Mountain City High since I was born, but loved to grumble that carpentry and construction work was his true calling, which had been thwarted by the social expectations of others.

Also—and he couldn't stop reminding me of this—Oak Ridge would be a healthful change of pace for him because no alcohol was allowed on the premises.

I was as willing for him to go as he was chafing to be gone. Nonie's removal had altered things between us. The "put-upon" note in his voice, which Nonie had her ways of quelling, was now directed at me, who only seemed to exacerbate it.

I had not known how wobbly things were at Old One Thousand. I barely knew what a mortgage was. Hitler had committed suicide in his Berlin bunker, and the European part of the war had ended in early May, which was supposed to have made everybody happy, except it didn't. All sorts of qualified young men with talents or important connections would be coming home soon to wrest away jobs from the "old guys" like my father, who was forty-five.

We got on each other's nerves. One minute he was treating me like a child and then the very next was complaining that something I had said or done was "downright childish." My worst offense had been at a coffee hour after church. President Roosevelt had died only a few weeks after Nonie, and some people my father didn't like but who were influential in the community were saying wasn't it sad that FDR hadn't lived to see V-E Day. My father stood looking over our heads, encased in his laconic reserve, and I felt that somebody in our family needed to point out that Nonie hadn't admired FDR all that much.

One evening there was a curse and a thud, and I found my father passed out on the kitchen floor. While I was kneeling over him, wiping the blood from his forehead, I prepared myself to receive fatherly praise for being just where I was needed with the wet cloth. But he cracked open an eye and slurred, "Get the fuck away."

His June first departure meant I would have to stay with a friend during the week before Flora arrived. I had three friends in fifth grade. My favorite was Annie Rickets, with her wild imagination and her gleeful malice. She speculated outlandishly about what was going on behind the scenes in the lives of people we knew. Both her parents worked for the phone company and, she darkly hinted, had access to equipment that could breach any secret, local or national. Also she was witty about sex. Nonie had provided me with an overview of how things worked, but Annie contributed specific anecdotes garnered from her frank-talking mother and her own salacious speculations. Her gleeful malice occasionally went too far, like when she said my grandmother looked like an upright mastiff driving a car. I found a picture of a mastiff in a dog book and didn't speak to her for a week. From then on Nonie was off-limits. But Annie shared a walled-in sleeping porch with her two younger sisters and couldn't have overnight guests.

Then there was Brian Beale, a late-born child who looked like a young prince in an old-fashioned storybook. His father was dead, and his mother, who cochaired the altar guild with Nonie, was raising Brian to be a classic actor. He was taking elocution lessons from an English lady in town to get rid of his mountain twang. Brian and I were allowed to go to afternoon movies by ourselves, and he liked to drawl in his new-fledged British accent, "When we are older, Helen, I shall probably ask for your hand." Brian had stayed at our house two years before, when his mother had an operation, and when I told him about Flora not being able to come till the second week in June, he said, "You'll stay with us, of course." I thanked him and imagined myself already there, though Mrs. Beale was an awful worrier and wouldn't let us do much. But then Lorena Huff phoned and said she and Rachel were counting on my staying with them. My father left it up to me, and guiltily I chose the Huffs. I lied to Brian that my father thought it was more proper for me to stay with a girl. Rachel Huff, who had moved to town with her mother at the beginning of the war, was less fun than either Annie or Brian. Also she asked rude personal questions and was usually in a grumpy mood from being forced by her mother to excel in so many things. But they had a huge house and a good cook and a pool, and Rachel had twin beds with canopies and her own bathroom and a maid who picked up your discarded clothes. Mr. Huff was up in Washington doing something so important for the war that he could never come home. But he was always sending contraband items like steaks and Hershey's bars, and Mrs. Huff admired me. She said I was a good influence on Rachel. She was also partial to my father. Nonie had enjoyed teasing him about this.

When he dropped me off for my week's stay with them, there was Mrs. Huff's usual cagey flirtation to get through while they had their drinks.

"Tell me, Harry, what are they really making over there in Oak Ridge? One of Huffie's sources says it's a new kind of fuel, so the planes can go on longer raids to bomb the Japs."

"That's as good an educated guess as any, Lorena, but I can only tell you what I'll be doing. Overseeing the construction of a new complex and making sure the men on my crew show up for work. I wish I could do that sort of thing all year round. I'm not cut out to be a school administrator."

"You'd be good at any kind of work you chose, Harry, but I'm a little hurt with you. Helen could have perfectly well stayed with Rachel and me the whole summer. We have everything here. You had no need to import some fancy governess from out of town."

"Flora is my wife's first cousin. She's training to be a teacher, but she's hardly a fancy governess. I thought it would be better for Helen to stay in her own home. She's had enough upheaval as it is."

"Wasn't she that emotional girl reading your mother's letters to everyone after the funeral? Well, you know best, but if for some reason it doesn't work out with Flora, my offer stands."

"That's very generous of you, Lorena, but I see no reason why things shouldn't work out."

The week with the Huffs turned out to be a torment. Everyone had a schedule but me. Rachel and her mother were on the tennis court before breakfast. I lay in bed hearing their back-and-forth *thwocks*, interspersed with Lorena Huff's criticisms and Rachel's sullen groans. Then the cook started her breakfast sounds, and here came the gardener's truck rattling up the drive, and after that began the various parcel deliveries, which seemed to go on all day. Ladies arrived to see Lorena Huff, and they sat on the screened porch and tinkled ice and planned charitable events. Twice a week a man came to the house to teach Rachel piano (she was on John Thompson's book two), and every afternoon at three a mannish woman in jodhpurs drove Rachel away in a jeep for her riding lesson.

"I want you to treat our house like a resort," Lorena Huff said. "Swim in the pool, have little talks with Rachel, and show up for meals. We'll take care of the rest. I want you to consider Rachel and me as your family until that cousin of your mother's gets here."

Wasn't it a contradiction in terms for a family member to treat her home as a resort? But what made me far unhappier than my lack of any schedule was the sense that life at Old One Thousand was going on without me. *It* had a schedule and needed someone there to register it. I did my best to patrol its rooms and porches in spirit. Nonie seemed always to be there waiting, just around a corner or on the other side of a door. Sometimes the Recoverers were there, the ones from her stories, discussing their rates of improvement as the sun passed over the house.

Around three o'clock this time of year, as Rachel was being driven away for her riding lesson, they would be gathering up their books and cards and migrating from the south porch to the west porch. And in the background, doing whatever he did in his consulting room (sometimes he wrote poetry: ". . . 'midst our cloud-begirded peaks / on this December morn / a boy is born," he had begun his ode on the occasion of my father's birth), presided the watchful spirit of my grandfather Doctor Cam.

Rachel and I swam and had I-bet-you-can't-do-this contests in the pool while her mother lay in the sun in her two-piece bathing suit, her skinny brown midriff baking to a crisp, her face concealed by a picture hat, leafing through magazines and turning down pages when she saw something she wanted. Rachel and I had a thermos of cold lemonade, and Rachel's mother had her own thermos, which Rachel said was "spiked," and eventually Lorena Huff would rise from her deck chair, wiggle her fingers at us coyly, and sway unsteadily toward the house.

Every morning, Rachel and I crunched down the sparkling white drive to the mailbox, Rachel toeing up as much gravel as she could, and by the time we had walked back with the mail, Rachel would have gotten in at least two of her embarrassing questions. These ran the gamut from "Which is worse, having your mother or your grandmother die?" to "Don't you want to know who your father will marry to look after you?"

I grew more desolate as the week went on. I felt I was neglecting an important duty and losing more of my identity every hour I stayed apart from the rhythms of Old One Thousand. There were times when I was sure that, if I could be there at that very moment, Nonie would find a way to speak to me, and maybe even to appear, which made me all the more desolate.

Flora was to arrive on a midmorning Saturday train from Birmingham, after a long layover in Columbia, and Mrs. Huff kept warning me that the poor girl would probably be exhausted after sitting up all night and would need to rest before beginning her duties. "Your mother's cousin is welcome to come back here, Helen. We'll keep the resort going for you two awhile longer. We can provide everything you need."

"Thank you, but I really need to get home." Lorena Huff meant well, but I was starting to feel bludgeoned by her hospitality.

The Flora who emerged from the train looked uncharacteristically in charge. In a simple gray suit sprigged with tiny white flowers, her hair secured in a businesslike knot beneath a little hat with a demure veil, she could pass for the fancy governess Mrs. Huff had accused my father of hiring. I could see Lorena Huff revising her estimate of the emotional girl she had seen reading Nonie's letters at the funeral reception.

I ran to Flora and flung my arms around her.

"My goodness!" she exclaimed, surprised. "You seem glad to see me."

"Let's go *straight home*," I hissed into her neck.

"Well, of course," she said. "Where else would we go?"

"Just don't accept any invitation, okay?"

"Okay," she repeated, giving my shoulders an encouraging little shake before stepping over to greet Mrs. Huff and Rachel. The dreaded invitation was offered, and I was impressed at how maturely Flora got out of it.

"No, I'm not at all exhausted," she said. "I brought Mrs.

Anstruther's letters to keep me company during the trip. They always inspire me. I read them over, and it was like hearing her voice tell me what to do next. Helen's grandmother and I corresponded for six years, you know. You've taken such good care of Helen, Mrs. Huff. Just look how brown these girls are! But now I want to get her right home and settle us into our summer routine."

However, Flora's arrival that day was to mark the high point of my faith in her.

IV.

My one solace during the week at the Huffs' had been planning the historical tour of the house I would give Flora the day she arrived. I had played it back and forth in my head, room by room, hearing my own narrating voice. First thing, we'd head straight up to settle her in her room. Flora had slept in this room on her two previous visits to this house, first when she stayed on after my mother's funeral and then back in March, when she came up for Nonie's funeral. She had already been told we called this upstairs front room, which opened out on the west porch, the Willow Fanning room, after a Recoverer who had stayed in it a year and a half while convalescing from a nervous breakdown. But there were other layers to reveal, the sort you wouldn't tell a regular guest, not even a cousin visiting for family funerals. I had planned to drop a few hints about my father's attachment to Willow Fanning when he was sixteen, maybe even going so far as to foreshadow their ill-fated elopement. My father shouldn't mind, he was "an old guy" now, as he kept saying, and if he did mind, well, too bad. It was he who had chosen to make Flora an intimate of our family for the summer. I would tell just enough to make her feel she was being inducted into a private family story, and if she proved a worthy listener I would dole out more details. I might also allude to other noteworthy Recoverers on Flora's first day. The point was to draw her into the ways of Old One Thousand and make her my ally in keeping things going the way they had always been. And what better start than Flora's having just reread Nonie's letters on the train!

But Flora completely derailed my plans by making us stop first in the kitchen, where she proceeded to unpack her luggage. Out of an old carpetbag, whose threadbare state had embarrassed me when Lorena Huff was lifting it into the back of her station wagon, came a sack of flour, filled mason jars, and an entire ham. And then from her suitcase Flora parted a meager layer of personal garments and lifted out a sack of cornmeal, which she held in one arm like a baby while she plucked out tea bags, a tin cake box, and some wax paper parcels of what looked like dead grass. With a sigh of fulfillment she deposited these items on the counter.

"You didn't need to bring tea bags," I said. "And we already have flour and cornmeal."

"Well, I wasn't sure. And I never go anywhere anymore without my self-rising flour. In a pinch, you can make biscuits with it and mayonnaise. I baked them for my teacher-training group last winter and they came out perfect every time. And this cornmeal is stone-ground at a mill near where we live. Now, Helen, you'll have to show me where everything goes."

"What are those dried-up old things in the wax paper?"

"These are Juliet's famous herbs. For spaghetti sauce and to enhance our everyday dishes."

"Juliet who?"

"Juliet Parker. Don't you know her name? She raised your mother and me."

"You mean that old Negro who lived with you?"

"There's a lot more to Juliet than that. And she's not old. Now this apple-cured ham is from your uncle Sam. He picked it out especially for you."

"Uncle Sam owns the meat market and has been separated from his wife for ages and ages," I said.

Flora needed to know that I was familiar with the names that mattered in my mother's past.

"Well, he's the part owner with his friend Ben Timms. Ben and your uncle Sam and my daddy worked in the iron mines together when they were young. Uncle Sam is getting remarried. I mean he and Aunt Garnet are going to get remarried. They were never divorced, but they want to renew their vows and make a fresh beginning. Isn't that sweet?"

I stared at Flora, still wearing her little hat with the demure veil, so proudly unloading all this foreign food and all these people with their complications into our house.

"Is everything all right?" she asked. Something in my face must have sapped the confidence she had brought with her on the train. Already I was learning how effectively she could be managed by a simple look of disdain.

"I was just thinking where all this stuff should go," I said.

"Juliet and I wanted to be sure I brought enough to give you wholesome meals over the weekend. We'll order whatever else we need from the grocery store on Monday."

"Why do we have to order? We can go and get whatever we need in Nonie's car."

"Oh dear, I thought your father would have explained. I don't drive."

"Do you mean you can't, or what?"

"I never learned. None of us did. We didn't have a car, so there was no need."

"But how are we going to get anywhere?"

"Your father has set up an account for us at the store. They make lots of deliveries because of the gas rationing. All we have to do is make a list and call up. We don't even have to pay when they bring it. It's all been arranged by your father, isn't that nice?"

"But how will we get to church?"

"I thought maybe we could go down that shortcut your grandfather built for his patients, so they could walk to the village. Your father said you'd show me."

"That's impossible! That shortcut is completely grown over, it's dangerous!"

What had my father been thinking? In its heyday the steep path down through the woods to the bottom of the road had dispensed with a mile's worth of Sunset Drive's hairpin curves. My grandfather had had the stepping-stones brought in from a quarry at his own expense; the residents on lower loops of the road, who would also profit from the shortcut, had granted him rights-of-way for his project. But that was almost thirty years ago, when my sixteen-year-old father and Willow Fanning had used it for their getaway. Surely he was not still remembering the path as it was *then*. Many of the stones were now upended or missing and the pine railings rotted out. Where had I been when my father was dispensing his obsolete information to Flora?

After we got the Alabama foodstuffs put away (Flora was thrilled to discover some empty cocktail olive jars in the pantry, just the right size for "Juliet's famous herbs"), we climbed the stairs and went down the hall to her room at the front of the house. I had lost all enthusiasm for my tour. It occurred to me now that it would be wiser to keep our family stories separate from Flora's. I lolled in the doorway of the Willow Fanning room and let Flora prattle on as she hung up her few garments and deposited the rest of her things in the freshly papered drawers that Mrs. Jones, who cleaned on Tuesdays, had prepared. Next to her underwear, Flora slid in some hand-sewn satin envelopes.

"What's in there, handkerchiefs?" I asked.

"Sanitary napkins. You know what those are, don't you?"

"Good grief, yes," I said, offended. "My grandmother told me about all that stuff years ago."

Presently I saw Nonie's pile of letters go in the top drawer and determined to have a secret look at them as soon as an opportunity arose.

"Are those all the clothes you brought for the whole summer?"

"Oh, no, honey, Juliet is mailing me the rest. We decided it was more important for you to have the right meals for the weekend."

When the phone rang in the hallway, I was sure it was my father calling from Oak Ridge to see how we were getting on. Adopting Nonie's ironic deadpan, I would be able to tell him about all the food in the luggage without Flora knowing we were making fun of her. But it was Lorena Huff.

"Helen! Guess what Rachel just found under your bed in her room. Your new blue Keds!"

"Oh, I'm sorry."

"Not at all, sweetie. Don't you know when you leave something behind, it means you want to come back? I'll bring them over. Do you need them today?"

"Not really."

"Oh."

"I'm helping Flora get settled in."

A pause. "Everything's going okay, then?"

"Yes, ma'am, we're doing just fine."

"In that case"—a shade more formal—"I'll drop them off tomorrow."

"We might not be home. Tomorrow's church."

"Well, look, Helen." Now there was a chilliness, a touch of hurt. "I'll drop them by when I'm over that way next. No need for anyone to *be home.* I'll just leave them inside the screen door, okay?"

"Okay." Then, realizing I had forgotten to say the proper things when she and Rachel had brought us home, I burbled out my thanks for the week at their house. "Everything was just wonderful, Mrs. Huff. Thank you for having me."

"You're welcome, Helen." She sounded tired. "If you need us, you know where we are."

"Yes, ma'am."

"Please give my best to your father next time you talk to him."

"Yes, ma'am, I will."

V.

When I returned to Flora, she had changed out of her traveling outfit into some wrinkled pedal pushers and a sleeveless blouse that showed where her tan stopped just above the elbows. "You know what, Helen?" she said, wriggling her bare feet into scuffed brown loafers with pennies in them. "After I give you a light lunch, why don't you show me that shortcut of your grandfather's anyway? Maybe it's not completely out of the question. When was the last time anyone used it?"

"I have no idea. I'm not supposed to mess around down there by myself. But we can walk down and look at it now if you want. I'm really not hungry. Just remember I said it's dangerous."

As we tottered down our horrible driveway, she acted pleased each time I grabbed for her hand, but I did this to keep my balance. ("Everyone still on *board*?" Lorena Huff had cried as her new Oldsmobile bucked a nasty rut today.) I had grown used to hearing Nonie complain about the ruts ("Goddamn sinkholes," my father called them), but I was in the car at those times. After several of Flora's apologetic little yips when she stumbled, I did a pretty fair imitation of Nonie's voice reassuring her that we were going to get this road seen to as soon as the war was over.

At last we reached the paved road. Then you had to walk down Sunset Drive until you reached the big curve, which doubled back on itself and was so dangerous that the town had put up hairpin curve signs in both directions and a streetlight, which unfortunately got shot out at least once a month by ruffians. They came from the other side of town to shoot out this streetlight, Nonie said. When I asked her why they didn't shoot out the streetlights on their own side of town, she said wryly, "They already *have*, darling."

Just before that curve, in the woods sloping off to the right, began the shortcut that my grandfather had made to take his Recoverers down to the next paved loop of Sunset Drive, and then down a continuation of the path through more woods to the final loop, which opened onto the street of neighborhood shops if you turned south, and toward our church if you turned north.

"This is *it*?" asked Flora, when we reached the shortcut. "But I don't see any path at all."

"I told you, it's grown over."

"How odd. Your father made it sound—"

"Well we're here now," I said irritably, "so we might as well look for where it used to be." I plunged ahead into the overgrowth, exulting in every clawing bramble and slapping branch that came my way, a yipping Flora following close behind. Something ripped at my arm, but I crashed on, hoping it would bleed. At last I found a few of my grandfather's descending steps, which ended abruptly at a crater deep as an open grave, bristling with roots and wild vegetation. The crater looked perfectly terrifying, and I was elated.

"Well, there's our shortcut to church," I said.

"Oh dear," said Flora, coming up beside me. She was breathing hard, and I could smell her underarm perspiration. "My church shoes certainly wouldn't make it down *that*. But, I mean, when did your father last use this path?"

I was on the verge of relenting about Willow Fanning when Flora wailed, "Oh, no! Your arm is bleeding!" First she tried to doctor it with a leaf and some of her spit, and then she went into what I would come to recognize as a typical Flora flagellation. It was all her fault, she should never have suggested this outing, what a fool she was—"and on the very first day of my taking care of you!"

"Don't be silly," I said. "It's just a little blood. It's good we saw it up close. I needed to see it, too, instead of just driving past it. My father was probably thinking of how it was a while ago." Though it was gratifying to hear my voice reassuring her, I was feeling less reassured myself. Beyond my resentment at the idea of her "taking care" of me rose an unsettling thought: what if there were ways I was going to have to take care of Flora?

As we walked back to the house she asked what kinds of things I had done while staying with the Huffs.

"Oh, they had all their *activities*. Rachel had her tennis and her riding and her piano lessons and Mrs. Huff had her sunbathing and her magazines and her spiked lemonade." Nonie or my father would have picked up on my sarcasm at once and joined the game, but Flora went earnestly on.

"But what did *you* do, Helen?"

"Oh, I swam with Rachel and things, but mostly I just thought about being back home."

We walked uphill some more. I could feel her working up to her next question. "And, what things were you wanting to do back home?"

While I was at the Huffs', the life of our house was going on without me. I needed to be there to register it. I felt the longer I wasn't there, the more of myself I would lose.

Of course I didn't say this. While I was still concocting a normal-sounding reply that would satisfy her, Flora jumped in with "Helen, I know everything has changed for you since your grandmother passed away, but it would help if I knew what in particular you like to do."

She had interrupted my concocting process. I couldn't come up with a single thing to say I liked to do.

When we got back to the house, Flora observed almost regretfully that it was still too early to start supper. "What did you usually do on Saturday afternoons, Helen?"

Well, if Nonie hadn't "passed away" she would be taking her nap on her three pillows about now and I would be upstairs on the Recoverers' west porch, reading a book or gazing at the non-view of hectic branches. But now, for the whole summer, Flora's room opened onto this porch and so it was off-limits to me.

"Sometimes I just read in my room." It was time to squash this dogged inquisition. "I know what," I said, calling on Nonie's voice again. "Why don't we each go to our own room and replenish ourselves?"

Flora seemed tempted. "Would you like anything first? A glass of milk or a sandwich?"

"No, thank you. We ate at the Huffs' before we went to the train station."

"Well, you have only to ask, Helen. That's what I'm here for. And don't worry about church tomorrow. We'll go in a taxi. I've got the money for that."

The angle of light in my room was different from when I

was usually in it. Nonie often remarked that every one of us needed to get away from other people and replenish our personal reserves. I felt my room's resentment at my untimely entrance. To disrupt its personal replenishment as little as possible, I crept quietly onto my bed with the library book I had taken to the Huffs' and never opened.

This author produced a continuing string of novels, all featuring a girl and a house and a mystery. There was always a historical angle as well. The librarian had told Nonie and me they were "like Nancy Drews for the more sophisticated reader."

This novel opened in a place where it had rained heavily all day, but now at the sunset hour the clouds parted and a breath of spring air wafted through the window of a muddy little sedan car just entering the town. The driver was a girl of sixteen, and her alert Irish setter sat beside her. Piled into the rear of the car was a mound of baggage.

A girl in her own car arriving at her destination with her alert and faithful dog, her luggage, and her plan—this author's girls always had plans, usually involving historical or family research and requiring dangerous snooping. It was the kind of story I craved, but something nagged at my peripheries. Outside the window beside my bed the sun was highlighting an unsightly row of weeds that had sprung up against the closed doors of the garage. Inside the garage was Nonie's car. To keep the battery charged, my father had alternated driving it with driving his own, but what would happen now? Not only had he been shockingly out of date about the shortcut we were to take to church but he had gone off without making arrangements to keep Nonie's battery alive.

* * *

FLORA, I WOULD learn, went into a kind of trance when she prepared our meals. She would never come right out and tell me to hush, but if I talked she would simply hum or nod, remaining inside her bubble of chopping or stirring or turning meat in the pan. Could she not do two things at once, or did she need to tune out all distractions to remember how she'd been taught to cook?

The first evening I was all set to be sociable, as I had been with Nonie and more recently my father when they were making our meals, but I soon saw that it didn't matter much to Flora whether I kept up a running commentary or stayed quiet. I wondered whether she might be the slightest bit slow-witted, and even anticipated with a superior thrill how I would have to get us through the summer without outsiders suspecting.

We ate in the dining room. At the last minute my father had removed the papers that were piled there. We had answered all of the condolence notes that had come in so far. Except, of course, the one from the old mongrel, which my father had crushed in his pocket. On Monday the postman would bump up our driveway with more mail, and maybe a letter from my father. Already I was fast forgetting his unsavory side.

It would soon be the longest day, and with the sun pouring through the dining room's west windows, we didn't light the candles, though Flora recalled how Nonie had always done it with such gracious ceremony.

"Didn't you have candles at home?" I asked.

"No," said Flora, "but I remember when I was little how Daddy and Uncle Sam ate their breakfast by the light of a candle in a mustard jar."

"You mean in the winter when the mornings were dark?"

"Oh, no, all year round. Even in summer, they left the

shades down. They got in the habit of eating breakfast in the dark when they were younger and worked in the iron mines."

"Why would anyone want to eat breakfast in the dark when they're going to spend the whole day down in a dark mine?"

"That's what I thought when I was little. But Daddy said miners prefer it. Later, Juliet told me Daddy and Uncle Sam also liked it because it reminded them of before they had electricity and their mother still made their breakfast."

"That was my other grandmother?"

"No, she was your mother's grandmother. That would make her your great-grandmother."

"Did you ever know her?"

"No, but your mother remembered her. When she was a little girl she had to help take care of her and it wasn't pleasant. The old lady was bedridden and couldn't even go to the bathroom. She should have gone to a nursing home but back then families didn't do that and also our family was too poor."

"It's just as well, then," I said, cutting Flora off before she said any more about going to the bathroom at the table.

"What is, honey?"

"That I had just the one grandmother, who was wonderful."

"Yes, she was. I don't know where I would have been without your grandmother's support. You were so lucky to have her, though it's a shame you couldn't have had Lisbeth, too. I was thinking on the train coming up, I had more time with your mother than you did. Lisbeth was a little mother to me." Predictably the tear ducts opened. What would it be like to produce such easy evidence of your feelings? Yet I also felt superior to Flora in my habit of restraint.

"Could I ever read those letters?"

"Well, honey, they were private, you know."

"You read them aloud to everybody after the funeral."

"That probably wasn't such a good idea. At least your father didn't think so. But I meant it as a kind of tribute. And I didn't read any of the really personal parts."

VI.

Sunday began badly with the taxi driver and would get a lot worse.

"Y'all better get your dad-blamed driveway fixed before somebody busts an axle and prosecutes."

"Oh!" yipped the adult-in-charge to whom this rebuke had been addressed.

"We are having it seen to, now that the war is over," I piped up in my grandmother's voice.

"Oh, *seen to*!" he imitated in falsetto, jolting us sideways to avoid a rut.

We were driven in hostile silence down Sunset Drive. It was a sultry, overcast day. I got an uneasy sensation as we passed the spot where my grandfather's shortcut lay in ruins. There was a familiar smell in the taxi that reminded me of my father. At least he was spending the summer in a place where sobriety was enforced.

"We will need a taxi to take us home after church," Flora humbly ventured as she clumsily selected coins with her gloves on to pay the driver.

"I'm off duty now, lady. Just call the number."

"We can get a ride home with Mrs. Beale and Brian," I said as we headed up the sidewalk to the church.

"You go first, Helen." Flora nudged me ahead of her into the nave.

I led us to our family's usual place in front on the pulpit side. Nonie liked to be up close so she could do without her glasses. Too late I realized that whatever Flora did wrong would be seen by everybody behind us.

"Are the Beales here yet?" she was anxiously whispering before I could sink to the cushion for silent prayer.

"They will be. You better kneel down."

I didn't remember how Flora had comported herself here during Nonie's funeral, but it wouldn't have been so noticeable that day, with so many people from other churches bobbing up and down at the wrong times. Today she dutifully mimed my actions. When it came time to follow in the prayer book, she kept leaning over to see what page I was on. During Father McFall's sermon she turned red trying to suppress a cough until an imperious hand from behind tapped her shoulder and shoved a lozenge at her.

I made her go up for communion, because by that time I was so distressed it mattered very little to me whether she was eligible to take the sacrament or not. At the conclusion of his sermon, Father McFall had asked us from the pulpit to join him in saying the Prayer for a Sick Child. Brian Beale, he announced, had come down with polio over the weekend.

Father McFall himself drove us home. "When I saw you from the pulpit, Helen, I realized you hadn't heard about Brian."

Flora sat in front with the rector, who was diplomatically grilling her. He began by saying that he had been among the listeners when she was reading Mrs. Anstruther's letters. Next came cordial inquiries about her Alabama life, her plans for the future, and her summer plans for the two of us. ("Though some activities may have to be forfeited, with this polio outbreak.")

Brian had gone swimming at the municipal lake, which was now closed; one other child, a little girl, had been stricken and was in an iron lung.

"But his mother never lets him go to the municipal lake," I protested from the backseat. "Mrs. Beale is scared silly of diseases."

"Well, this time, rightly so. But it was a hot day and Brian was lonely and bored, so she gave in and took him and even went in the lake herself. She has scarcely left his bedside at the hospital."

"Does this mean Brian is going to be crippled?"

"We're taking it a step at a time, Helen."

Though it gave his old Ford sedan a severe shaking, Father McFall allowed himself no comment on our driveway. I remembered to say, "Won't you come in?" as Nonie always did when people brought me home, but he said he had hospital visits to make.

"Will you see Brian?"

"I'm headed straight there. Do you have a message for him?"

"Tell him I said please get better soon."

Tell him I'm sorry. It was my fault.

"I'd like to visit you two during the week, if that's all right. I'll phone first," Father McFall said in parting.

Inside the screen door, we found my Keds tied together with a ribbon. There was no note.

It was a hot day and Brian was lonely and bored.

If I had been there, he wouldn't have been either of those things. We would have been in our outdoor sanctuary under the trees in his fenced-in backyard, which was visible enough from an upstairs window for his mother to spy on us. We would have drunk her iced apple juice and played Brian's favorite game, in which he was either auditioning before a hard-to-please New York director (me) for a lead role or being coached by the director in his role.

If I had stayed at Brian's last week rather than languishing in luxury at the Huffs', he would have been in church this morning. As I passed his pew, his princely little profile would have swiveled just enough to beam me a possessive greeting: didn't *we* have fun this past week? After church, the Beales would have driven Flora and me back to Old One Thousand and maybe Mrs. Beale would have let him stay overnight. Flora would have made hot biscuits to go with the ham, and for dessert there would have been more of the pound cake she had brought in the suitcase from Alabama. After supper, Brian would have sat down at our out-of-tune piano and picked out some show tunes, and Flora would have praised him and remarked happily on what a nice evening we were having, and then she would have excused herself and retired to the Willow Fanning room. And Brian and I, as we had done since we became spend-the-night friends back in first grade, would have separated to undress and then reconvened in either my room or his, which was my grandfather's old consulting room. We would have snuggled hip to hip in our pajamas on top of the spread, covering our knees with a quilt, and taken turns reading aloud. I was the faster sight reader, but Brian liked to practice his delivery and his English accent. Sometimes we read from the books we had outgrown for the sake of doing the parts. He was always Eeyore and Piglet and I was always Pooh.

All Sunday afternoon Flora kept watching me mournfully

as though another member of my family had died and she was expecting me to fall to pieces any minute. "Let me know if I can do anything, honey," she kept saying.

"Don't *you* have anything you need to do?" I was finally driven to ask.

She looked hurt, then recovered herself and said she had been hoping to use her time off to prepare sample lesson plans for whichever job came through. She had interviewed for three: one for sixth grade and two for fifth.

"Then why don't you go and do that?" I said.

But as I prowled around downstairs after getting rid of Flora, I felt the house ignoring my existence. I kicked open the kitchen screen door, noticing for the first time that the bottom board, where my foot always landed, had split.

I decided to walk completely around the house and force it to acknowledge me. The day was still under that stubborn haze that withholds either rain or sunshine.

When was the last time I had walked all the way around this house? It seemed that for years we had climbed into our cars and gone somewhere and come back and gone into the house. When was the last time *anyone* had walked around this house? This made me think of Brian, who might never be able to walk around his house again. Other thoughts came. I pushed them away until all that was left was the forlorn scene I was walking through. Everywhere things were falling apart. Peeling paint, missing roof tiles, an unattached downspout swinging tipsily out from a roof gutter. The former "front lawn" had become a weedy slope ending in unkempt woods, where two broken old trees had collapsed against each other and were rotting together. Did I really remember a lawn green and smooth enough for me to roll down, over and over again? Who had been with me? A woman dressed to go somewhere else, looking off into the distance. There was discontent in the air. Was it mine, or hers, or just the day in general? Was I remembering my mother or was my memory as unreliable as my father's memory of my grandfather's shortcut to town? It seemed hard to believe that when the Recoverers took their constitutionals on this lawn they could have looked out through healthy, upright trees and seen the mountains. Yet a charming recovering drunk, Starling Peake, had painted a small canvas that hung on our living room wall, testifying to this lost view. "Poor Starling," Nonie would say. "He let us down, but he was happy the day he painted that picture."

What had my mother seen when my father brought her to Old One Thousand for the first time? "It must be wonderful to live in a house like this": those were her first words to my grandmother. Could the house have disintegrated that much in twelve years, or had my mother been being polite, or had she been more worried about the impression she made and not really noticing what was in front of her? Or had it seemed like a grand house, compared to what she had been used to? The way Flora talked, the Alabama house seemed far from grand.

At last I reached the garage, where yesterday, from the window of my room, I had spotted the unsightly new weeds blocking the entrance. Now, as I wrenched open the garage doors, I imagined those weeds shrieking as I crushed them flat. With a heavy sigh I climbed into the driver's seat of Nonie's car and laid my face down on the steering wheel. The dull heat pressed in. Spit trickled out of my mouth onto the hot leather. I began to feel funny, but something told me that I would have to endure it if I wanted anything to change. I had never fainted before, but Nonie had often described what it felt like. Then

I must have lost consciousness for a second or two. The next thing I knew, I was sliding down from the seat and leaving the car.

That's right, darling. Now close the garage doors. You'll come back later when it's cooler and shear those nasty old weeds flat to the ground with the kitchen scissors. We can't fix everything at once, but this will be a gesture in the right direction. And I want you to move into my room. It was my place and now it will be yours. When Mrs. Jones comes on Tuesday, ask her to prepare the room for you. Tell her I came to you in a dream and said to do this. Mrs. Jones respects dreams and is partial to the supernatural. Remember how provoked I was when I found out she was telling you those stories about her little dead daughter, Rosemary, and that uncle who kept speaking to her through a crow. But then you and I had a little talk, you couldn't have been more than five at the time, and you said, "Don't worry, Nonie, I don't believe in her ghosts, but I do like the stories." And I said, "All right, then, as long as you know the difference."

VII.

When I told Flora at supper that I was going outside to cut down some weeds with the kitchen scissors, she merely asked did I want her to help.

"No thanks, I need to do it by myself." I was sitting at the head of the dining room table, Flora having insisted it was my rightful place when my father was not here.

"Okay, honey." She got up and started clearing the dishes, and that was that.

I felt as though I'd gotten away with something. Every other person in my life at that time, adult or child, would have made some remark about my intention or the impracticality of the scissors, but not this literal-minded cousin. In all the years since, I have come across few people who can keep their personalities out of your business. I haven't been one of those exceptions myself. Someone I once wanted badly told me at the end of his patience with me, "I have yet to find a person willing to let me do what I have to do without making clever comments or saying what I ought to do."

I say Flora was literal-minded. Was that it? Was she inclined to take things at face value because she was prosaic, unimaginative, lacking in cunning? I recall her being all of those things at various times. Once when I was mad at her, I called her simple-minded, and she bowed her head modestly, as if I had paid her a compliment, and said, "I expect I am." Later that summer I told someone Flora was simpleminded, but he said he thought I must mean simple-hearted.

Something had been left out of her, but was that something her virtue or her deficit? Was she *single-hearted* (not an attribute you hear mentioned much anymore, as in that old dismissal prayer that exhorts us to go forth "with gladness and singleness of heart"), or was she a member of that even rarer species, the pure in heart? I am still making up my mind.

It was getting dark when I sheared through the last clump of weeds in front of the garage door. My fingers ached from gripping the scissors. The weeds had been more resistant than expected. They had squashed easily, but were tough to cut. Every time I made another trip to the woods to dump their remains, I could hear them jeering, "We'll be back, little girl, twice as many of us: we'll be growing over your grave."

Flora was listening to the radio in the kitchen and making a list of the groceries we were going to order tomorrow.

"Helen, sit down a minute and tell me what kinds of meals Mrs. Anstruther fixed for you."

"Oh, just normal everyday things."

"Such as?"

I was still outside with my slain weeds. And hovering just beyond them was a hospital door I wanted to keep closed. Behind it was Brian, transformed into a cripple because of my selfishness.

"What did she make for breakfast, for instance?"

"Oh, cream of wheat, oatmeal. French toast if we weren't in a hurry."

"No eggs?"

"French toast *has* egg in it."

"But I mean—"

"And I had hard-boiled eggs in my school lunches." Nonie always put in an extra egg for Brian. He enjoyed having to peel them. Nonie worried he didn't get enough food in its whole state. His mother cut off the crusts on his school sandwiches, and carved smiley faces into his radishes.

We moved on to suppers. Yes, Flora said happily, she could do meat loaf and cube steak and macaroni and cheese. And she was sure she could make creamed chipped beef if she knew what kind of beef you used. Had my grandmother kept a box of recipes?

"No, it was all in her head. She cooked for her father until he married again."

"Yes, the awful stepmother. That's when she packed her bag and ran away and a handsome doctor stopped his carriage and said, 'Young lady, can I take you somewhere?' "

"No, he said, 'Can I *carry* you somewhere?' And it wasn't a carriage, it was a cabriolet."

In all those letters, it would have been natural for Nonie to have related parts of her history to Flora, but that didn't keep me from wishing she hadn't. How many people could repeat accurately the things they were told? Look at that game, Gossip, where the sentence whispered into the first ear is unrecognizable when it reaches the last. People didn't listen. Or they heard what they wanted to hear. Or changed it to make a better story.

"My grandfather was from South Carolina," I explained to Flora, "and they say 'carry' down there instead of 'take,' when offering a ride. And he was thirty years older. She saw him as elegant, not handsome."

Flora took these corrections with good grace. "If my fifth or sixth graders are as smart as you, honey, I will have my work cut out for me."

I was teaching Flora how to play advanced jacks when my father phoned from Oak Ridge.

"Not much happening here on a Sunday night. Harker and I walked down to where they're building some more houses for workers with families. Harker is my roommate. I'd say it was like being back at college, except Harker wouldn't have been at college. But he suits me. He's a master welder, deaf as a post, and laughs at everything I say. What have you girls got to report?"

"Brian Beale and a little girl have come down with polio. She's in an iron lung and he may be a cripple for life."

I had flung down this dramatic offering to get the attention of the parent I had not spoken to since he left me with the Huffs, but I soon regretted it.

"Where is Flora?" he asked.

"On the floor. We were playing jacks."

"Let me speak to her."

After she had imparted the information he wanted (the lake, the hospital, the little girl, Father McFall says we'll have to take it a step at a time with Brian), she was reduced to monosyllabic yips in response to my father's instructions. Then she passed the receiver back to me.

"Okay, Helen, here's the deal," he said curtly. "You're staying on top of that mountain. I've been where I forbid you to go. Are you listening to me?"

"Yes, sir."

"As of right now you're quarantined. Worse things than having to stay at home can happen to little girls. Like iron lungs, or death, or shriveled legs. I was luckier than most with the leg.

At sixteen I had my full growth. You are only ten—okay, going on eleven—and I forbid you to risk becoming a woman with the shrunken limbs of a child. Flora has her orders, and I depend on you to help her carry them out. Do I make myself clear?"

"Yes, sir."

Flora went straight to pieces after talking to my father. She was indulging in the kind of panic adults were supposed to hide so as not to worry children. She stumbled around blindly, tripping over our abandoned jacks, wailing a litany of her many failings, which I tried not to hear word for word because it was too upsetting: she should never have taken this job, she was not good enough, smart enough, she could never fulfill my father's expectations, she should never have agreed to take care of me.

How could I put her together again? What would Nonie do? First she would make you sit down. She would say something soothing and reasonable, though always retaining her edge of authority, and convince you that the crisis, whatever it was, could be managed. I told Flora we should go sit on the sofa in the living room so she could relay my father's instructions while they were still fresh in her mind. He had said he depended on me to help her carry them out, but to do that I was going to need a list of what we were supposed to do and not do. While everything was still fresh in her mind.

We sank together onto the faded yellow silk cushions that held so many associations of "talks" it was like sitting down on my past, and I coaxed my father's injunctions out of Flora. We were not to go into the shops, not even the ones in our immediate neighborhood, or take the bus to town to go to the movies or to any place where people gathered, not even to church.

I was not to go to my friends' houses or have them to mine, and I was not to visit Brian in the hospital.

"We might as well curl up and die!" I would have screamed if there had been a guaranteed adult there to talk me down. But Flora was the one who needed to be talked down, and it was gratifying to see the influence I could wield on a person twice my age. My father had gone overboard because of his own history, I explained, but he would come around, she would see, next time he called he would loosen the restrictions; meantime we had to keep him calm so he could do his job and bring home some much needed funds at the end of the summer. As she could see from the state of the place, we could use some repair money. The pay was fabulous at Oak Ridge, especially when it was someone valuable like my father who was used to keeping order and knew about blueprints and building things. I told her if he chose to work there year-round he'd get double his salary as high school principal. And then, saving my clincher for last—or so I thought—I revealed to her that my father himself had been a victim of polio.

At this Flora perked up. "Oh, yes, Mrs. Anstruther wrote about it in the letters. Suddenly she had the two of them to care for, the doctor with his stroke and her son with polio and everyone else running out on them. But she rose to it, your grandmother did. She cooked the meals and cared for her dying husband and massaged Harry's legs. Your mother called your father's limp endearing in the note she sent with the wedding announcement."

"You must mean the engagement announcement," I corrected.

"No, honey. We didn't even know she was dating someone

till we got the wedding announcement with her note. And then I'm afraid we thought—well, never mind what we thought—but later on, Daddy figured that Lisbeth hadn't asked us because we wouldn't have done credit to her. Lisbeth was very proud—well, she had every right to be, she was so superior."

Thanks to my efforts Flora had regained charge of herself. Now I was the one floundering among misgivings. I couldn't have said exactly what in her version of things unsettled me. I knew my parents had been married quietly in our church because, as Nonie said, Lisbeth didn't want to put her uncles to the expense of an Alabama wedding. There was an elegant reception afterward at our house, after which my father and mother took a short wedding trip to Blowing Rock in Nonie's car, which was brand-new then, and returned to their school jobs the following week.

I also knew what Flora had stopped herself from saying, having been apprised by Nonie of the facts of life through her resourceful use of the "Social Hygiene for Girls" pamphlet that had brought my father and mother together. She doled out supplements to this story as I grew into an age to handle them: what *exactly* the pamphlet had said, which parts had struck Nonie and my father as amusing or outdated when they read it aloud to each other over cocktails. ("It was a sad little production, full of unintended slipups. One I particularly remember was the misprint *impotent* when *important* was meant. And parts of it were insulting. It claimed that though a few well-brought-up young women were trained to safeguard their morals by the age of sixteen, most were not. I bristled at that. What was 'well-brought-up' but a code for privileged? I don't claim to be more than a farmer's daughter, but I was perfectly capable of safeguarding my morals at age sixteen.")

The uncles in Alabama had thought Lisbeth and Harry had started a baby and had to get married fast. But when I didn't come along until a full year and a month later they had to find another reason they hadn't been invited to the wedding.

It was a short courtship for my parents because from the very first evening, when they were playing cards, Lisbeth had felt she was part of our family. It was understandable, Nonie said. Lisbeth had lost her mother when she was eight, and the nearest thing she'd had to a female to care for her after that was the Negro woman who lived with the uncles.

"Well, I lost *my* mother when I was *three*," I would remind Nonie.

"Yes, darling, but after that you had *me*."

"I think Lisbeth returned my love first," Nonie would muse. "You know how your father often strikes new acquaintances as somewhat acerbic. I was the one who brought her out, made her feel at home. She liked me, she liked my style, and she liked the way we lived. Why, that first evening, she said she'd bring her poker chips next time she came—and then blushed to high heaven because she had invited herself back—it just showed how comfortable she already felt with us. We settled into our weekly threesome—I want you to know I became an excellent blackjack player—and it wasn't long before Harry looked across the card table and realized this was the woman he'd been waiting for all along."

I had been considering telling Flora how my father had caught polio when he ran away with Willow Fanning, but she had preempted my story with this information about my parents' marriage, which I now had to find a place for.

That night I went to bed in my old room. The garage voice had said I should move on Tuesday, when Mrs. Jones came to clean. I was to tell her what "the dream" had said and that she should make up Nonie's room because I would be moving into it permanently. She was a great respecter of the supernatural, Mrs. Jones was. Her little dead daughter had spoken to her at the cemetery. "Momma, you don't need to take the bus out here anymore, I'm not under this stone, I am at home with you." The spirit of her uncle Al had begged Mrs. Jones's forgiveness for wrongs he had done her as a child. "Say you forgive me, sweetheart," he had said, "then open that window and let my spirit fly free." Mrs. Jones had said aloud to him in her kitchen: "If you say so, I forgive you, Uncle Al, but you were always kind to me." Then she had opened the window, and felt a great whoosh of air, and the next morning there was a big crow on the branch outside fixing her with its yellow eye. Mrs. Jones threw bread crusts out to it for several days, remembering how Uncle Al always brought her treats, and then one morning it made a strange triple caw that sounded exactly like "Bye, sweetheart," looked her straight in the eye, and flew off for good.

Tonight and tomorrow would be my last nights in this room of my childhood, and the room seemed to feel this because it wasn't being unfriendly anymore. Its wistful sadness was like that of a friend who knows you've outgrown the friendship and need to move on.

VIII.

After breakfast Monday morning Flora checked over our list for Grove Market.

"Would you like to call it in, Helen?"

"Not really."

I wished I'd said yes as soon as she began speaking to the person on the other end, who could not have been grouchy Mr. Crump because he would never have put up with such dalliance. Why couldn't she just coolly read off the list, with pauses to let the other person write things down?

"What, no fresh corn? We would have corn by now in Alabama. But then we planted our garden very early down there: corn, okra, spinach, peas, runner beans. I guess you wouldn't have any okra this early either. No, I thought not. Too bad, we'll have to do with canned corn, then. And does your meat market have something called chipped beef? Oh, in jars. How big are the jars? Maybe two jars then. And remember now, this all goes on Mr. Anstruther's tab, he's away doing important war work over in Oak Ridge, Tennessee. We're going to be ordering whenever we need something, is that all right? He doesn't want my little cousin to go into public places because of this polio outbreak. Oh, and two quarts of milk for my cousin, she's still growing—wait, let me see if she wants anything else. Helen, can you think of anything else?"

I had gone beyond embarrassment. "Maybe some candy."

"What kind?"

"Clark bars."

"How many?"

"Five," I risked.

"Five Clark bars," Flora relayed without batting an eye. "And can you tell us approximately when your delivery person will be coming? Not that we expect to be going anywhere! And you ought to know our driveway is a tiny bit rough."

Our big event of the morning was the walk down our tiny-bit-rough driveway to fetch the mail. Flora had two letters, I had nothing. She kissed the handwritten envelope ("Dear Juliet, at least somebody loves me!") but ripped open the typewritten one first, scanned the contents, and began to cry.

"What?" I said.

"I expected it. But still—"

"What?"

"They said no, and it was my first choice." Bravely she replaced the letter in its envelope and scrubbed her eyes with her fists like a child. "They *say* it's because I don't drive. The thing is, someone offered to drive me to that interview, but it would have been in a truck and I thought I'd make a better impression if I arrived alone on the bus. It was this darling little school in the middle of a field. Fifteen sixth graders. I could have handled it real well."

"But you had three interviews, so you still have two more chances."

"I wonder if I had told a lie about the driving— I could

have learned to drive later. But this was probably their way of letting me off nicely. If I had said I could drive they would have had to have come up with some other excuse for not wanting me."

"You have to start thinking better of yourself, Flora."

"That's exactly what Mrs. Anstruther said in her letters."

"Well, it's true. Others judge you at your own estimation."

"Her exact words! You're so lucky to have had her, Helen. I'm such a mess. Not like your mother. Nobody had to tell Lisbeth to think better of herself. Maybe you have to be born with it. Were you born with it? I don't know. But, being her daughter, your chances are better than mine."

"Who cares whether you were born with it?" I asked. Yet Flora had set misgivings buzzing in my head. "You have to at least *act* like you have it."

"That's just what your grandmother would have said!" crowed Flora, almost knocking me down with a hug.

Father McFall telephoned to report that Brian was "holding his own" in the hospital and that he had conveyed my message. Annoyingly he kept skirting around my questions about Brian's condition. "But I'm still hoping to drop by and visit with you and your cousin this week." He offered it like a consolation prize for not telling me anything I wanted to know.

"My father said we can't have any visitors. He said we can't even go to church." I was glad to be able to punish Father McFall in this small way.

The phone again. This time it was Annie Rickets, my favorite acid-tongued little friend. "Can you talk?"

"Sort of."

"Is she around?"

"Upstairs in her room."

"The dear old Willing Fanny room."

"Oh, Annie, I've missed you."

"You're going to miss me a lot more."

"What do you mean?"

"Just joking. How is it going with her?"

"Okay, I guess."

"Except for—?"

I lowered my voice: "Kind of naïve. *Huge* inferiority complex. Not that we'll be going anywhere for people to notice. My father has quarantined us to the house. Did you hear about Brian?"

"I heard he was pretty bad. His acting career's probably over, unless he does wheelchair parts. But at least he's not in an iron lung like that little girl. So how was your week with the high-living Huffs? Did you get lots of *swimming* in?"

"I'd have gotten in a lot more if I'd known the summer was going to turn out like this."

"I heard a really odd rumor about him."

"Who?"

"Mr. Huff. Some people think he doesn't exist."

"That's crazy. He's always sending packages."

"You can send packages to yourself."

Though I knew Annie's best rumors originated inside her own fiendishly inventive head, that didn't make them any less appealing. They always had a rightness about them, like the rightness of what ought to happen next in a good story. "I don't suppose you're going to tell me where you heard this rumor," I said, and waited for her usual answer.

"Well, when you've got not one but two parents working for the phone company, you hear a lot. You can listen in on anything if you have the right equipment. Which brings me to my exciting news. We're being transferred."

"Wait a minute. Is this some more of that joke?"

"What joke?"

"What you said a few minutes ago about how I was going to miss you, but then you said you were joking."

"It's no joke. I just wasn't ready to tell you yet. They're moving us to this boring little town in the flatlands. Daddy will be regional manager and make lots more money and Mammy will stay home with us. She'll probably die of resentment and boredom or kill us first, I haven't decided which yet."

"When?"

"Daddy's already down there looking for a house. We're supposed to move in three weeks. They're paying for the Mayflower van and we don't even have to pack up our own stuff. My rotten little sisters will share a bedroom in the new house and I'll get one all to myself."

"You sound awfully pleased." Two out of three friends cut down in two days. I was on a losing streak, like Flora with her jobs. Only she still had two out of three left.

"You can come visit. It's only a bus ride down the mountain. You'll be able to stay over at my house for a change. Maybe I'll give my room a name like the rooms at your house."

Then she ruined everything. "But the truth is, and we're both smart enough to know it, Helen, we'll probably never see each other again."

SLOWLY IT CREAKED into afternoon and I was beginning to see how the whole summer was going to be. Meals and Flora.

Flora and meals. We couldn't go anywhere and nobody could come to us. To escape Flora, who was already preparing supper, though we had hardly finished with lunch, I had gone to the garage to sit in Nonie's car. I had been waiting very quietly, trying to summon back the voice from yesterday, when a motorcycle roar shattered the stillness. I slammed out of the garage in time to see it buck over the crowning bump of our hill. It was a three-wheeled affair with a storage trunk behind. A skinny man with pointy features and close-cropped bright orange hair dismounted, mouthing my father's worst obscenity. But when he spotted me, he quickly socialized his face and called, "You folks have one holy terror of a driveway." He wore khakis, the pants stuffed inside high lace-up boots.

"We're having it seen to, now that the war is over," I said haughtily.

"Well, it is and it isn't."

"What?"

"The war. We still have the Japs to beat." He looked past me into the open garage. "Oldsmobile Tudor touring car. Nineteen thirty-three."

"How do you know that?"

"I worked on cars like this before I joined up. My name is Finn. I'm your grocery deliverer. One thousand Sunset Drive. Sounds like a movie."

I started to shake hands but remembered my father's warnings. This person had been all over town delivering groceries. "My name is Helen Anstruther," I said.

"The one who likes the Clark bars."

"How did you know that?"

"I heard her ask you when I was taking your order. I fancy them myself."

He wasn't a foreigner, but he wasn't a local either. His speech was different. On his sleeve there was a patch with an eagle's head.

"Were you in the war?"

"I was, I was. I was supposed to jump on D-Day but I got sick in England and they had to ship me back to the military hospital here."

"It must have been your lungs then."

"Now how did *you* know *that*?"

"It's their specialty. My grandfather helped them start that hospital. He was a doctor. This house used to be his convalescent home where people could finish recovering from lung problems. Or sometimes mental problems."

His high-pitched laugh resembled a cry of pain. "The perfect place for me."

"How do you mean?"

"I had a collapsed lung and then later came the mental problems."

Then here came Flora flying out of the house, apologizing for having been upstairs, as if her presence were required before any two people could start an interesting conversation, apologizing for "our" driveway, and oh, what a cute machine, but such a hot day to be outside riding around bareheaded.

"This is Finn, who'll be delivering our groceries," I cut her off. I introduced her simply as Flora, leaving off the cousin part.

Flora plunged into a handshake, all polio warnings forgotten, and said she hoped we hadn't weighed him down by ordering too much, we would try not to order too often.

"Oh, I have people who order every single day," said Finn.

"My goodness, every day?" exclaimed Flora, sounding foolishly impressed.

"Many of our customers don't have refrigeration."

"We didn't have refrigeration back in Alabama when I was growing up," Flora eagerly volunteered. "Just this one little icebox in the cellar with a block of ice. The iceman brought us a new block twice a week."

Shut up, I was thinking, but Finn only smiled at her. "I've got this one lady," he said, "who doesn't hesitate to phone the store whenever she remembers something she forgot."

"She must be a rich lady," I said sarcastically.

"Ah, no," he said. "She's a lonely old lady who's losing her memory. But I always fit her in. It's no trouble at all." (He sweetly pronounced it "a-*tall*.") He seemed like a kind, good-humored person, if a little odd-looking. It was certainly kind of him to pretend not to notice what a fool Flora was.

Somehow we got the grocery bags into the kitchen without her embarrassing me again, though she did keep calling me her little cousin and had started up again about the okra. I made sure Finn got a good look at our Frigidaire, which was more up-to-date than anything else in the house. This was not Flora's Alabama. It would have been interesting to hear about his collapsed lung and even more about the mental problems, but I needed to get him away before he started dreading his future deliveries to these two isolated females at the top of their holy terror drive.

"WHY DO WE always have to eat at six?" I asked Flora, when she started rolling out her biscuit dough.

"Because that's when people eat."

"We never used to eat at six. We ate at all different times. My father and Nonie had to have their cocktails first."

"Well, you and I don't have any cocktails." She looked very proud of her clever reply.

"But it's still afternoon outside."

"Go outside then. I'll call you when it's ready."

"Did that Negro maid make biscuits every day *back in Alabama*?"

"I've told you, Juliet isn't a maid. She's part owner of our house."

"That's the stupidest thing I ever heard."

"Well, it's true. Many a time she's had to make the whole mortgage payment by herself. When Uncle Sam dies, it'll be all hers."

"What about you?"

"What about me?"

"Aren't you your uncle's next of kin?"

"I'll have a job teaching by then. I can make a down payment on my own place if I want one. I might even be married."

"Married?"

"Don't look so surprised. So far, two people have asked me."

"What was wrong with them?"

"Why should anything be wrong with them? Because they wanted me?"

"No, no! I just meant—"

"I know, honey. I was teasing. One was a lawyer. The other owned a farm. He's the one who offered to drive me to that interview in his truck. Maybe I'd have done better to let him. The subject of my not driving might never have come up."

"What about the lawyer?"

"He was too old, for one thing—he had two grown children. I worked for him one summer and he was very nice to me. But I wasn't really attracted to him." She giggled. "He had little hairs growing out of his ears."

I recalled the hairs growing out of my father's ears. Rachel Huff's mother had told her that with Nonie gone my father would probably want to marry again.

During supper, I thought about Finn, but kept him to myself. Then Flora said brightly, "I hope we didn't go against your father's wishes by letting that nice delivery boy carry our groceries in. Do you think we did?"

"Did what?"

"Go against your father's wishes. But your cleaning woman is coming tomorrow, isn't she? Mrs. Jones. *She* must have been going in and out of all sorts of public places, too. We can't be expected to live completely in a vacuum, can we?"

"We're doing a pretty good job, if you ask me."

IX.

Mrs. Jones arrived at nine on Tuesdays, bringing back the clean sheets and towels she had dropped off at the linen service the week before. She had been cleaning this house for thirty years. She remembered the doctor in his final years, and my father as a teenager before his polio. She remembered the Recoverers and she remembered my mother and she remembered me before I could remember myself. Her own little Rosemary had been alive when Mrs. Jones started coming to our house. She still brought her lunch in Rosemary's old school lunch box, a thermos of hot tea (which she said kept her warm in winter and cool in summer), and her own table-model radio, which she carried under her arm and plugged into the wall sockets of the different upstairs rooms as she went about her work. Starting with the kitchen, she did the downstairs rooms in the morning. She didn't like to be talked to when she was scrubbing the kitchen floor because she said being on her knees and the rhythm of the arm motions made it the ideal time for going over her life. She didn't play the radio in the morning, radio was for the afternoon upstairs. *Guiding Light* and *All My Children* were for the Willow Fanning room; then a silent break for the Willow

Fanning half bath and the front upstairs bathroom (she considered tiled floors with their proximity to water unsafe for plugged-in devices); then on to *Ma Perkins* and *Pepper Young's Family* in the Hyman Highsmith room; then *Stella Dallas* and *Lorenzo Jones* for the two nameless Recoverers' rooms, whose guests had been more forgettable, except for the one who had let us down. *When a Girl Marries* was for my grandfather's consultation room, and she finished her day with *Portia Faces Life* in his half bath, which had a wood floor.

"I admire that woman," Nonie said. "Despite all her adversities, Beryl Jones manages to stay in control of her days. How many people do you know who can do that?"

On this Tuesday, Flora took it on herself to welcome Mrs. Jones to the house. "I'm Helen's first cousin once removed. Her mother and I grew up together in Alabama. Sometimes she was like my big sister and sometimes she was like a little mother. Did I meet you at the funeral reception, Mrs. Jones?"

"No, ma'am, I wasn't able to make the reception."

"Oh, please, call me Flora. And whatever I can do to help you, just let me know. I'm Helen's caretaker for the summer while her father's away, but I've got plenty of free time for housework."

"Oh, my routine more or less runs me," said Mrs. Jones. "I would get all turned around if someone was to try to help. I do the downstairs in the morning, and then if it's warm like today I eat my lunch upstairs on the south porch, and in the afternoon I turn out the upstairs rooms."

"Well," said Flora, "in that case, I guess I'll go up and work on some lesson plans. I start teaching school in the fall. I'm in the Willow Fanning room."

"Yes, ma'am, I know. I do that room first, after I've swept the upstairs porches."

"Well, don't worry, I'll make myself scarce. I have some shelf reorganizing I want to do in the kitchen. But I already went and stripped my bed for you."

"That was thoughtful, but there was no need."

I lurked about while Mrs. Jones scrubbed the kitchen floor on her knees and went over her life. I tried some more of my library book, but my own life seemed more urgent and mysterious than the girl researching someone else's old house. I walked around our house, forcing myself to acknowledge more signs of decay, and fantasized that we would somehow come into money and make everything nice again. I heard my father forbidding me to risk becoming a woman with the shrunken legs of a child, and pictured Brian Beale's ten-year-old legs withering this very minute beneath the covers of his hospital bed. I knew I should be writing a note to him in time for postman to take it away, but couldn't make myself do it. I thought of Finn, with his pointy features and carrot crew cut, rushing over to the lonely old lady on his motorcycle whenever she remembered something she'd forgotten to order. He'd roar up in front of her modest little house that didn't have a refrigerator and tell her it was no trouble "a-*tall*." I prepared some interesting things I would say to him next time—if I could get them in before Flora interrupted and brought things down to her level.

I materialized when I heard Mrs. Jones starting on my grandmother's room.

"I can still feel her in here," said Mrs. Jones, holding her feather duster aloft in front of the blinds like a conductor raising his baton.

"I had this dream." I got right to the point. "She told me she wanted me to move into this room. She said you would understand."

Mrs. Jones clasped the duster to her breast. "She mentioned me?"

"She said, 'Mrs. Jones respects dreams and is partial to the supernatural.' Those were her exact words."

"Dear me if that doesn't sound just like her. The dead can speak to you anytime they like, whether you're awake or asleep. Whether you listen or not is up to you."

"She said I was to ask you to make up her room for me."

"Did she say we should empty out drawers, or what?"

I considered a moment. "No, just make up the bed. I'll go through her things myself."

"That's what I did with Rosemary's things. I went through them a little at a time and let them bring her back."

"You know, I think I am growing up," I said.

"Well, surely you are." Mrs. Jones had laid aside her duster and started on the bed, as though being guided by Nonie.

"No, I mean I'm understanding things this summer that I couldn't understand even this past winter."

"Like what, dear?"

"Well, like Rosemary's diphtheria and my mother's parents in the flu epidemic, all in the same year. Before, I just couldn't get my mind around it. Your seven-year-old daughter and those people from such a long time ago. It was the same year, 1918, but I just couldn't see how they could all fit into that same time period."

"That's the thing about the dead," observed Mrs. Jones happily, lifting up the mattress pad and giving it a vigorous shake. "They make you understand that time isn't as simple as you thought."

She let me help make up the bed. "It's the right thing that you should have this room," she said. "You're the lady of the house now."

"But I'm not going to tell Flora about the dream." Here I had to remind myself that Nonie had considered the whole truth too much even for Mrs. Jones. Even I had almost forgotten that Nonie's voice in the garage told me to say the instructions came to me in a dream.

"Well, that's up to you, dear."

"Flora is very—" I hovered between wanting to betray and wanting to appear loyal. "I'm not sure she'd be able to understand. I'm just going to tell her moving in here was something I decided to do and leave it at that."

"Well, like I said," Mrs. Jones reiterated, "you're the lady of the house now."

AT SUPPER I let Flora go on about all she'd accomplished while Mrs. Jones had been cleaning the house. In the morning she'd answered Juliet Parker's letter and walked it down to the box just in time for the mailman, which made me feel guilty because I hadn't written my note to Brian. Then she'd worked up some fifth-grade geography lesson plans and created a behavior chart for her class: "You know: neatness, courtesy, self-control, so they'll know what I expect from them."

In the afternoon she had reorganized the cupboard shelves and the refrigerator. "I kept thinking how that nice delivery boy said so many people still don't have them and I felt positively luxurious."

"His name is Finn."

"Is that his first name or his last?"

"He just said Finn. He was in the war until his lung collapsed, so he's not exactly a boy anymore."

"You two really had a conversation, didn't you? I heard you

talking a lot with Mrs. Jones, too. You miss your friends, don't you, honey?"

"Mrs. Jones was helping me move into my grandmother's room."

"Oh, well, goodness, that's a change." I could see she was taken aback.

"It's something I decided to do," I said. I quoted the voice in the garage: "It was her place and now it will be my place."

"It certainly is a nice big room," said Flora, "if you're sure it won't make you sad."

"I'm sad already, so I might as well be sad in there."

I COULD HARDLY wait to go to bed that night, but there were amenities to be gotten through first. Flora said I wasn't getting enough exercise for a young person, so after supper while it was still quite light we pitched into the rutty driveway, giggling and steadying each other, and walked down to the hairpin curve on Sunset Drive where the thick woods sloped off to the right and my grandfather's shortcut reproached us with its unsightly neglect. "Wouldn't it be great if we could *repair* the path, somehow," said Flora, "and surprise your father when he gets back. Only I wouldn't know where to begin, would you?"

"You'd have to cut down *years* of overgrowth," I said. "It would take really serious tools. And the handrails are all rotted, they're dangerous even to touch. And someone could fall into that crater and be badly hurt. It would have to be filled in and for that you'd need to get dirt from somewhere." I was sounding like the adult, talking the child out of an impractical idea.

Tuesday evening there was a mystery program Nonie and I liked, and Flora and I sat curled on the sofa with our shoes off, listening to the cabinet radio with the big speakers. We agreed not to turn on lamps so we could be more scared. This one was about a little girl who gets separated from her mother in a department store. They look and look for her, the store detective, the manager, the police, but she just isn't anywhere to be found, and night comes and the store has to close, and the distraught mother lets herself be convinced that the girl wandered out of the store and the police will have to continue an all-night search through the town. But the little girl has fallen asleep behind some crates in a stockroom and when she wakes up she's at first frightened because her mother is gone, but then all these nice, elegant, well-dressed people, even some well-dressed children, come out from the shadows of the department store and befriend her. By the time daylight comes, she has decided to accept their offer to become one of them because they have convinced her it's a better world. In their world, they tell her, she can never get lost or feel abandoned again.

"Oh, God," cried Flora, wriggling and hugging herself in the gloom, "I knew that was going to happen! I just knew it."

In the final scene the mother comes back to the store with the police next morning. And in the children's department, she sees a group of child mannequins and one of them resembles her daughter so much she goes into hysterics. But the police and the manager soothe her and assure her they will find her little girl before the day is over.

"Look at my arms," said Flora, rubbing them up and down. "They've got goose bumps. Oh, honey, I hope this won't give you bad dreams."

The program made my heart long for Nonie. There were things about it to discuss that she would be so good at. But I would have to wait until bedtime to figure out what those things were.

X.

The way my days registered seemed to change after I moved into Nonie's room. Events stopped marching forward in a straight, unselective procession and began clustering themselves into bunches, according to mood and subject matter. There were the things Flora said and did that slowly compiled a picture of what I could expect from her. There were my retreats into the sanctuary of my new room, where I seemed to merge with Nonie and came out thinking and speaking more like her. Was this shift in perceptions something my memory has imposed? Well, what is anybody's memory but another narrative form?

The shift may have begun that morning, when I told Mrs. Jones I was growing up because I could now understand how her little Rosemary and my mother's parents could have died in the same year.

Lying in Nonie's high, roomy bed, freshly made up for my occupancy, I felt it was inviting me to stretch my legs and arms into its extra adult space and to observe life from a larger field of vision.

I was still thinking about the radio program. Flora had

ingested the story at its obvious level of horror and gone to bed triumphantly caressing her goose bumps and worrying that the story would give me bad dreams. For Flora, the little girl had been turned into a mannequin, the mother saw the resemblance and went to pieces, but the policemen talked her around to believing the child was still out there in the real world and that was the end of the scary program. But there were scarier levels of the story that could exist within the bounds of the everyday world. That's what Nonie was good at: digging down to those levels. Though she was a skeptic and had nourished such leanings in me, she was a skeptic with great regard for the suggestive powers of the imagination. That is why she could tolerate Mrs. Jones's respect for the supernatural and allow me to listen to the stories about little dead Rosemary and the uncle once I had assured her that I did not take the ghosts literally.

If Nonie had listened to the program about the little girl, she would have enjoyed the scariness as much as anyone, but she would have seen into other aspects that were just as scary.

"Don't you wonder, Helen," she might have mused, if she had been lying next to me, "what would have happened if the little girl had *turned down* the mannequins' offer? After all, they didn't force her, they didn't just high-handedly turn her into one of themselves, did they? They gave her a choice and she chose to go back with them to a place where you can never get lost or feel abandoned again. Does such a place exist, do you think? And if it doesn't exist, what options did she have other than to stop being human?"

FLORA'S BOX OF clothes, sent by the ever-faithful Juliet Parker, arrived. As I watched her unpack her summer wardrobe with little yips of recognition, I felt she was filling our house with more inferior stuff from Alabama. When the garments were all laid out on her bed in the Willow Fanning room, I realized that I had already seen her most presentable things: the suit she was wearing when she stepped off the train, the blue dress she had worn at Nonie's funeral, and even the few changes of clothes she had allowed herself in the luggage crammed with the Alabama foodstuffs so I would have "proper meals" for the first weekend.

Then the contents of the box had to be ironed, with Flora's commentaries.

"This skirt came from an old dress of your mother's, Helen. I loved that dress on her. She gave it to me when she got tired of it, she always got tired of her favorite things, but when I got old enough to wear it my bustline was way bigger than hers, so Juliet cut off the top and made it into a skirt. Now, *this* skirt I made myself. It isn't very successful, but I think it will be fine just around the house, don't you?"

"Where else are we going to be but just around the house?"

Though nobody was forcing me to hang around for Flora's ironing and chattering, I felt a perverse compulsion to watch the room become adulterated with her belongings. I had always known this front upstairs room in its uninhabited state, kept bare of anyone's personal clutter, except for that of the occasional overnight guest. Who knew what possessions had surrounded the perfidious Willow Fanning, what flimsy or "not very successful" garments had to be whisked away from what surfaces before my sixteen-year-old father could recline upon them and continue falling in love with a woman twice his age? Nonie's stories of those last days of Anstruther's Lodge had been grim narratives of denouement and summing up; there was no place in them for asides about what anybody wore.

("So there we all were, going on with our routines, in the summer of 1916. Your father was and always will be the age of the century. I was the majordomo of the operation, as by then we could afford a cook and a cleaning woman for our patients, which we called the Recoverers. In Doctor Cam's first establishment we could take up to ten Recoverers, but when we moved up here to one thousand Sunset Drive we never had more than four; we didn't need to by then, they were so well paying. They had graduated from whatever sanatorium they'd come here for in the first place, which is to say they were officially mended in lungs or mind or destructive habits, but weren't yet ready or willing to go back to where they came from. Some of them ended up staying for years.

"A majordomo? Well, she's kind of a combined butler and housekeeper. She organizes the household, sees what needs attending to or repaired and finds the proper person to do it, though I always kept the accounts myself and ordered the food and picked up people at the train station. Your grandfather never learned to drive an automobile, which I always thought was a shame; he looked so elegant driving a horse and buggy.

"He had struck up a friendship with one of the longer-staying Recoverers, Hyman Highsmith—we called him High—who had briefly studied medicine in Vienna before he was called home to Georgia to run his family's button factory. He and Doctor Cam were roughly the same age and they were fascinated by this new field called 'psychiatry.' High ordered every book on the subject he could find, regardless of price, and whenever time permitted your grandfather would go away with him to lectures and seminars.

"When your father ran off with Willow Fanning, who had been with us a year and a half by then, your grandfather and

High had gone by train to New York to hear someone who had been hypnotized and cured by Freud. I was left with one other guest, a sweet recovering inebriate named Starling Peake, and the cook, and Beryl Jones. But by the time your grandfather and I brought Harry home from the hospital after his polio, Starling and the cook had fled because of the polio, and then your grandfather had his stroke and that was the end of Anstruther's Lodge and the Recoverers. Only Beryl Jones stayed on, bless her. Let's see, her Rosemary would have been five at the time. Poor little Rosemary. Poor all of us, really.")

Flora was ironing barefooted. Her habit of going without shoes in the house I found somewhat obscene because her feet were childishly shapeless and uncared-for. I thought of Nonie's visits to her chiropodist to have her long, narrow feet soaked and sanded and the corns on the knobbly joints shaved away and her almond-shaped toenails blunt-cut and buffed to a high pink sheen, though nobody was going to see them but us. I would wait in the reception room, leafing through the latest issues of ladies' magazines with their mailing labels addressed to the chiropodist's office. If there were other women waiting I surreptitiously examined their shoes and, on lucky occasions, their feet, some of which were beautiful and others grotesque. I would share my findings with Nonie as we drove home, and in turn she would report what the chiropodist had said about her feet. He once told her she had "haughty toenails," which had made her laugh, but I could tell she was pleased.

Flora's toenails were the opposite of haughty. They turned up like they were making too much effort to be friendly. This led me to wonder about my mother's feet, which I had no memory of ever seeing. I was sure they had been different from Flora's, just as her "bustline" had been different.

After the ironing board was put away and the motley assortment of Alabama clothes hung in the closet, it was time for Flora's two predictable questions: "What do you think you could eat for supper?" (as though cajoling a languishing invalid with a picky appetite) and then, when that had been decided, her infuriating follow-up: "So, Helen, what are your plans for the day?"

"How can a person have plans when there's nothing to do?"

"What did you do before?"

"Before *what*?"

"Well, before I was here."

It was just amazing how she walked into these traps over and over again.

"Before you were here I was at Rachel Huff's and they had a pool. And before that, I was still in school. And before *that* . . ." I paused before delivering my coup de grâce—"my grandmother was still here."

Flora seemed about to bestow her gift of tears, but then actually said something new. "You've had such a strange childhood. I keep forgetting. You were with her so much. She was like your best friend. Tell me what kind of things the two of you did together."

Now it was my turn to feel my eyes tear up. "We drove around, we went to movies, we went to her doctors, we shopped."

"How about when you were here in the house?"

"We talked. Or she would go to her room and replenish herself and I would read or do homework. And then when she was rested we would talk some more."

"You didn't go out to play?"

"Around here there was nobody to play with."

"Well, don't children have little imaginary friends?"

"Did you have little imaginary friends?"

"It was different with me, with us, I mean, when your mother was still living at home. We had to help out. Lisbeth got the worst of it because she was older. I told you how she had to take care of our grandmother—"

"Yes, the bedpans. We don't need to go into *that* again."

"Well, I'm just saying. There wasn't time for us to have imaginary friends. And even with the big difference in our ages, we had each other."

"I'm going for a walk," I said.

"Want me to go with you?"

"No. I'm going out to look for an imaginary friend."

"Well in that case," Flora said, my sarcasm seeming to wash right over her, "I think I'll sit on my porch and write some letters and work on my lesson plans. What a luxury, to have a porch right outside your bedroom."

XI.

Nobody until Flora had called my childhood strange. Even Annie Rickets had never implied that. And what right had Flora of all people, dumped in her infancy by a runaway mother, growing up in a house partly owned by the maid, to pronounce on what was strange? Every time she opened her mouth about the Alabama life she had shared with my mother, out came something I wished I hadn't heard. If, according to Flora, my mother always got tired of her favorite clothes and her favorite things, what would have happened to me if she had lived? That is, if I had been among her favorite things. Which would have been worse? Never to have been a favorite or to become an ex-favorite, cut in half and passed on to someone left behind?

As I crept down our treacherous driveway in my blue Keds, I tried not to feel terrible about hurting Mrs. Huff's feelings. I also wished I could recall a time I had walked down this driveway with somebody other than Flora. Our two recent walks had somehow turned it into a Flora thing, displacing better walks, walks with Nonie to the mailbox, or possibly even further back, with my mother when I was two or three. Did my mother ever hope for any mail? For years Flora's letters had lurked in our mailbox, her young, indiscreet letters that Nonie had destroyed after reading. Before that, Flora had probably written to my mother, saying how she missed her, splashing adolescent tears on the stationery. It was sickening to think of the younger Flora's fat envelopes arriving year after year, biding their time until she had outlived both Lisbeth and Nonie. Now she was in our house, awaiting envelopes addressed to herself in our box, hanging her clothes in our closets, the awful truncated dress being the worst: the upper half of my mother cut away because Flora's "bustline" was way too big. Lisbeth, in her few unsmiling photos, was wand-thin and had no bust to speak of, but now I worried which way I would go. Would I soon be pooching out in front like Flora? So far, my chest was flat, but one of Annie Rickets's boobies, as she called them, had risen under the nipple like an insect bite. "What if the other one never pops out?" she had said and laughed. "Do you reckon they'll put me in the circus?"

Though I knew it was too early (Old One Thousand was last on the postman's route), I checked the mailbox. A black ant inside sped off in a snit. Maybe later today there would be a letter from my father. ("Hope I wasn't too fierce about the quarantine, Helen, but I want you to grow up to be a beautiful girl with nice straight legs . . .")

Though *beautiful* was not a word my father used about people. He liked his compliments to have room for reservations. Flora had become a "looker," he'd said, "but certainly not in your mother's style." Did he think I was becoming a looker, which, when he said it, carried a faint whiff of vulgarity, or was I developing in my mother's style—which was what? Mrs. Huff, a commenter on everybody's looks, was always telling Rachel if she would hold herself like me she would convey "a certain something." Conveying a certain something sounded more like the style my father would approve of, but it didn't mean you were good-looking. Mrs. Huff had also said, "You take after your grandmother," and Annie Rickets had said my grandmother looked like a mastiff driving a car. Brian Beale, during his asking-for-my-hand proclamations, regarded me with complacent possessiveness, but had never actually mentioned looks. (It was painful to think of him, especially since I still hadn't written any letter.) "That certainly suits you," Nonie would say in the store. "It's very pretty on her," the saleswoman would chime in. "It's *smart*," Nonie would emend. "It's *elegant*." When one front tooth came in sticking out a little, the dentist said, "If Helen can get in the habit of pressing her finger against that tooth when she's reading or studying, we can most probably avoid braces." A year later he pronounced that our tactic was working and that "my beauty" would not be compromised. But he said it in a jocular way.

How would my father describe me to someone? ("Yes, I have a daughter, Helen; she's going on eleven. She's—") For instance, to his roommate, Harker, the master welder, at Oak Ridge. But the roommate was deaf and laughed at everything my father said.

I had no plan for my walk. Walking was not something I normally did. None of us walked, really. The main reason I was doing it was to escape from Flora and get some of myself back. I headed downhill because that was the way we always headed in the car. The other way, uphill, soon turned into unpaved road through forest being thinned but still undeveloped, a road mostly used by loggers, which eventually joined up with a county highway on top of the ridge.

But I was not getting myself back. To the contrary, I felt

myself slipping away. A veil seemed to rip and through it I could see Sunset Drive going on exactly the same without my needing to exist. This thought made me queasy.

What would happen if I didn't return? Flora would slide and scuttle down the driveway, yipping at the ruts, until at last she would come upon me, standing like a statue on Sunset Drive. "There you are, Helen! I was beginning to get *worried.*" And then she would come closer and see that my eyes were blank, like a statue's. There would still be my features, but my life spirit would have departed. I'd be like the little girl who turned into a mannequin.

Then I was so close to the rip in the veil that I was more on the other side of it than I was in myself. It was like being conscious of losing my mind at the exact moment I was losing it. I reeled and felt faint. I couldn't even find words to think about what was happening to me.

Move over in the shade, darling. You still know what the shade is, don't you? That's right. Now sit down on the ground and let everything go.

There was a back-and-forth shushing of leaves, like a broom tenderly sweeping a floor. I was able to hear the tender sweeping without needing to know if I existed. Then a loud roar drowned out the gentle shush and there were footsteps and someone said, "Hello, hello? Is anyone there?"

Finn's boots creaked as he squatted down in front of me. A strong, sweaty smell came from him. His narrowed green eyes scrutinized me with concern. Parked across the road was his three-wheeled motorcycle with its storage trunk.

"We didn't order anything," I said.

"You didn't, no, but I was bringing you something anyway. What the bejesus were you doing?"

"I was just . . ." I started pushing myself up from the ground. His strong hands hauled me the rest of the way.

"When I came around that curve, you didn't look up or move a muscle. You were like a catatonic."

"A what?"

"Someone who's been shocked so bad they sit staring at nothing all day. I've seen soldiers like that."

"I was just thinking, is all."

"And were they productive, your thoughts?"

He was smiling now, the skin around his eyes had little crinkles, and it struck me how sadly timed things could be. Here I had been planning for days what I would say to him when he came again and wishing Flora and I would run out of things so we'd have to order again. But just now I was trying to hold on to the voice that had spoken of shade and called me darling, and the scary thing that had preceded that, the horror of losing myself, which was already fading. And here he was, actually asking me about my thoughts, which nobody had bothered to do since Nonie. But as they were not thoughts I could tell anyone, I made up something.

"I was thinking about my grandfather's path through the woods—it's just down there. He had a shortcut made for his patients so they could walk to the village without having to go round and round on the road. Only we didn't call them patients, we called them our Recoverers. And I was thinking whether we could repair it to surprise my father when he came home, but it's all grown over and there's this dangerous crater right at the beginning. We would probably need a tractor or something to fill it in."

"Will we go and take a look at it?"

It was a strange way of putting it, like he was consulting the future.

"Don't you have to deliver people's groceries?"

"Like I said, I was bringing you something."

"Me?"

"Well, the both of you. I found some okra."

"Okra?" I repeated stupidly.

"She was so disappointed when we didn't have it the other day."

"They grow it down in Alabama," I explained, wanting to encourage him to keep our families separate. "That's where Flora comes from."

"Ah, Flora." He sounded relieved to have been supplied with the name. "They must grow it up here, too, because they were selling the first crop at the farmers' market this morning."

"I could show you the shortcut," I said. "It's just down there, around the curve. But it's awfully rough in there, so we'll have to be real careful."

"Well, you lead the way . . . em, how do you like to be called?"

"Just Helen. I don't have a nickname." Too late it came to me that he hadn't remembered my name, either, and was trying to get around it. "What do *you* like to be called?" At least I had not said his name.

"Finn is fine. It was all last names in the Army and I'm used to it. My birth name is Devlin. Devlin Patrick. Devlin was my mother's brother who died and Patrick was the saint. There are slews of Patricks in Ireland."

"Are you Irish?"

"Born Irish, but I'm an American citizen now. How else would I be wearing U.S. Army Parachute Infantry boots? My father's cousin adopted me when I was ten. They were Finns who'd settled in Albany, New York, and did well for themselves."

"Did your parents die?"

"No, but they had five kids and no money, and my father's cousin and his wife had money but no kids, and they asked if they could have one of us boys."

"You mean your parents sold you?"

"It wasn't a term anyone used, but there were benefits to both sides."

"But how did *you* feel about it?"

"Oh, I was thrilled to be the one chosen. I couldn't wait. Everyone wants to go to America."

We scuffed on downhill toward my grandfather's shortcut, Finn half-smiling at his parachute infantry boots and probably remembering things while I imagined what I would feel if my father suddenly said, "Helen, I've got a proposition. How would you like to go to America and live with ———?" But I was already in America, where everyone wanted to go, and the only cousin I had was Flora—and my father was paying her to live with me.

"You were ten, like I am," I said. "Though I'm going to be eleven in August. Didn't you miss your *house* in Ireland?"

He laughed his high-pitched laugh that sounded like a cry being squeezed out of him. "What house? My brother and I shared a room with my father in town, and the girls, who were still little, stayed with my mum and her people in the country."

"Didn't you miss your brother? Was he jealous when he didn't get chosen?"

"Ah, that's another story," he said, looking suddenly unhappy, "and that's enough about me."

When we got to the hairpin curve I told him about the ruffians who came from the other side to shoot out the streetlight and he fell into the same trap I had with Nonie. "Why didn't they stay on their side of town and shoot out their own streetlights?" he asked. "Because," I said wryly, "they already *have*," making him laugh.

"Remember it's all grown over," I warned, when we were at the entrance of the shortcut. "Don't expect to see a path or anything. And just a little way in, there's this horrible crater. I should probably go first."

"I see the path, it begins here," he said, diving ahead of me into the brush, "then it follows that old fallen railing and down there it dips out of sight."

"Watch out for that crater. Flora couldn't see anything when I brought her here."

"That's because she didn't spend two years of her life studying the ground and learning how to use it to keep yourself alive."

I followed behind his fast-moving boots, wondering what it would be like to be a boy.

"Now your grandfather," he called back, "why was it he built the shortcut?"

"So the Recoverers could walk straight down the mountain to the stores without having to walk miles of extra circles on the road."

"The Recoverers were the patients?"

"Well, they weren't really patients anymore. They had finished with their treatments at other places in town, like Craggy Bluff, if they were inebriates—"

"Now that is a lovely word I haven't heard for a while: inebriates."

"—Or if they had had TB they would have been at Ashland Park, or, if they had TB and money, up at Highmount. And if they had mental problems, they would have been treated at Appalachian Hill. When they came to us they were pretty much recovered, but they still weren't ready to go back to where they came from."

"Like me." He laughed. "Did you know any of these Recoverers?"

"Oh, no, they were all gone before I was born. The last one left in 1916, when my father was sixteen. I don't think the shortcut's been used much since. My father is the age of the century, so it's easy to remember his age."

"The year of the Easter Rising."

"The what?"

"Some very bad Irish history that happened in 1916. Nobody talked about anything else when I was a boy."

"You better be careful." I had to pant to keep up with him. "There's this crater just—"

But, uttering a sort of war whoop, he had already disappeared over its edge.

"Mr. Finn?" I crept closer, fearful of falling in myself. "Are you all right? Did you fall?"

"Of course I didn't fall," came his voice from below. "I jumped. Jesus, Mary, and Joseph, if this isn't the mother of all foxholes!"

I peered over the edge to see him dancing a little jig on the floor of the crater, his arms pointed skyward from the elbows, a silly, ecstatic grin on his upturned face. The crater was wider than I remembered from when Flora and I had seen it. Maybe because there was more light in it at this hour.

"Come down," he called.

"No, I can't."

"Yes you can. It's fabulous down here." He was still dancing the jig with a look of mad ecstasy. From where I stood above, the hair on his head looked like sharp little orange spikes sticking up in a field of flesh. For all I knew he might still have mental problems.

"Come on, I'll help you. See that young sassafras? Grab hold of it and swing down until you're standing on the root below."

"I really *can't.*" I wondered whether it might not be wisest to run away and leave him there.

"You can, you can. Come on, it's great!" He had stopped the dancing, and his sunlit green eyes glittered up at me. He raised his arms, beckoning with his fingers. "Trust me, I'll catch you." It seemed important to him that I trust him. He would dismiss me as a child if I ran away. My hand was already on the young sassafras. How did he know to call it that? I didn't know anything but the limited world of my "strange childhood."

"Now keep hold of it and step onto the root—"

One blue Ked on the root, then the other. Two blue Keds. What would Mrs. Huff think if she were watching me right this minute?

"Now grab my hand and ye're down."

My knees were wobbly, my heart was thumping, yet somehow I gripped his hand and was down.

"Good girl." He shook my hand before releasing me. "I'm proud of you."

The whole thing felt overdramatic. It was not *that* far down, really.

"Now what?" I tried to act blasé, though I was still shaking.

"What do you mean, now what?"

"What do we do now that we're in this hole?" I sounded just like my father.

"What do we do?" he cried incredulously. "We admire it. Man, what I could have done with this hole. And I didn't even have to dig it. It dug itself. Just imagine, all those days and nights and years since the uprising, since your father was sixteen, this amazing thing was quietly creating itself, slowly sinking and shifting and forming itself into this lovely shelter. Why, a body could set up housekeeping here. There's spaces for little side rooms, and that lovely moss for the floor, even some little flowers for natural wallpaper, and twining vines for curtains. And smell the lovely earth odors, all the odors coming from the pores of the earth. And so dry. In a foxhole like this I would not have come down with pneumonia."

I was getting worried. Not only was I standing in a hole in the woods with a man I barely knew but he might be crazy. He'd admitted himself he'd had mental problems after the collapsed lung.

"Well, I don't think my grandfather had it in mind to create a foxhole," I said, taking on the voice of reason. "Or even a future foxhole. This would all have to be filled in if we were going to fix the path."

Elation and playfulness drained from his countenance. "Ah, yes," he said. "Your wanting to surprise your father. I got somewhat carried away, didn't I?"

"Oh, no . . . I can see . . . I mean, if someone's just come back from having to dig their own foxholes in the war, this must seem like . . ." I trailed off, unable to think of a comparison. "I better be getting back," I said. "Flora will be worrying." For good measure I added untruthfully, "She gets really upset if I go out of her sight."

With relief I watched him reassume his adulthood. "Then, up you go," he said, giving me a boost till my foot was firmly on the root. I grasped the slim trunk of the sassafras tree, and realized I could probably climb up and down by myself whenever I wanted. It would be fun to show someone. Like Brian, who I was sure had never climbed into or out of a hole in his life. But Brian would probably never climb anywhere, up or down, again.

We hurried along the paved road to Finn's motorcycle. "I hope we won't have upset Flora too much," he said.

"We'd better not say anything about going in the crater," I said. "It'll worry her and she'll cry. My cousin has the gift of tears."

"God forbid we make your lovely cousin cry," he said. "If you ride behind me on the seat, we'll get you home that much faster."

"Oh, I couldn't possibly—"

"Ah, you can do anything you set your mind to, Helen. I've seen you in action now. So climb up and hold on tight."

XII.

How are you settling into your new room?" Mrs. Jones asked. It was Tuesday again and I was helping her change the linens on Nonie's bed.

"Oh, fine."

"Have you . . . dreamed anymore?"

I knew from her wistful tone she meant had I dreamed about Nonie. The answer was yes, but, as it had been a hideous nightmare, I weaseled.

"I've heard her *voice* a couple of times. And one night I woke up really sad and so I did this strange thing."

Mrs. Jones smoothed down the top sheet on her side and companionably waited.

"I got her new hat out of the closet. She was trying it on when she had her heart attack, you know."

"That's right."

"Then I put it on. I sat down in front of the three-way mirror and pinned it on. It still had her hatpin in it. She always carried this pin in her purse in case she felt like trying on hats downtown."

"How did it look on you?"

"Well, I tried it different ways but none of them looked right and then I saw if I scrunched down far enough so I couldn't see my shoulders, it was just the hat on a person's head. And it was like she was there."

Mrs. Jones sighed.

"It was like she was showing me how she looked just before she died. I mean how she would have looked if I had been standing behind her."

We each plumped our pillow in its fresh case and then together folded the counterpane over them.

"That's wonderful about that hatpin," she said at last. "What did you do with it?"

"Oh, I put it right back in the hat afterwards and put everything back in the box."

"That's exactly what I would have done!" Mrs. Jones raised her eyes to the ceiling and seemed to be recalling some precious item belonging to Rosemary that she had cared for in a particular way. After a minute she added, "That little girl died, you know."

"What little girl?"

"The one who came down with polio the same time as your friend. It was in the paper. How is your friend doing?"

"They may let him go home, but it will be a long road to recovery." I was quoting Father McFall. The rector had "dropped by" the house on his way to the hospital and sat and talked to Flora while I finally wrote a letter to Brian that he could hand-deliver. "He has been asking about you," Father McFall explained, just short of scolding, "and I know you'll both feel better if you send him a few lines on paper. Something he can keep and reread."

"Unlucky little fellow," said Mrs. Jones. "And they're saying now it was just the two cases, not an epidemic. They may even reopen the lake for the fireworks on the Fourth."

Would my father lift our quarantine when he heard there was no epidemic? Somehow I doubted it. He liked us where we were. "Getting on a-okay here," he had scrawled on the back of a postcard of the American flag. "I am much more suited to this kind of work. You and Flora stay on your hill. That way I know you're safe. Will try to call soon. Harry."

Flora had received a second rejection and spent that day in tears, but the following day she was offered a job teaching fifth grade in a county school in Dothan, Alabama, and was now making lesson plans upstairs on the porch outside the Willow Fanning room. After my great adventure with Finn, we had had the okra fried crunchily in egg and bread crumbs and she had bemoaned her "stupid mistake" of being in the tub when Finn had brought me home. I hadn't believed my luck when Finn had helped me down from the motorcycle and Flora hadn't come flying out the door, but I was beginning to think it might have been better to get it over then. Because now she wanted to go over and over everything that had been done and said in my first free hour away from her.

"Now where was it you two met up on Sunset Drive . . . ?"

"Just before where the shortcut is." Naturally, I didn't tell her about starting to lose myself and having to sit down.

"And so you showed him the shortcut. Did you walk or ride to it?"

"We walked there and back and then we rode to the house." Of course I didn't tell her we had gone down into the crater. That was Finn's and my secret.

"And he told you he was Irish, then adopted by Americans."

"By his father's cousins who had done well."

"Did he say how?"

"How he was adopted?"

"No, how they had done well."

"No."

"Did you offer to pay him for the okra?"

"No. It was a gift."

"Did he say that? Did he say it was a gift?"

"He said he was bringing it because you had sounded disappointed when the store didn't have any. That sounds like a gift to me."

"He said I was disappointed? How sweet. Maybe we should ask him to dinner, or would that be wrong?"

"Why would it be wrong?"

"Because he's the person who delivers our groceries and also there's your father's orders about staying away from people."

"Well, Mrs. Jones comes to the house every week and Father McFall came to the house and he goes to the hospital to visit a polio patient, and Finn's already *been* in the house when he carried our groceries in."

"Then maybe we should ask him."

"Will you ask him over the phone or wait until he comes with more groceries?"

"I've been thinking about that. The phone might be the easiest. When I'm calling in our next order I could ask him."

"But someone else might be taking orders when you call in."

"Well, if it's him, I'll ask. Or would you rather do the asking?"

"No, no, no!"

"But what should I cook?"

"Everything you cook is good."

"Oh, Helen, thank you for that. We're not having too bad a summer, are we?"

"Not too bad." I felt I should agree.

"I could do Juliet's rationed pork dish. It always turns out well."

Alabama again! But at least it was something to look forward to.

THIS IS WHAT I dreamed after Finn brought me home on his motorcycle. I can remember every detail of it still. It is one of those dreams you can spend a whole life deciphering.

I was going down my grandfather's ruined shortcut, leading the way to show someone the crater. The person behind me was someone my age. I didn't know if it was a boy or a girl. I was being very bossy and superior and giving directions. "Now I know it looks scary from above, but it's easy if you're careful." I showed how to grab hold of the sassafras tree. ("You can tell it's a sassafras because it makes this shushing sound that no other tree makes. Then once you have a good hold of it you put one foot down on this big old root. Like this, watch me.")

Then without turning around I knew who was behind me and it was the most wonderful thing. It was Nonie as a girl my age, when she was still Honora Drake who lived out on the farm, only she was visiting me for the day. In the dream I knew the old Nonie was dead, but this was even better. Mrs. Jones had been right when she happily proclaimed, "That's the thing about the dead. They make you understand that time isn't as simple as you thought."

I had been sent this new Nonie exactly my age to play with

and she was going to be better than any of the others, smarter and more fun than Rachel in her wildest dreams, sharper-tongued than Annie, more adoring of me than Brian. I felt an ecstasy in body and heart. I felt I had been set free to do anything I wanted. Without turning back to look at her, I called triumphantly: "Just wait, there's a whole house down there, with little side rooms and living flowers growing out of the floor. So set your first foot firmly on the root, the way I'm doing, and then slowly bring your other foot down, and—"

But there was a shriek like a big bird and something dark flew over my head and landed in a sickening thump below me. Only it wasn't a bird, it was an old woman all in black and she wasn't in one piece. Parts of her lay flung all over the floor of the crater. There was one leg turned sideways in a thick stocking and its black old-lady shoe. I can still see that shoe, its black lace in the lace holes, the perforated design on its vamp, its clumsy raised heel. And then Nonie was calling to me from somewhere among those flung-down parts: "Quickly, darling, go in my purse."

"We didn't bring a purse!" I knew she meant her little vial of pills, but how could we have brought a purse when the girl behind me had been too young to carry a purse yet? Her voice was fading now, still calling for the purse, leaving me to wake with the knowledge that I had utterly failed to save the person who loved me most.

Not a dream I could tell Mrs. Jones. I had told her simply that I had waked up one night feeling sad, and then about the hat. The sad part came after I had waked up in Nonie's bed. It had felt as though my own body had been flung down dismembered in the crater. But Nonie's bed did the job I could not accomplish for her in the dream, it put me back together. I felt the life flowing from the center of me into all my extremities, and was soon brave enough to turn on the lamp.

Nonie's purse was still in its place on the dresser—Mrs. Jones understood it needed to stay there—and I went over to it and took out the vial and shook out one tiny pill and swallowed it. Maybe I would die. I was still enough under the influence of the dream to feel this would be a fitting end for me. I ran back to the bed and lay down, but nothing happened. So I got up again and headed to Nonie's closet. My own clothes hung inside now, and my shoes were on the floor. Hers were still there in their boxes. She was particular about her shoes and wouldn't have been caught dead in those old-woman shoes from the dream. She preferred I. Miller pumps, size 8AA, in black or gray, with a three-inch tapered heel and a V-shaped vamp to accommodate her high instep. Her bedroom slippers were always narrow suede Daniel Greens. I checked a few boxes to make sure some evil nighttime thing hadn't substituted the old-woman shoes.

Then I took down the shiny new hatbox with the horse-drawn carriages going round and round it. At first I planned just to stroke the hat, but when I carried the box over to the bed and lifted the hat out of its tissues and saw her hatpin in it I felt compelled to sit down in front of the three-way mirror and try it on myself. Experimenting with different angles I found that if I slouched down in a certain way I could visualize how she might have looked if I had been standing behind her in the store.

XIII.

I had to flee the kitchen in embarrassment when Flora was inviting Finn to dinner after placing our order. She was going on too long, making it sound like we never had people to dinner—which we never did, but why did she have to tell things like that? I couldn't stand it anymore when she started discussing the menu with him, making sure he liked pork and of course bringing in the marvelous Juliet, who had discovered how to bathe wartime rations in a wonderful sauce.

I shut myself in my old room. Its window was brighter for daytime reading, and also I felt I was making amends to it for my abrupt desertion. I lay on top of my old silk baby quilt Brian and I had used for reading, but didn't open the book yet. Mrs. Jones had brought it from the library when she returned the one I hadn't finished. This one, *Hitty*, didn't look too promising—it was about a doll—but Mrs. Jones had chosen it herself, after consulting with the librarian, and I knew I would have to at least skim enough that I could "report" on it so her feelings wouldn't be hurt.

Finn was coming to dinner on Sunday. Flora had invited him for six o'clock. I had heard that much before she started in on how nice for us some company would be and launched into Juliet and the wartime pork. I was reminded afresh that my biggest fear concerning Flora was how her lack of reserve would reflect on our family. How, people would ask, could someone as picky as Principal Anstruther go off and leave his daughter, who had just lost her irreproachable grandmother, with a young woman who didn't know any better than to read letters from the dead woman to the funeral guests? How exactly was this Flora related to the Anstruther family? Well, she was first cousin to Helen's mother: the two girls grew up together in Alabama. Oh, her *mother,* I see."

So far, only Lorena Huff had pronounced on Flora as "that emotional girl" who had read the letters, and Father McFall probably had his own reservations after quizzing her during the drive home from church. If Flora would only show more reserve, I could cover for her, but she would babble the most embarrassing things when least expected. It was bad enough when we were alone, but who knew what she might say to Finn?

At least she had been offered a job and had accepted. What if all three letters had said no? Would my father have felt sorry for her and found it a convenience for himself to keep her on? After having given it some careful thought, I no longer dreaded he might marry her. He was too critical, she wasn't his type, he would always be rolling his eyes and leaving the table and carrying fresh drinks up to his room. The idea of them sharing a room was preposterous. But my father was perfectly capable of keeping her with us to serve his needs. She could cook. (When I finally came around to admitting that Flora cooked better than Nonie, it made me think less of cooking.) My father would teach her to drive Nonie's car and it would be Flora who picked me up from school. Lorena Huff would be right, after all: I would have a live-in governess.

But now it wasn't going to happen because Flora had a job and she had written to accept and they were going to send her the schoolbooks and schedules so she could start planning. She would be gone from Old One Thousand the last week in August and my father would be back with his burnt grilled cheese sandwiches and his cocktails, complaining about his job kowtowing to small-town faculty egos and waiting to be replaced by some younger man with connections.

And why should I care about what Finn thought of Flora? From the beginning he had been "my" person, someone I had connected to before Flora flew out of the house. I looked ahead to more conversations when he would ask me about my thoughts and to future adventures when he would teach me more things and praise me for my bravery. Yet I was sophisticated enough already to perceive that he was something of an outcast type himself. He had admitted to mental problems (I was eager to hear more about those), and if you looked at him critically, as someone like my father would certainly do, he was a little ridiculous, with his sharp, pointy features and orange spikes of hair and skinny body, dancing a jig in a hole in the woods. And on the motorcycle, when I had held him around his waist and laid my face against his damp back, his rank male smell made me screw up my nostrils.

My father liked to trap people in epithets. Brian was Little Lord Fauntleroy and Annie was Lady Uncouth. Nonie's stepbrother, in tears at the funeral home because he couldn't "see Honora," was the Old Mongrel. What would my father's epithet for Finn be?

Nonie preferred an indirect approach to judgment. "Is she

the kind of person we'd like to invite to dinner?" she had asked my father on the evening he brought home the girls' hygiene booklet Miss Waring said she could not teach. What would Nonie have said about Finn? I couldn't hear her initiating a dinner invitation, but suppose Flora had said to her as Flora had said to me, "Maybe we should ask him to dinner, or would that be wrong?" Nonie would have responded exactly as I had done (this realization cheered me): she would have first asked, "Why would it be wrong?" This response, I now understood, would have given her more time to think about the rest of her reply. And what would that have been? Here I drew a blank, though in time I would become so proficient at channeling Nonie's responses that they would become inseparable from mine. Or rather, from what mine would have been if I hadn't had Nonie inside ready to speak for me before I knew what I wanted to say.

But still, I was impatient to see Finn on Sunday. If only I could be sure Flora would not ruin everything with her eagerness and disregard for what should be left unsaid.

In the new library book, a doll was writing a memoir of her first hundred years. I had to remind myself that Mrs. Jones's Rosemary had still been in the doll-playing stage when she died of diphtheria. The librarian had told Mrs. Jones that all the books in the series I liked were checked out and said this doll one was suitable for readers through the age of twelve. If all the books in my series about girls and houses with mysteries were checked out, the fickle librarian must have been recommending them to other people besides me.

I leafed through the illustrations again, the first one of the doll (Hitty) taking up a quill pen to begin her memoir. Hitty had a square face, a thick neck, goggle eyes, and an ill-natured smile. I had been able to deduce from the chapter titles ("In

Which I Travel," "In Which I Am Lost in India") that this was one of those books grown-ups dote on because it sneak-feeds young minds with plenty of history and geography.

I heard the phone ring, but it couldn't be my father because he called in the evening. Maybe it was Finn calling back to say he couldn't come on Sunday. I imagined him hanging up the phone at the store and thinking, *I can never get through a dinner with that excitable woman who sounds desperate to have company. If it was just Helen and me it would be different.*

Flora was knocking at my door (at least someone had taught her to knock). "Helen, it's for you."

"Who is it?"

"It's your friend Annie. Why don't you talk to her on the upstairs phone? I've got things to do in the kitchen and you'll have your privacy."

"She doesn't sound so bad," said Annie as soon as Flora had hung up downstairs.

"Oh, Annie." My sigh spoke volumes.

"Just thought I should let you know I'm leaving town this afternoon."

"This afternoon!"

"They're cutting the phone off in a few minutes, and I didn't want you to call me up and hear 'That number has been disconnected.' Not that you *have* called me up a single time."

"I didn't realize you were leaving so soon!"

"I guess time runs differently up there at Shangri-la. I said three weeks, and it'll be three weeks on Monday." There was a frosty tone beneath her usual teasing.

"Oh, Annie, things have been so— Oh, I don't know what to say."

"You don't have to say anything, Helen. Actually, I called to say a few things to you."

"What?"

"Remember our lemon squeezes? You would tell me what I did that really bothered you and then it would be my turn to tell you. One time you told me I chewed with my mouth open."

"We haven't done a lemon squeeze since third grade."

"No, but I remembered it and I make sure nobody sees the inside of my mouth anymore. In fact, I was having a moment of gratitude toward you just now because when I'm making my new friends in the flatlands I'll know not to do it. So, thank you."

"You're welcome, but—?"

"So I've decided to do you a favor and tell you a few lemon-truths before I ride out of your life forever."

Where was this heading?

"I don't have long, so here goes. Mammy saw Mrs. Huff downtown and Mrs. Huff said your behavior had really hurt them."

"My behavior! What did I do?"

"It's not so much what you did as what you didn't do. You stayed in their house for a whole week. You slept in Rachel's room and swam in her pool for an entire week and haven't called her since. You never even sent a thank-you note."

Oh, God, I hadn't. Counterattack was my only defense. "Have *you* always remembered to send thank-you notes?"

"It's not your turn, Helen. I haven't finished. You were always—" She stopped and then made a new start. "You're smart, Helen, and I used to consider you my best friend, but your trouble is you think you're better than other people. Mrs. Huff told

Mammy that you got it from your grandmother. Who we all know went around with her nose stuck up so high a bird could have pooped in it."

"Mrs. Huff said that?"

"The bird-poop part was me, but the rest was her."

"That's not fair! She's dead!"

"Yes, and you've got a few more months of people feeling sorry for you. But after that, you'd better take a good, long look at yourself in the mirror."

I could hardly breathe I was so hurt, but something told me to snatch what lemon-truths I could out of her before she rode out of my life forever. "What do you think is wrong with me?"

"What do I think? Well, it so happens I've thought a lot about it. Other people don't exist when you're not with them. We're like toys or something. You play with them and examine them and then you put them on a shelf and go away. We don't have lives, we're just your playthings."

Was this true? The idea struck home somehow. Yet there was something satisfying about others thinking of me like that. It put me out of the zone where I could get hurt.

Flora-like, my own eyes were leaking. Among other things, I felt I had not defended Nonie as she deserved.

"Listen," said Annie, "Mammy is hovering, saying I have to get off the phone so they can disconnect it. Are you still there?"

"Yes."

"Was I too harsh?"

"No, you were just being . . . lemony."

"I really liked you, Helen. It's just that—"

"I'm going to hang up now, Annie. Good luck with your new friends. And remember to keep your mouth closed when you chew."

I hung up quietly and sat for some minutes at the wobbly little phone desk in the upstairs hall. It had been in the same spot ever since I could remember, though the phone models had changed. I was glad she was leaving town. She wouldn't be around to blab her findings to anyone else.

But Mrs. Huff would. She was probably standing on some street corner right now, waiting to tell another mother about my bad behavior. If Nonie had been alive, I would have written the thank-you note and I would have written to Brian before Father McFall forced me into it. It was true I had been counting on people feeling sorry for me and overlooking my lapses because I had lost my grandmother.

I could hear Flora downstairs (she sounded as though she was in the living room) humming "Begin the Beguine" in breathless, hopping snatches, while she scrubbed something with a brush. What had she found to scrub that Mrs. Jones hadn't already scrubbed?

All the unoccupied rooms were left open to keep them, Mrs. Jones said, from getting that shut-up smell. ("Empty rooms need to breathe so they can stay connected to the rest of the house.")

The doors to the two front rooms, my father's and Flora's, were closed. I suppose Mrs. Jones felt that my father, as living head of the household, occupied the Hyman Highsmith room in spirit even though he was away at Oak Ridge. This was the room my father and mother had shared. It had its own porch entrance, to the south porch, just as Flora's Willow Fanning room had its own porch entrance to the west porch.

I entered my father's room, which smelled of furniture polish. It was the barest room in the house. After some recent falls from too much Jack Daniel's, he had rolled up the handsome

Persian area rugs and bestowed them on the two lesser Recoverers' rooms. That left the bed that he and my mother had slept in and the bookcase he had made and an old Victorian flattop desk he had found at a sale and refinished. The bookcase held only books about carpentry or furniture and was more empty than full. Mrs. Jones had outdone herself on the bare wood in this room because there was more of it here than anything else. Trophies from my father's public life were on display at the other end of the hall, in Doctor Cam's old consulting room, which Nonie had made into a family shrine room. Harry's college diploma was in a frame next to my grandfather's medical credentials. His bound senior thesis in history ("The Decline of Southern Honor After Appomattox") leaned against Doctor Cam's bound volume of handwritten poems ("midst our cloud-begirded peaks / on this December morn / a boy is born"). The family photos were also in the shrine room (a stiff-looking Nonie in long skirts holding the newborn Harry, a studio portrait of a younger Doctor Cam before he met Nonie, Lisbeth and Harry and Nonie on my parents' wedding day, and lots of me in all my stages to date. There was this one photo of my mother in a fur coat squatting beside me in my snowsuit. She looked strained by her squatting position but determined to pose like a mother enjoying the snow with her child.

"Isn't it about time," Nonie had cheerfully suggested to my father not so long ago, "we started calling the Hyman Highsmith room the Harry Astruther room? You've been living in it, except for college, since you were sixteen."

"Oh, let's keep it the Hyman Highsmith room," my father had said. "Harry Anstruther doesn't live in it."

"Then who does, pray tell?"

"You tell me."

Downstairs, Flora, still erupting little snatches of "Begin the Beguine," was scrubbing something more distant than whatever she had been scrubbing before. I had no hesitation in crossing the hall and entering her room. I had done this in imagination already and had progressively worked out the kinks in my plan. I opened the top drawer. The packet of letters now faced downward and the ribbon that bound them was looser than it had been when I first saw her place them in the drawer. She must have been reading them. I was able to slide the face-down top letter from its envelope without disturbing the ribbon. When you are doing something behind someone's back, you feel slightly cheated if they make it too easy. You may even feel they deserve it. Heart thudding, I quietly let myself out of her room, crossed the hall, reentered my father's room, closing the door, and went outside to the south porch. Shut off twice, I felt twice protected.

I read the letter standing at the rail, which was prickly with peeled paint. It took me several tries before I calmed down enough to register what was in it. It was clearly Nonie's first reply in the famous correspondence, which meant Flora probably kept the letters in chronological order, with the first one at the bottom. I was disappointed. Nonie didn't come through as strong and wise as I had expected, and what she conveyed was more confusing than enlightening. I was mentioned only once, at the very end—almost like a dutiful afterthought.

I couldn't wait to retrace my furtive route and get the thing back in its envelope, though I resolved to read more of the letters whenever opportunities arose. Meanwhile I would be thinking up ways to make those opportunities.

November 4, 1938

Dear Flora,

Your news has distressed us. My heart goes out to you. It is a terrible thing to lose a parent and all the more devastating when you only have the one to lose. In the short time we were with your father, it was clear how much he loved you and looked out for you.

Of *course* I don't mind your writing to me. The truth is we have been worrying and wondering ever since you left. We never heard from you after the week you stayed with us following Lisbeth's funeral.

Yes, it is doubly hard for you, as you said, to have lost the two people you loved most within a single year. Though it has been almost a year since Lisbeth's death, I am still fairly reeling from the loss of her. You had her when you were a child and I had her when I was old enough to be her mother. But she was more than "like a daughter" to me. She was the better, cooler young woman I wished I had been, and I loved watching her grow in self-confidence. She was one of those people who flourish best under a certain amount of protection, and I like to think we provided her with that protection. Lisbeth and I were not demonstrative women, but we treasured each other's company and admired each other. I had things to teach her and she had things to teach us. I miss her more than I can say.

It wasn't kind for those girls at school to say you should just tell people your father died of "lead poisoning." Of course, as you say, it was in the papers and everyone knew about the card game and the shooting. But you know, Flora, in future when you meet people all you need to say is that your father died when you were fifteen. That is enough.

Harry joins me in sending his deepest sympathy, and little Helen would, too, if she were old enough to understand. She is my joy and my responsibility now.

Do write to me whenever you feel like it. I will always reply.

Yours truly,
Honora Anstruther

XIV.

Flora and I argued about everything on the Sunday that Finn was expected for dinner.

"I'm making those cheese straws you like," Flora said, "and a pitcher of lemonade for when we are sitting in the living room getting acquainted. How does that sound?"

"We always offer cocktails to our company," I said. "Even Father McFall has his gin and limewater. And my father always has his drink before dinner."

"Or drinks," said Flora.

"You shouldn't criticize my father."

"Well, I'm not, honey. It was just a statement of fact."

Then it was how we were going to serve the meal. Flora wanted us to help our plates in the kitchen so the food would stay hot.

"Why can't *you* serve the plates in the kitchen and bring them to us at the table. That way, things would stay just as hot."

"Well, if you think—"

"It would be more elegant that way," I said.

Then there was the matter of where Finn should sit. "He

should sit on your left, Helen. You'll be head of the table as always."

"But the guest of honor always sits on the right."

"Well, but on your left he'll get the view of the sunset over the mountains. On your right, it'll just be the wall."

I could tell she had given a lot of thought to this and felt I should give in, especially since I had gotten my way about her serving the plates, which was how I had been picturing it.

Then there was the fuss over what each of us should wear. "My good suit seems too dressy, especially when I have to tie an apron over it."

"Just wear one of your regular dresses," I said.

"Or I could wear that nice skirt, the one Juliet made from your mother's dress, with a simple blouse—"

"No! Just one of your regular dresses."

"What about you, Helen? Have you decided?"

"I'll wear the dress I wore to church. I like it." It was one of the last dresses Nonie had bought for me: a small blue and white check with a white piqué collar that had a single red emblem on it like Chinese writing.

"Well, that's the main thing, isn't it? A person wants to feel comfortable."

But when I stepped into the dress and started to button it up the front, there was a nasty surprise. It wasn't exactly that I had started sprouting new parts, but when I forced the top button, I looked like a little girl who had outgrown her dress. But I had worn it to church. How could this have happened? Cursing Flora and all her tasty meals, I tore the dress off and stuffed it into the darkest corner of the closet, behind Nonie's shoe boxes, and, after some exasperating wrong choices, settled on a plaid pleated skirt and school blouse.

Finn, wearing a suit, roared up on his delivery cycle on the dot of six. He looked kind of weakened without his paratrooper boots, and there was something about his hair that made him resemble a puppy run through a bath. He'd brought us flowers from the farmers' market, which Flora made a great deal of ceremony about arranging in a vase, and as he passed through our kitchen he said the aroma was enough to make a man swoon. His feet in civilian shoes were small and dainty, like a dancing master's. How sad that all of us had gone to so much trouble and none of us looked as good as we usually did. Flora had obeyed me and worn an unobjectionable dress, but she had done something extra with her makeup that made her eyes and mouth too sultry.

The cheese straws and the lemonade awaited us in the living room.

"Now, Helen tells me cocktails are always offered to company in this house," Flora said, "so, honey, what are his choices?" Though she was honoring my wishes, she also managed to make it sound like a concession to a child.

"Ah, thank you, no," Finn said before I could begin my recitation. "I've been on the dry ever since my little set-to with the lungs. However, that lemonade looks grand."

"Sometimes," I said, "we'd get a Recoverer who'd just been cured of TB and was dying for a drink. My grandfather said this was a tricky proposition."

"Oh, why was that?" asked Finn, interested.

"Because the drink was like a reward but it might be just the thing to start him down the road to having to be cured of something else."

Accepting his glass of lemonade, Finn laughed and looked at me admiringly. "Were all the Recoverers men?"

"Oh no," Flora jumped in. "For instance, my room, the room I'm staying in for the summer, is called the Willow Fanning room. I don't know much about Willow Fanning, but Helen's grandmother told me she was quite a handful for such a delicate person and they came to regret taking her in."

"When did she tell you that?" I demanded.

"It was probably in one of her letters," said Flora. "Or, no, I seem to remember her saying something the first time I stayed in that room." To Finn she explained, "The first time was when I came up for Lisbeth's funeral. Lisbeth was Helen's mother. We were raised together in Alabama, Helen's mother and I. Lisbeth was twelve years older, but we were real close."

"He doesn't want to hear all that," I said.

"I do, I do," Finn insisted. "I find your whole setup fascinating. You two cousins up here on your private hill. And those Recoverers! You make me wish I were one of them."

"Oh, they were long before our time," said Flora.

"Yet she speaks of them as though they're still in residence," said Finn. "If I had been one of them, Helen, do you think they would have named a room after me?"

"The Devlin Patrick Finn room," I tried it out.

"Oh, what a beautiful name," cried Flora. "Why didn't you tell me that, Helen? I wish someone had given me a middle name."

"We can give you one now," said Finn warmly, leaning forward to touch her on the arm. "What name do you fancy?"

But his sudden intimacy seemed to fluster Flora and, murmuring that she'd need to consider it, she fled to the kitchen to check on something.

The living room was filling with a nostalgic orange light, which made everything look less shabby and more historical.

You couldn't see the snags on the arms of the yellow silk sofa, which Finn had been sharing with Flora. The carpet was a warm blur of soft-patterned flowers and not a mange of threadbare spots. The windows were open to the sunset in progress and a gentle breeze ruffled the sheer curtains. The scrubbing sounds I had heard the other day, I now realized, had been Flora's washing the insides of the windowsills.

I had chosen Nonie's wing chair for myself and was gazing demurely down at my lap because I thought Finn was studying me, but it turned out he was looking at the little painting that hung above my chair.

"Did one of you do that?" he asked.

"No, it was one of the Recoverers," I said, and went on to quote Nonie: "Starling Peake let us down, but he was happy the day he painted that picture." I explained that it was the view from our house before it got blocked out.

"You could have it back, the view," Finn said. "All ye'd need to do is top some trees."

"It would cost a lot of money," I said.

"That would depend on who you got to do it. I might be able to help you."

"I would have to ask my father," I said, like an ungrateful little prig.

"Well, of course, naturally you would," Finn replied sportingly, though he blushed with embarrassment.

I was relieved when Flora stood over us, taking charge like an adult and directing us to our seats. "I will bring your plates from the kitchen," she announced, rosy with her cooking, "so that everything will stay as hot as possible."

Greed rose in my throat at the sight of the steaming food on the plate, but this was immediately followed by dismay at the recent image of myself pooching out of my favorite dress. Flora had been stealthily turning me into a fatty with her meals. Unless I was vigilant and changed my habits, my father wouldn't recognize me when he came home. Finn ate like a hungry man who had been taught not to bolt his food. He praised each item and asked Flora how she managed to have everything including the biscuits come out at the same time, and that, unfortunately, set off an accolade to the person who had taken Flora in hand when she could hardly reach the stove and taught her everything about cooking. It was Juliet Parker this and Juliet that, until I felt I needed to put in that this was their colored maid back in Alabama.

"No, not our maid," said Flora. "Juliet lived with us. She raised me and Helen's mother. She was a full member of the household. Why, she's even—"

"Where do *you* live, Finn?" I interrupted like a rude child, but it was better than having Flora say what I was sure was coming next: that Juliet Parker was part owner of their house.

"I live in an attic storeroom above Mr. Crump's store. Its washing facilities leave much to be desired, but it's convenient to the job. They only charge me for linens and utilities, so I can put away a bit."

"What about your American parents? Will you ever go back to them?"

"That's a lot of questions, honey," Flora mildly protested.

"No, no, I don't mind," said Finn. "You two have told me something about your lives and now it's my turn. I get on very well with Grace and Bill. Sure they would love to have me back. Bill would make me a partner in his auto parts business, but I'd like to try my wings first. I'm twenty-two—"

"We're the same age!" cried Flora. "When is your birthday? Mine was May."

"Ah, mine was last November, and there's already the next one looking over my shoulder, so I'd better get cracking."

"How will you try your wings?" I asked, keeping to the subject.

"I'd like to study engineering or maybe industrial arts."

"And you've got the GI Bill!" cried Flora. "The government will send you to college."

"Well, I'm not so sure of that," said Finn. "We'll have to see how things fall out."

"But it's a sure thing," insisted Flora. "I know several boys in Birmingham who are going to take advantage of it as soon as they're discharged."

"But, you see, I'm already discharged. Because of the lung . . ." Finn tapped his chest. "And then I developed this other complication." He tapped the side of his head. "Which made me act a bit daft for a while. They dealt with it out at the hospital, but I have to stay here in town and see a doctor out at the hospital once a week until he says I'm my old self again."

"Was that your mental problem?" I asked.

"Helen, honey—" began Flora.

"It's all right," Finn assured her. "It happens to a lot of soldiers. Meanwhile, this mountain air is good for me, and I get to know people like yourselves. How would I ever have met the two of you if I hadn't been your deliverer?"

The phone rang. "Excuse me," I said, getting up. "That's probably my father. I'll take it in the kitchen."

"May I speak with Helen?" a voice asked faintly. It was Brian Beale.

"This *is* Helen."

"Oh. You sound different. I thought it was that lady who's living with you now."

"She's not *living* with us, just staying till my father comes back. Where are you?"

"Oh, I'm home. But I have to go away again tomorrow."

"Where?"

"I have to go to this place. But I wanted to thank you for your nice letter. Father McFall brought it to the hospital. It really cheered me up."

"Oh, it was nothing," I said bitterly, recalling my forced effort with shame. Without thinking, I added, "This has been the worst summer of my life."

"Same here," said Brian without the least hint of irony, which made me feel horrible.

"How—how *are* you?" I was venturing just as Flora whisked into the kitchen to take the pineapple upside-down cake out of the oven. "It's Brian," I told her. "He's out of the hospital."

"Am I keeping you?" Brian asked.

"No, it's just we have company for dinner."

"Oh, sorry. I'll get off."

"No, I was already finished eating. Why are you going away tomorrow?"

"It's this place where they work on you so you can get better. I'll be going to school there, too."

First Annie, now Brian. That left only Rachel, whose mother now hated me. It was while Brian was telling me that his mother was closing up their house and going with him that I realized he was talking in his old way, like before he had the speech lessons. The English accent was completely gone.

"Listen," I said. "Can I call you back in the morning so we can really talk?"

"No, that's okay, I just wanted to thank you for the letter. I'll be going by ambulance first thing."

"Ambulance?"

"It's the most practical, for now. My mother will follow in the car. Listen, Helen, you be good. I guess we'll see each other again sometime."

When I returned to the dining room, the lamps were switched on and Flora was serving out the cake. The way she broke off whatever she had been telling Finn made me sure she had been filling him in on my recent losses—"First her grandmother dies, then her little friend Brian gets polio, and her little girlfriend has just moved away . . ."—but she must have been telling about my father's polio, too, because as I came in Finn was murmuring that it was "no wonder, then, he was being extra strict, considering his own experience."

"Well, how is Brian?" asked Flora, who had never even met him.

"He's going away by ambulance tomorrow morning." A huge slice of pineapple upside-down cake, which Flora knew was my favorite, awaited me on my plate.

"I thought you said he was home from the hospital."

"He is but tomorrow he's going off to this other place where they will *work on him* some more. He won't even be coming back for school."

"Probably one of those Sister Kenny places," said Finn. "It's an intense regimen but they get results, I'm told."

"We're very lucky it didn't turn into an epidemic," Flora prattled on. "Mrs. Jones said they're going to go ahead with the fireworks on the Fourth. Though it's so sad about that one little girl. Did Brian say anything about his legs, Helen?"

"No, and I didn't ask. If he's going there in an ambulance, they're probably not in the best shape." I knew I sounded rude, but it was better than crying. Brian had spoken to me the way people do when they have already given up on you. I felt like giving up on myself. Flora always made sure I got a complete ring of pineapple in my serving of cake, and now its yellow eye glistened gelidly up at me: "Eat, little girl, and expand some more."

When we were having coffee back in the living room, Finn took a small sketchbook and pencil from his jacket pocket and asked if he might draw the room to send to his American mum. "Grace would love this. She has this way she wants her rooms to look but she says it's not the kind of look you can just go out and purchase."

We sat on either side of him on the sofa and watched the agile pencil, which seemed like an extension of his hand, bring to life Nonie's wing chair and the little painting above it, and then the eight-foot highboy looming in its shadowy corner, and then on to Nonie's desk, which faced the window that used to have a view of the mountains. Finn evoked the highboy's gloomy corner with hard, slanted lines that got closer together the darker he wanted the shadows. The branches that now obstructed the view he rendered with intricate wispy strokes. His shadows brought out the room's spooky potential, and the erratic clutter of his branches made you feel the sadness of everything going to pieces around you. He commented as he drew: "What Grace wouldn't give for that highboy. What a lovely little desk."

"My father refinished that desk for my grandmother," I said. "He likes working with wood a lot better than having to kowtow to faculty egos."

Which really made Finn laugh.

"She wrote her letters at that desk," Flora had to put in. "She wrote her letters to *me* at that desk." She was about to call on her gift of tears when I shot her a murderous look and she pulled herself up short and offered instead, "Six years' worth of letters. Those letters from Mrs. Anstruther have become my guide for living, why, they have saved me from—"

Who knows what she would have blurted next if I hadn't asked Finn where he had learned to draw like that.

"Oh, it was just this thing I started doing after I came to America. Bill liked me to draw scenes from Ireland. He had left as a baby and couldn't remember anything. And I drew the men in my company, each with some personal military object, like his helmet hanging on the wall, so they could send home war portraits of themselves."

"You can do people, too?" marveled Flora.

"Surely I can. Will I draw the two of you?" (That funny "will" of his again.) "How about the two of you sitting side by side on the sofa?"

"No, just draw Helen. She'll like it better if I'm not in it," Flora told him without the slightest hint of rancor. I can still hear her saying those words.

"Maybe I should sit over there in my grandmother's chair," I said.

"You get to know a person when you draw them," Finn commented after he had laid in a few strokes, interspersed by quick glances. He scrutinized me the way he had the furniture. Sitting close beside him, Flora squeaked encouraging little *mmm*s, which seemed to be more about the drawing than about me. Once she said, "Oh!"

"What?" I said.

"He got that look of yours when you're—"

"When I'm *what*?"

"Keep still," Finn commanded.

"Can't I even speak?"

"You can speak if you don't change your expression or move your mouth."

"*How* do you get to know a person when you draw them?"

"You catch some of their passing thoughts," he said. "Now, do ye think you can keep your face still and just lift one hand out of your lap and lay it on the arm of the chair?"

"Which hand?"

"The right . . . no, I mean your left. So it'll be the one on my right. Now unclench your fingers and let them hang loose over the edge of the chair, and would it be too much to ask you to lose the frown? Good girl."

THE YOUNG EX-SOLDIER'S pointy face, sharp nose elongated by the shadows of the lamp-lit room, made him look like a skinny magician growing out of a myth as he drew the frowning girl-child self-importantly arranged in her late grandmother's wing chair. I made much of the shadows and the history of that shabby room in "Impediments," the title story in a collection of stories about failed loves. In the story, the young man is awed to be in the house and he is trying to impress the young woman sitting beside him by drawing her grumpy little cousin. He is deeply attracted to the young woman, she is different from the usual pretty girl, she has a natural, unspoiled warmth and an endearing determination to make you feel appreciated. But the young woman goes away at the end of the summer and the soldier is left with his unrequited love. Yet this evening of lamplight and shadows in the arrogant, crumbling old house on top of a mountain will serve him all his life as a source of his art. It, more than any other source, is responsible for the elegiac, "lost," overlay that haunts his canvases and wins him fame and fortune. Years later, he sees a frowning woman sitting in a wing chair across a crowded room. She is balancing a glass of champagne rather primly on her lap and staring into a space that seems far from this room. The vision instantly fires up in him the old, trusted elegiac spark and he goes over to her and says, "I'd like to sketch you, just as you are, in that chair." And she comes back from whatever far-away place she has been in and looks at him closely and says, "But you already have." He thinks she is speaking symbolically or trying to charm him by being mysterious. But she lets him sketch her, just as she is, balancing her glass of champagne primly on her knees. Soon a crowd has gathered around the wing chair: who can resist the spectacle of a famous artist on one knee in front of a chair, sketching an unknown woman? He says, "You are a very good model. You keep still, but you don't hide the flow of your thoughts." She responds with a distant half smile. He signs the drawing and offers it to her, but she says, "No, keep it to remember me by," and stands up, puts down her undrunk champagne, and walks out of the party. The reader knows that she has loved him since she was ten and has measured all men since then by his memory. But she has also, over the span of years, grown into her father's cynicism and is hardened enough not to try for a belated romantic ending.

XV.

I was helping to strip Nonie's bed. It was the day of the week I felt sanest. Mrs. Jones had known the Recoverers and Doctor Cam and my father when he was sixteen and the elusive Lisbeth. She knew what I had lost in Nonie. Her Tuesday appearances attached me to my old world.

Each week she took away bundles and the following week she brought back separate flat packages labeled by room. Each piece was marked in India ink so the laundry would know which room it belonged to when they made up the packages. Nonie's linens were marked MASTER; Flora's were marked FANNING. My father's were marked HIGHSMITH.

"I reckon I'll be going to those fireworks tomorrow night they're having down at the lake," said Mrs. Jones.

"But you *hate* fireworks."

"Not hate. It's just them going off unexpectedly makes me jump. But this time I'm going for that little girl who died from polio. It was Rosemary's idea."

I waited the way Mrs. Jones had shown me how to wait when we were beginning this kind of conversation.

"Rosemary always was one for remembrances. She loved

little ceremonies. For people who had passed or for a neighbor's pet. I woke straight out of sleep and she was saying clear as anything, 'Mamma, go down to the lake on the Fourth and every time a pretty firework goes up in the night sky say "Stella Reeve, you are not forgotten."' That was the little girl's name. It was in the paper. She was from Georgia. Her aunt was driving her to camp. It was so hot, the aunt said, and they saw this lake and decided to stop there for a swim."

"You'll go all by yourself at night?"

"I usually am all by myself."

"I wish I could go with you."

"That would be nice. But you have to mind your father. He has his reasons."

"I can't wait till school starts, even if all my friends are gone."

"You'll make new friends. How are you liking that library book I brought?"

"Oh, it was fine."

"You already finished it?"

"There's not a lot to do up here."

I was prepared for some discussion of the book about the traveling doll to back up my lie, but Mrs. Jones simply nodded and said she'd take it back and bring me another one next Tuesday. "Maybe this time she'll have one of those in that series you like."

"We had someone to dinner on Sunday," I told her.

"That was a change for you."

"It was only that Finn who delivers our groceries. But Flora thought we should ask him."

"Was it nice?"

"Yes, but I ate too much. Nonie never made such huge

meals. After dinner, he drew a picture of our living room to send to his mother. And he drew this portrait of me." I got it out of the top drawer of Nonie's dressing table to show.

"Why, it's good enough to frame."

"Do you think it looks like me?"

"Well, it makes you look older, but they're your features and you look that way when you're . . . pondering something. Why weren't you wearing your nice dress?"

"Oh, it seemed too formal," I said. For an extra reason I almost added that he was only the person who delivered the groceries, but I stopped myself in time. What if Mrs. Jones were to think I wouldn't have dressed up for her, either, as she was only the person who cleaned the house? I was going to have to be more careful of people's feelings. I had lost enough friends.

The outgrown dress was back on its hanger in the closet, a little rumpled from its punishment on the floor, but looking like any dress waiting to be put on again.

AS JULY BEGAN to crawl forward, I fantasized that my father would show up for my birthday in early August, even though it would fall on a Tuesday this year. He wouldn't announce it in his postcards, the latest being of a black bear and her cub standing in a meadow ("Greetings from the Great Smoky Mts. Nat'l. Park") with its less than satisfying message: "Thought you and Flora would like these two, whose ancestors were among our state's first settlers. Lots of construction going on here. Will phone soon." He wouldn't hint at it in a phone call, either. His car would just drive up sometime around the middle of the seventh, raising a cloud of dust and . . . what would he do then? I couldn't recall very well what he had done in former years, because Nonie always did so much. She treated the day like a national holiday. Last year, for my tenth birthday, a huge gift-wrapped box waited on the dining table all through the day while Nonie and I went to lunch at the Downtown Cafeteria and then to a wonderful Gene Tierney movie in which she fools people into thinking she's been murdered. Afterward Nonie drove us out to the Recreation Park, where we both rode the merry-go-round and had ice cream sundaes. When we returned to the house I opened her presents, but we left the big package on the table for when my father got home because it was supposed to be from him, though I knew she had probably chosen it and wrapped it herself.

It was dusk when my father finally came in and made himself a tall Jack Daniel's. When I opened the package and thanked him he raised his eyebrows at the white Samsonite suitcase with my initials, H.D.A., in gold and said, "Ah, now you're one of us."

At first I thought he meant because my initials were the same as theirs, Honora Drake Anstruther's and Harry Drake Anstruther's.

But then he added, "Now you can run away."

"Why would I want to run away?"

"Oh," he said, smiling into his glass, "it seems to run in the family. Doesn't it, Mother?"

It was later that evening, after supper, when he had refreshed his drink and stumbled up to bed, that Nonie told me the fullest version yet of Harry's running away at sixteen with Willow Fanning.

("It was a sad thing, darling. She tricked him because she wanted a man to travel with her. By then Harry had his full growth and looked more like twenty than sixteen. And then, when they got to where she wanted to go, she dumped him. He caught polio coming home on the bus. At least she had paid his fare."

"Where did she want to go?"

"To meet up with another man."

"But how did she trick my father?"

"By making him think she adored him. Young men are pushovers for coquettes. And an invalid coquette is hard to resist. I often worried she'd ruined all women for Harry. But then your mother came along, the very opposite of a coquette.")

FLORA GOT ALL the mail. Packages from the school where she would teach fifth grade. Today she had a letter from a teacher at her school who said he would be glad to teach her how to drive so she wouldn't need to be dependent on the bus.

"That's very kind of him, now all I need is a car," remarked Flora, but so good-naturedly it could not qualify as sarcasm. "He was right nice, he was on the committee that hired me. Who knows, Helen? Maybe I'll follow in your mother's footsteps."

I knew where this was going and did not respond.

No week went by without a letter of several pages (on both sides) from the faithful Juliet Parker. ("She says the blight got the first tomatoes but luckily there was still time to replant . . . Oh! Uncle Sam and Aunt Garnet are going to wait until I'm back for their remarriage ceremony, isn't that sweet?")

And then one day Flora looked up beaming from Juliet's latest letter and announced, as if a prize were being bestowed on both of us, that "they" would so much like it if Flora could send them a recent picture of "Lisbeth's girl."

"There aren't any," I said.

"But surely—didn't you and Rachel Huff snap pictures of each other? No? Well, I'm sure we can find *something* recent. How about a school picture?"

"No," I said.

"No school picture?"

"Just no. Not that I can send down there. I don't want my picture passed around by people I don't even know."

Flora's face went through some drastic changes before she turned her back on me. I thought she might be cranking up for a crying spree, but then, still turned away, her voice, cold and dry, said, "You sound exactly like her."

"Like who?"

"Like Lisbeth when she was being cruel."

"Cruel how?"

Flora heaved a great sigh and made as if to throw herself forward into some kitchen project for next meal.

"Cruel *how*?"

"That's enough said. It's more than enough."

"You can't just stop there."

"I'm sorry I brought it up."

"You've got to tell me or *you'll* be cruel."

Flora turned around and treated me to what was for her a scathing once-over. "One time—it was your comment about your snapshot that reminded me of it—she went into the family album and cut herself out of the picture of all of us Daddy had taken with his new camera. Just scissored it out with manicure scissors and put the picture back in the album. It wasn't discovered till much later and Daddy asked her why she had done it."

"What did she say?" I could not imagine myself doing such an extreme thing, though I was thrilled by it.

"She said it was because she looked particularly nice in that shot and she wanted to have just a picture of herself without the rest of us around."

"That's not exactly cruel."

"Oh, there were other— No, I've said enough. I've said too much. It's just that you were so like her when you said, 'Not that I can send *down there*.' Like it was beneath you. And yet you were hardly three when she died. She wouldn't have had enough time to turn you against us."

"Why should she want to turn me against people I didn't even know?"

"Because we weren't the kind of people she could be proud of. Sometimes at night when I would wake up and throw my leg over her to make sure she was still there, she would get mad and say mean things. Oh, this has gone *beyond* far enough, Helen. Now go away and put it out of your mind." Again she turned toward some kitchen duty that could save her.

"You might as well tell me what she said, because I'm *not* going away. You're stuck with me until the end of the summer."

"I didn't mean for you to go away, Helen, I only meant—"

"She would get mad and say *what* mean things?"

"Oh, that my mother was trash and Daddy got left holding a package that wasn't his, and how her father had been the only brother smart enough to leave the state and better himself, but then along came the influenza and dumped her right back to start all over with the people her father had struggled to get away from. When she was a little girl, she said, she used to lie awake in Florida and hear her father and mother make fun of them back in Alabama, imitating their accents. Her father had worked hard to get rid of his. Both he and her mother had acting ambitions. Now, aren't you sorry you made me tell you such things?"

"Not really." I was elated rather than sorry. Flora had given me two vivid snapshots of the woman I couldn't remember.

AFTER FLORA'S EXPLOSION, or the nearest she had ever come to one, I felt things between us had seriously shifted. If I was going to get through the rest of the summer successfully (rather than abjectly), I was going to need new tactics.

In the daytime, walking around the house and its dilapidated grounds, or lurking on the Recoverers' porch on my father's side pretending to read a book while I waited for opportunities to steal across the hall and plunder Flora's drawer for the next letter, I forced myself toward a subtler kind of thinking. Sometimes I was sure I could actually feel my brain stretching to make room for more intricate and convoluted paths. Not just stopping at the first old I-am-furious-so-I'll-lash-out point, but letting it branch and divide into other possibilities. I could lash out and make her cry and get some instant satisfaction, or I could hold back and see what benefits came from my holding back.

After Flora's outburst I went away and checked myself over for wounds and then added up the pluses and minuses. What was lost was that I now knew Flora didn't adore my mother as much I had thought, but so what? How important was it that someone like Flora should adore my mother? What had been found were some valuable pointers to what Lisbeth really was like, and out of that finding branched another: that I saw myself not only capable but willing to behave as my mother had behaved under the circumstances. No, Lisbeth herself had not lived long enough to "turn me against them," but poor Flora in her anguished disclosures had certainly made some headway. To the deplorable list of a father shot between the eyes during a poker game and a live-in Negro maid who owned half the house were now added a trashy mother and a father left holding a package that wasn't his.

However, I was stuck with Flora for the rest of July and most of August. "You're stuck with me!" I had shouted at her and rendered her instantly on the defensive. Being stuck with Flora, how could I make the most of my stuckness?

For a start, there were still those unread letters from Nonie in Flora's drawer. I needed to find more reasons to be upstairs during the times while Flora was safely occupied downstairs. And what else could be wrested from this jail sentence with Flora? Well, I could squeeze more out of her about my mother. This would require a more subversive approach because, guilt-ridden over her loss of control, Flora was on guard against it happening again.

I worked on these things during my pitiful daytime rounds of our house and in bed at night, burrowing into Nonie's sheets and hoping for further instructions from her. Her high-shouldered black purse (faithfully gone over with a cloth every Tuesday by Mrs. Jones) watched over me from its same spot atop the dresser. Her Easter hat lay in its tissues storing up its powers for those extreme situations when I would be driven to put it on again and angle myself just right in the mirror so I could evoke the back of her head.

When I needed to, I spoke aloud, in a husky undertone that couldn't reach the type of person who might shamelessly crouch outside doors—and Flora, to give her credit, was not that type. The things I said, or asked, came out in a kind of automaton's chant, as if I were being cranked up from inside and "played":

Round and round but what else is there?

And then I would stop and wait (in midstep if I was walking around the house in daytime, in midbreath between the laundered sheets marked MASTER in Nonie's bed at night) in case there was an answer.

I had lost all desire to walk down to my grandfather's shortcut and explore the crater by myself. That whole experience had been ruined by the subsequent nightmare of a dismembered Nonie lying at the bottom and the old-lady shoes.

Round and round the house, "remembering" it when it had flower beds and a view painted by a recovering inebriate who bolted at the first whiff of adversity ("We could have named it the Starling Peake room, but how can you name a room after someone who ran off without paying?"); when it still had a grassy bank I rolled down over and over again while a woman turned her head elsewhere in restlessness or disappointment: the culmination of my outdoor rounds being the pilgrimage to the garage to sit in Nonie's Oldsmobile and lay my cheek on the steering wheel and wish her voice back.

Occasionally it came, though not like the first time, when she told me to cut down the weeds, and not like the day I was walking down Sunset Drive feeling strange and she told me to sit down in the shade and let everything go. If it came through now, it wasn't immediate and visceral like those first two times. It was becoming more like my memory of her voice—or worse, my ventriloquism of it. Unlike Mrs. Jones, I couldn't accept with unconditional certainty that my dead one was speaking to me.

XVI.

How many did you have in fifth grade, Helen?"

"How many *what* did I have in fifth grade?"

"Oh, sorry. How many children were in your fifth-grade class?"

I had to stop and count. "Twenty."

"That many," she said.

"Why?"

"They say I'll have ten. Maybe twelve. It's a rural school. I just wish I knew what they were going to be like so I could prepare better!"

"There'll be some smart ones and some dumb ones."

"You were one of the smart ones. Mrs. Anstruther used to write that your report cards were pure joy."

"And there'll be some you like and others you wish you could hit."

"Oh, I would never do that."

"I said 'wish.' "

"I just hope they'll respect me. And like me, too, of course."

"Well, they will if you . . ."

"If I what? Really, Helen, I'd be grateful for your advice. What about your teacher?"

"Which one?"

"The teacher you had this past year for fifth grade."

"We had different teachers for different subjects."

"Oh, I'm going to be teaching mine all their subjects. Which teachers were your favorites?"

"That depends on whether you mean like or respect." I knew I was edging into my smarty-pants mode, but it worked so well on Flora it was hard to forfeit the advantage. "I didn't always like the ones I respected and I didn't necessarily respect the ones I liked."

"That's very well put, honey. Respect is probably the most important, though, isn't it? I mean, if you had to choose between being liked and being respected."

"Maybe you won't have to choose between them," I magnanimously predicted.

"Why did you respect the ones you respected?"

I had to stop and think. "They made you feel they knew things."

"What kinds of things?"

"The things they were supposed to be teaching you, of course—" But she kept goggling at me for the next wisdom I was about to impart, so I added, off the cuff, "And things about life in general."

"I sometimes feel I know nothing about life in general," Flora said despondently. "You know what I am afraid of, Helen? I'm afraid those kids will see right into me and despise me."

"Well, if there is nothing in there for them to see, they won't have anything to despise." My father would have smirked at this cleverness, but, alas, Flora was on the verge of tears and I knew it was time to jettison the smarty mode and do something to shore up her confidence.

"You know what we should do?" I said. "We should play fifth grade. You'll be yourself as the teacher and stand behind the desk and I'll be your fifth-grade class."

"But how can you be a whole class?"

"You wait and see."

"What desk should we use? Your grandmother's? But we'd have to turn it around so I could stand behind it. And then those pigeonholes would block my view of the class."

"We'll use my father's room upstairs. He has the perfect flat desk and the room's practically bare, so it will be easy to imagine what we need."

"Oh, I don't know, Helen, he might not like that."

"He's not even here, and we can't mess it up because we're not going to bring anything in."

"I might want to have a few of my books on the desk," said Flora, already into the spirit of things. As my guardian she seemed pleased and grateful that the two of us were getting along again, yet she was also like my contemporary who couldn't wait to play this interesting new game. For Brian I had made up our Auditions game, and Annie and I together had created our Bad Habits game, which we never tired of, in which we took turns imitating unfortunate habits of people at school—no one, from the janitor to the principal, was exempt—and having the other guess who was being mocked.

Flora would have begun right away, but I suggested we should start next morning so it would be like the first day of real school. I told her to wear a dress and put on her high heels to practice entering the classroom. I was eager to begin, too, but I needed some time to prepare. Not only did I have to be all those children, but also I was going to have to make up the action and direct it as we went along.

"How should we begin?" asked Flora next morning. After breakfast, she had dashed upstairs to put on her nice suit and her heels. "I left off my nylons, because I have to save them. I hope that's all right."

I was already seated on the bare floor in my father's room, about ten feet out from the desk. "You'll come in," I said. "No, not yet! You have to get in the proper mood. You're making your first entrance. This will be their first impression of you. Just remember there's ten of me here, in all shapes and—"

"They said there might be twelve."

"Well, for our purposes we're going to have ten."

Flora went out in the hall, and when I gave the signal she came in. Her walk was all right, but her face was bunched with nervousness. I decided to go easy, however, until she got into the part.

"Good morning," she said brightly after scurrying behind my father's desk. "My name is Miss Waring. I'll write it up here on the board." She turned away, and while she was writing in the air above her, I felt a strange pang. Miss Waring had also been my mother's name, the name she must have written on her classroom's board the first day she came to teach at my father's school.

Flora whipped around and gave me a shy look of triumph (see how well I imagined the board!). "Now I'm going to go around the room and have each of you say *your* name . . ."

Flora's torturous word arrangements could drive you crazy, but if I stopped her to say she sounded like she meant to *walk around the classroom* I might put a crimp in the confidence she was beginning to build.

But I couldn't let it pass when she pointed at me and said, "Will you say your name for me, honey?"

"No, no, *not* 'honey.' Just point to the person and nod in a cool, friendly way."

"Oh, okay."

"And they're only going to have first names. It's too complicated to think up family names, too."

"Good idea." Assuming a passable cool, friendly demeanor, she pointed and nodded.

"My name is Angela," I piped up in a saccharine voice, sitting up straight and clasping my hands over my tummy like a goody-goody. A class always needed one of those.

"Angela," she repeated, with a little too much gratitude, but I let it go. She pointed and nodded again to the next child.

I hunched over, emitting a dangerous growl.

"I didn't quite get that," she said.

I growled again, more angrily.

"I'm sorry, but I—"

"Don't apologize! He hates school and he wants to hate you. You've got to be firm and show your authority."

"You will have to speak up, young man," Flora said firmly.

"Jock!" I bellowed.

"Jock," she repeated calmly, not rising to the bait. "And you there, next?"

I undulated my shoulders suggestively. "I am Lulabelle."

Flora tittered.

"What's funny? You're not supposed to laugh at people's names."

"I'm sorry, Helen, it's just that you're so good at this—"

"You have to stay in character, *Miss Waring*, and for Pete's sake stop saying you're sorry."

"Oh, I'm sorry—"

Then we both started giggling. Flora became my age for a minute. It made me wonder, almost sadly, whether she had played enough as a child.

After the coquettish Lulabelle came dumb and timid "Milderd," who couldn't pronounce her own name.

"Is that *Mildred*?" suggested Miss Waring tactfully.

"Yes, ma'am. Milderd."

"All right. And—" She nodded at the next student.

"Brick," I said in a strong, masculine voice, already seeing his potential as a leader.

"Can someone be named Brick?" asked Flora, derailing the whole thing.

"Parents sometimes give their children family names for first names. His mother's maiden name was Brickstone," I improvised, "which is on his birth certificate, but everyone calls him Brick."

Next was Suzanne, alert and confident, with an assertive ponytail, the kind of girl you hoped would pick you as her friend. Then came Timmy, who had a chronic snivel and cough and would maybe die during the school year. After that was Ebenezer, a sly young mongrel who took things that weren't his, like Nonie's stepbrother, Earl Quarles. Then there was Jason, who would be either a positive or a negative influence on the class, I hadn't decided yet. And last of all was a definitely negative girl named after that homely doll in the book I couldn't read. Hitty's ill-natured smile would spook the teacher until Miss Waring started wishing she could slap her.

"You are so good at this," Flora would say, shaking her head in awe. Not during our class practices anymore, because during those I had pretty successfully weaned her from lapsing out of character. "I feel I know these children. I want to keep them interested. I love what we did with Alabama history, having them be the Indians and then the Spanish and French and so on. I lie awake at night and think about them, I think up ways to help them improve. For instance, what if I asked little Mildred to practice using the word 'dread' in different sentences? 'I dread the dentist,' and so on. She might find she could pronounce her own name after all."

"Better not use that example, though. If she doesn't dread the dentist, it might make her start."

"Oh dear, you're right. You know, maybe it's just as well, Helen, that I won't have someone like you in my real fifth-grade class."

"Why is that?" I asked, though I could tell she was going to say something flattering.

"You're just so quick and imaginative I couldn't keep up with you, that's why."

"But how do you know there won't be someone— I mean, it's possible that you'll have someone like Brick or Suzanne," I deflected modestly.

"No," said Flora. "*You* made up Brick and Suzanne, whereas this is a rural school and . . . oh, I don't know. Your mother used to say Alabama's education standards were woefully behind. That's why she practically starved herself so she could finish college at Chapel Hill and get a North Carolina teaching certificate."

"How do you know she starved herself?" This was the first I'd heard of it.

"Because we all had to help her out. I mean, not me, I was still a child, though I contributed little candies for the food packages. But everyone sent money orders, even Juliet. And, even then, Lisbeth had to go to bed early so she could do without the dinner meal."

"How did you know this?"

"Well, Lisbeth still wrote to us fairly often in those days, and she would describe what it was like to go to bed on an empty stomach. She said she would curl up in a ball so she felt fuller in the middle and then pull the blanket over her head to keep out the sounds of other students heading off to dinner. It made Daddy cry to think of her suffering like that for an education. Juliet said that was when he started going out and playing cards for bigger stakes."

I, too, lie awake at night now, when I am older than Nonie ever became, and think about those children, the only fifth-grade class Flora ever got to teach. Brick and Suzanne and Lulabelle and Ebenezer and Jock and Jason and Hitty and Timmy and Angela and little "Milderd." I round them up in whatever order they present themselves on that particular night and meditate on whatever pattern they want to form. It might be winners and losers. It might be who improved the most, or who disappointed the most, or who got together with whom years later and revealed something heartwarming or shocking. The combinations seem endless. Or maybe I should simply say I have not reached the end of them yet because I always fall asleep before the possibilities are exhausted.

It has puzzled me how those ten imaginary students could have played such a comfortable, even comforting, role in my night life for so many years. Their continued existence has always stayed innocently parallel to the remorse that I am still growing into. Sometimes I think those classroom hours with Flora stay safe and separate from the rest of that summer because they were filled with hope and promise and mutual development and even closeness. We were making up a game that needed both of us. (Does anyone, of any age, make up such games anymore?) But right here, *right in here* somewhere, in what we were making together, is located the redemption, if there is to be any.

[undated]

Dear Flora,

Here is a quick reply before today turns into one of "those" days. Harry is under the weather and taking a day off and I'm going to pick up Helen from school and take her to the movies so my son can have a quiet house.

I was so relieved that you had nothing to worry about, after all. I found myself almost wishing you had kept the worry to yourself. I knew a girl—this was of course many years ago—who *did* discover she had something to worry about. It was not her fault, she was forced, but, as I say, this was ages ago, another lifetime, really, and I was to lose touch with her. I have often wondered how things turned out. I think I remember hearing through the grapevine that she married someone older and I like to hope things worked themselves out.

Since you asked my advice, even though your little crisis has passed, I will say to you what I've said before. Keep yourself to yourself until you've got a ring on your finger and even then don't tell everything. Especially not then.

I would just add it's a smart habit to destroy correspondence. Old letters can fall into the wrong hands. I have to admit that I shuddered when you mentioned *rereading* my letters. I do wish you would deposit their main message—that I care about you and want you to be your best—in your heart and then destroy the letters.

Take care, now.

Yours truly,
Honora Anstruther

XVII.

Though our Fifth Grade game brought Flora and me closer and gave us something to plan for each day besides the next meal, it also gave me shamelessly easy access to Nonie's letters across the hall in Flora's drawer. After we'd finished, Flora, flushed with her successes—of which she had more and more, because she obeyed directions well—would gather up her books and say now she'd better get down to the kitchen and earn her board and keep. She would ask me what I would like for dinner and cheerfully offer tasty suggestions when I said I didn't care.

After our classroom hour in my father's room, I would fling myself flat on the floor, my arms and legs outspread like a prisoner on a rack, and dramatically declare myself worn out. And Flora would say, "Well of course you are. That imagination of yours must just *guzzle* energy." At last she had stopped asking what I was going to do with the rest of my day. This was partly due to my ungracious replies during the first weeks, but the tide really had turned when I was able to say, lying on my back on the bare floor, "I'll stay here awhile and plan tomorrow's class while everything's fresh in my mind, and then I'll go out on my father's porch and read." The perfect child who knew how to keep herself quietly occupied. And Flora would cross the hall and change out of her teacher dress and high heels and scuttle downstairs on her funny bare feet with the upturned nails, humming one of her tunes.

On a subsequent raid of the drawer I'd had a setback. The letters were no longer in their neat packet with the earliest conveniently at the bottom. The ribbon had been untied and cast aside and they were scattered all over, some detached from their envelopes. It was as if another unauthorized person, more careless or more desperate than me, had been plundering the drawer. I realized that of course it had to be Flora rummaging around for some remembered advice to help her get through something.

The new disarray allowed me to snatch up a letter at random and retreat to safety without having to spend time making the packet look untouched. But it destroyed my plan of reading the letters as they had been written. I had been hoping to construct a chronicle of how Nonie had been lured into the correspondence and what she might have revealed to Flora that she hadn't had a chance to reveal to me before she died.

Forced to read the letters (some undated, often the ones missing envelopes) in this haphazard fashion, during which Nonie gamely responded to Flora's various crises, I wasn't sure whether Flora was sixteen or eighteen or twenty when she was having them. I wasn't even sure what some of them were: Nonie could be maddeningly oblique. I needed Flora's side of the correspondence because she was sure to have spilled all, but hadn't I watched those letters disappear into Nonie's pocket, doomed to the place of no rereadings? And she had surely taken her own advice and destroyed them as soon as possible.

I also felt let down by the, so far, few mentions of me in

the letters. I had yet to read about the little girl whose report cards were such a joy and who was the chief reason for Nonie to go on living. "I'm going to pick up Helen from school and take her to the movies so my son can have a quiet house" was not a description of the person I thought I was.

"OH DEAR, I hope Finn is all right," Flora said after ordering our groceries.

"Why shouldn't he be?" I asked, though I had been wondering about him myself but didn't want to be the one to bring it up.

"It was this impatient man on the phone. He kept cutting me off before I finished my sentences."

"That was Mr. Crump. He owns Grove Market. I wouldn't take it personally. He's just in a bad mood generally."

("Poor Archie Crump," Nonie had said, when we were driving home from the market. I had been complaining that Mr. Crump looked straight through me as though I wasn't there. "He does that with all children," said Nonie, "I wouldn't take it personally. Things didn't work out for him as he expected." "What things?" "Well, Archie started off as a stock boy at Grove's—he was in high school with Harry. Then he married Mr. Grove's daughter, but after Mr. Grove died and Archie inherited the store, Serena Crump went off to live by herself at the beach." "Why?" "Well," said Nonie, pausing to assemble an answer, "maybe she came to realize she hated groceries." This sent me into hysterical laughter. Nonie continued to face front, behind the steering wheel, her nose uplifted—so high in the air a bird could poop in it, Annie would say—but she allowed herself a wry smile. "It's not you particularly he ignores," she added. "He just doesn't notice children in general." "Maybe we make him sad because he never had any," I suggested. "That's a sweet thought, darling," she said, reaching over to pat my hand.)

"I just hope Finn's not unwell," Flora went on.

"He was probably already out delivering groceries," I said. But now she had me worried. Could his lung or his mental state have collapsed again? Could he have displeased Mr. Crump and gotten fired? I was surprised at the alarm such prospects raised in me. Ever since his evening with us, I had been plotting how, as soon as Flora left, my father and I would ask Finn to come and live with us. "You can be our honorary Recoverer," I imagined myself saying to him. I had Starling Peake's room picked out for him, with the nicest of the oriental rugs my father had discarded, and we could put in a desk where he could draw views from the window, after he had topped the trees, which he had already offered to do. He would drive me to and from school in Nonie's car and we would run errands as Nonie and I had done and my father would pay him "something," as he was paying Flora "something." Finn's joining us would improve life for all three of us. In the evenings, the two men would have their drinks together and I would serve them Flora's cheese straws, which I was going to have her teach me to make. And by the time Finn came to live with us, I would also have learned to cook a few meals whose aromas could make a man swoon.

But it was Mr. Crump in the Grove Market van who arrived with our order in the late afternoon. Flora got off to a bad start with him by flying out barefooted and asking where Finn was.

"Day off," said Crump with a scowl. "That driveway of yours is a liability."

"We're getting it fixed as soon as the war is over," I piped up, but he neither heard nor saw me.

"Here, let me help you with those boxes," said Flora.

"Better go back," he warned, looking her up and down. "You'll cut up your feet."

"Oh, they're tough as old nails," Flora said with a laugh, wresting a box away from him. But then, going triumphantly up the porch stairs ahead of him, she stubbed her toe and yelped, almost dropping the box.

"What'd I tell you," said Crump, with the nearest thing to a smile I had ever caught on his sour face. He held the door for her and set down his box of groceries next to hers on the kitchen counter. Then he took a deep breath and let out an animal-like groan.

"Are you all right, Mr. Crump?"

"Yes, ma'am. It was just—"

"Oh, please call me Flora. I'm Helen's cousin. Her mother and I grew up together in Alabama. Why don't you sit down a minute, Mr. Crump, if you can spare the time. I've got some corn bread ready to come out and it's never better than when you have it hot with a glass of cold milk. That's what I'm going to do, and it would be nice to have some company. Helen, how about you?"

"No, thank you. I'm going out."

I fled to the garage, to sit in Nonie's car and fume, but not before I'd heard Flora begin to confide how hard the summer had been for "poor Helen being cooped up with nobody but me, what with this polio scare and her little friend and she misses her grandmother . . ." Old spill-all Flora, even to such an audience as Mr. Crump. Had she really thought I was going to sit down at the table with that rude old man and let him ignore me some more?

I was disgusted by the whole scene between them. Why did

she show no discrimination about people? If it had been Finn (why had he taken a day off during the workweek?) I could see her inviting him to sit down for corn bread and company. But didn't she see how Mr. Crump had looked almost happy when she stubbed her toe? Even his own wife couldn't stand him and had to go off and live at the beach.

I sat in the car, rocking the steering wheel to the left and to the right. I turned an imaginary key in the ignition and heard the engine roar into life. "Now, back out slowly," Finn instructed from the passenger's seat. "There is no rush. No rush, a-tall, a-tall. I saw the way you made up your mind to jump, that day in the woods. You can do anything you set your mind to."

At last Flora and Crump emerged from the house. I could see them without turning my head. They were talking and looking toward the car. If they walked over, I would look right through Mr. Crump. If Flora addressed me, I would have to answer, but I would do it in a way to make Mr. Crump feel he wasn't there. I prepared it so well I was disappointed when I heard the grocery van start up and watched it bump down the drive. Flora went back into the house. I would do the next best thing, I decided. I wouldn't say his name to Flora no matter what. It would be like she'd been having the corn bread all by herself and there was nothing to talk about.

But Flora, in full dinner-making mode now, was eager to talk. "It seems Finn had some important meeting today with a medical board out at the military hospital."

I kept silence, not rising to my usual "How did you know that?"

"It seems," Flora went on, "the Army is reviewing his case. He may get an honorable discharge instead of a medical discharge, and then he'd be entitled to all the normal GI benefits."

"But he said he was already discharged."

"Yes, but evidently his father, who knows some senator, got involved and now they have to reconsider."

So far she had substituted "it seems" and "evidently" for a certain person's name. Was she tacitly obeying my embargo? Had all those hours playing fifth-grade class together sharpened her sense of me?

But over dinner (we were having macaroni and cheese, along with the milk a certain person had delivered and drank some of) she allowed herself some *he*s and *him*s.

"I'm so glad I asked him to sit down a minute. When he groaned like that I thought he was ill, but you know what it was?"

I narrowed my eyes at a heaped forkful of macaroni and cheese.

"It was the corn bread," said Flora. "He smelled the corn bread and it reminded him of his mother. He told me that after we had talked awhile. Isn't that touching?"

I filled my mouth with the heaped forkful and looked out the window.

"Oh, and he asked if your father was interested in selling the Oldsmobile. He wants it for his wife."

"His wife! She doesn't even live here!"

"No, but he said she had always admired Mrs. Anstruther's touring car. He was thinking he might drive it down to her at the beach and come back on the bus. If she had such a car, Serena—isn't that a nice name?—might be tempted to come home more. I gather there have been some differences between them, but, you know, Helen, differences sometimes get ironed out over time. Look at your uncle Sam and aunt Garnet in Alabama, getting remarried after being separated for twenty-six years. Wouldn't it be sweet if Mrs. Anstruther's car were to be the means of their reconciliation?"

"My father isn't going to sell my grandmother's car so the *Crumps* can get reconciled."

"Of course not, honey. I only meant . . . And besides, it's up to your father. I told him that."

XVIII.

When did remorse fall into disfavor? It was sometime during the second half of my life. As a child, I knelt next to Nonie in church and said alongside her sedate contralto: *the remembrance of them is grievous unto us; the burden of them is intolerable.* Then, for a long time I didn't go to church, and when I next said the General Confession it had been watered down to *we are truly sorry and we humbly repent.* If someone had really done you an ill turn and later came to you and said, "I am truly sorry," would that mean as much to you as "the burden of it has been intolerable to me"?

Remorse is wired straight to the heart. "Stop up the access and passage to remorse," Lady Macbeth bids the dark spirits, "that no compunctious visitings of nature shake my fell purpose."

Remorse went out of fashion around the same time that "Stop feeling guilty," and "You're too hard on yourself," and "You need to love yourself more" came into fashion.

"The summer I turned eleven," I might begin, and often have begun, "I was left in the care of my late mother's first cousin. She was twenty-two. It was for the most part a boring, exasperating summer. Such an isolated summer would not be possible today. We had the radio and the mail and the telephone (though few people wrote or called) and the woman who came to clean on Tuesdays and the man who delivered our groceries. Most days my feelings fell somewhere on the scale between bored / protected and bored / superior. But there were also times when I felt I had to fight to keep from losing the little I had been left with, including my sense of myself. Maybe I fought too hard. Anyway, the summer ended terribly (grievously?) and I have wondered ever since how much of it I caused."

After I have furnished some specifics, I am always told, in one way or another, that I am being too hard on myself. "You were a child, not even an adolescent yet. You had lost your model and your bulwark and were clinging to your foundations, such as you had been taught to perceive them, and you were ready to fight anyone who threatened them."

Or: "At eleven, your cerebral cortex was still growing and your cognitive powers hadn't finished developing. You were still floating in a continuum of possibilities and discovering what was in your power to do. But you weren't yet adept at foreseeing the consequences of what was in your power to do."

Or: "Then was then. Now is now. Put all that behind you, accept the person you have become through your particular gifts and failures. It is all flow, anyway. Disruption and regeneration. Forgive that child and go forth and sin no more. At least, try to do no harm in the years remaining to you."

Remorse derives from the Latin *remordere*: to vex, disturb, bite, sting again (the "again" is important). It began as a transitive verb, as in "my sinful lyfe dost me remord."

But now I say alongside Thomas à Kempis: "I would far rather feel remorse than know how to define it."

Mrs. Jones limped in on Tuesday with her right ankle taped to twice its size. She had turned it while out walking, she said. Flora made a huge fuss over her and begged her to sit down and let her make her a nice breakfast. "And then I can help with the cleaning, Mrs. Jones. Under your supervision, of course."

"Thank you, I've had my breakfast, and it don't hurt nearly as bad as it looks. It's only twisted, not sprained. I'll be able to do my work just fine."

"Well, I can certainly do my room and change my linens."

"That's thoughtful of you, but I would get all turned around if I didn't stick to my usual system. I've got to the place where my routine more or less runs me."

"At least let me make you a cup of tea," implored Flora.

"Oh, I've got my thermos of tea."

"Well, just please call me if you need anything," said Flora. "Will you at least promise me that?"

Mrs. Jones said she would. She had finally stopped calling her ma'am after Flora's repeated injunctions to call her Flora and now respectfully abstained from calling her anything at all.

Flora said she would work on her lesson plans upstairs until Mrs. Jones came up at noon to do the top floor. Naturally we couldn't play fifth-grade class when she was in the house.

I went outside to bide my time in the garage while Mrs. Jones scrubbed the kitchen floor and went over her life. I knew almost to the minute when it would be time to join up with her in Nonie's old room to change my sheets. The car had become my designated place for thinking about Finn and planning the details of his moving in with us. Also, I felt the car was more in need of my company and protection since the grocer had expressed his horrible intention to Flora.

Mrs. Jones told me she had turned her foot in the dark walking back from the lake after the Fourth of July fireworks. "It didn't start hurting till I got home. It throbbed and swole up something awful but I kept my feet elevated as much as I could."

"You didn't *go to the doctor*?"

"No, I could tell it wasn't broken or sprained."

"How could you tell?"

"You can tell a right smart lot about your body when you get to my age."

"Did you do that remembrance thing for the little girl?"

"I did. Every time a pretty firework went up over the lake I did."

"But there must have been lots of pretty fireworks."

"I waited for the ones Rosemary would have thought pretty. The ones in color, or the whirly ones."

"And did you say the thing aloud?"

"I did, even though some folks looked at me funny. Every time I said it, 'Stella Reeve, you are not forgotten,' I thought of that little girl, on her way to camp, but her and the aunt stopping for that swim. When I was walking back to the car after the fireworks, I stumbled in the dark and turned my ankle."

"But you carried out Rosemary's wishes." I aimed for the bright side. We had finished Nonie's bed and I wanted to keep the conversation going as long as possible.

"Well—" Mrs. Jones began, but could not go on. The trembly corners of her mouth seemed to be fighting against the stoic slabs of her cheeks and making them twitch.

I made smoothing motions with my palm on Nonie's

newly made bed and lowered my eyes. I knew better than to prod Mrs. Jones with my imperious *what?* which worked so well on Flora. I waited, wondering if I would at last see this stolid woman cry.

But after a ragged breath she went on. "The day after the lake, when I was resting with my feet up, Rosemary spoke to me. Only she sounded different. She sounded . . ."

A second ragged breath. "She sounded like a *much older girl.* 'Mama,' she said, 'I want you to listen carefully. Are you listening?'

"I said 'I always listen to you, you know that, deary.' And then she said—in this voice of a much older girl—'What I keep having to remember, over and over again, Mama, is that you are older now. You could have hurt yourself bad down there at the lake and there would be nobody to take care of you. I have to be more careful what I say. Maybe it would be better if I stopped saying anything.'

" 'Oh, don't do that,' I begged. 'I look forward to it so much. Please don't do that, deary. It would break my heart.' "

I waited until Mrs. Jones had picked up her polishing cloth and started in on the furniture, applying her respectful weekly swipe to Nonie's purse on the dresser. She was her steady self again, the one about whom Nonie had said, "I admire that woman. Despite all her adversities, Beryl Jones manages to stay in control of her days." But Beryl Jones seemed to have forgotten I was in the room.

"What did Rosemary say?" I finally burst out.

Mrs. Jones folded over the dust cloth to a clean place and began on a lampshade. The monolithic slabs of her cheeks lay perfectly still now. "I haven't heard a peep from her since." She gave an odd dry laugh. "But I've been talking a blue streak to *her.* I sat for the better part of two days with my feet elevated and I talked and talked. I said, 'You know what, deary? I'm not the only one getting older. You're growing up, too. I can tell it from your voice. You're getting to be a responsible young woman who wants to take care of me and I love you for it.' And, you know, I've felt her close by. And something else: the more I sat there and talked a blue streak, the more I could feel my ankle healing."

TUESDAY EVENING WAS the mystery program Flora and I liked. The recent ones hadn't been as good as the one about the little girl who turned into a mannequin, but we felt from the start that this one had potential. "I'm getting goose bumps already," announced Flora, curled up at the other end of the sofa from me. From the cabinet radio's big speakers came the sound of the ocean going in and out against mournful, eerie background music. A twelve-year-old boy, Julian, whose parents have died, has become the ward of his aunt who lives on an island. You could tell at once from the aunt's voice that she isn't going to be much comfort. She is an old maid wedded to her solitary schedule. She paints pottery with island scenes and sells it to the tourists, and her pet words are *livelihood* and *self-sufficient.* When she speaks of Julian's parents it sounds as though they have gone and died on purpose so she would be stuck with him. But a boy his age is lucky to get to live beside the ocean, she keeps reminding him, and he will have to be self-sufficient and find ways to amuse himself during the day while she earns their livelihood.

Julian takes long walks against the mournful, eerie background music, missing his parents, until one day he comes upon a ruined beach cottage with DANGER and DO NOT TRESPASS signs all around it. An old fisherman tells him there was a bad fire years ago and then the property kept changing owners who never got around to rebuilding it and now it's going to be torn down because it's become a hazard for children who want to play in it.

Of course, as soon as the fisherman leaves, Julian picks his way through the ruins and discovers to his delight and surprise that there is an old couple living quite happily in one small undestroyed room. They are just as delighted and surprised by him. Their names are Ethan and Peg, and they can't get enough of him. They want to know everything about his life and all about his parents, even the sad parts, and they tell him his aunt can't help but come to cherish him, he is such a fine boy. They once had a fine boy his age who died in the fire when this cottage belonged to them. The boy's name was Luke. Soon the cottage will be torn down and they will have to leave, they tell Julian, but it has been a privilege to stay on for as long as they have in this place where Luke was last alive.

Julian visits them every day. He is so eager to go out in the morning that his aunt grows curious and asks what he has been up to. She praises him for being so self-sufficient. He doesn't mention the ruined cottage because she might forbid him to go there, but he says he is really getting to love the ocean and he hopes he's not upsetting her schedule too much. And she says no, she's getting used to having him around and then confesses in a softer, new voice, "In fact, Julian, I would miss you if you weren't here."

At this point Flora buried her face in her hands and wailed.

Then the day comes when he heads for the cottage and you can tell by the urgency of the music that this time it is going to be different. The cottage has been demolished at daybreak. The old fisherman is on the scene and Julian asks him, "Did they get the old couple out safely?" "What old couple?" the old fisherman asks. Julian tells him about Ethan and Peg, whose son, Luke, was killed in the cottage fire. "Son, are you joshing me?" asks the old man. He tells Julian that all three of those people were burned to death in that fire back in the 1890s, the son *and* the father and mother. Everybody on the island knew the story and Julian must have picked it up from some old-timer who got the facts slightly wrong.

"But I saw them," says Julian. "I saw Ethan and Peg. We talked."

"Sorry, son, that won't wash with me. I grew up on this island and I remember how they looked when they found them. Try it on some newcomer."

Then Julian describes the couple, and finally the old fisherman says, "Lord, if that don't sound exactly like I remember them. Even down to his sideburns—they called them muttonchops in those days—and her way of asking people all about their business. But look here, son, there are some things beyond rational explaining. You say they were kind to you and got you through a bad time. Well, if I were you I would be grateful for that, but I would keep it to myself."

THE THEME MUSIC swelled, and now the announcer was reminding us that this program had been brought to us by a wine "made in California for enjoyment throughout the world."

"Want to turn it off?" Flora asked. "Or would you like to listen to something else?"

"No, no, turn it off. And don't turn any lights on."

"Okay." Flora wafted through the gloaming, and the orange fan-shaped panel on the big console went dark. Already the days were getting shorter. You could tell the difference between now and when we had listened to the program about the girl who becomes a mannequin. Then, as though she was intent on obeying my unspoken wishes as well, Flora returned to her end of the sofa and reassumed her knee-hugging position.

"Were you scared?" she asked.

"No. Were *you*?"

"Not scared, no." Her face merged into the surrounding blue dusk, but you could still make out the dark outline of her hair. She was close enough so I could smell her shampoo mingled with the perspiration at the nape of her neck. "I just thought it was perfect. How about you?"

"I did, too."

As darkness filled the room, we floated companionably in our separate thoughts. I was still enveloped by the kind voices of Ethan and Peg, and even the softening aunt, and vibrating with the strange possibilities aroused in me by the program.

"Oh, Helen, please tell me you haven't been too bored this summer."

"Not too bored," I conceded.

May 21, 1944

Dear Flora,

How sweet of you to remember me with a Mother's Day card. This is the first chance I have had to sit at my desk in relative quiet and answer your letter tucked inside it. Goodness, child! I hope I am up to all your faith in me.

Helen is spending Sunday with a favorite friend. She went home from church with him. And Harry is dashing around getting ready to drive over the mountain to Tennessee for a summer job. He's going to manage a construction crew for some top-priority war work at Oak Ridge. It's called the Manhattan Project and Harry says it's amazing how the minute you drop the name to the Ration Board they are all over themselves to shower you with permits for anything you want. It was one of those word-of-mouth opportunities that came about through our rector. The chaplain out at the Episcopal Academy had signed on, and he told Father McFall (our rector) that they were desperately looking for responsible people used to exercising authority who didn't have to work during the summer months. I haven't seen my son so excited for years. He can't wait to leave.

Now, Flora, where to start? You say you have no faith in yourself and you are afraid when you go out into the world people will "find you out." What are you afraid they'll find out? That you have no faith in yourself? Well, think what you'd be like if you *did have* faith in yourself and then act as though you are this person. The way she presents herself. The way she walks, enters a room, what she says—and what she does not say. I cannot stress the latter part enough. "Spoken word is slave; unspoken is master," as the old adage goes. Just keep in mind that people do not read minds. They judge by what they see and hear, and you are a well-favored young woman with a modest, unaffected voice. Just let those two things work for you. You will be surprised how far they'll carry you. Hold yourself like someone who sets value on her person and remember that a simple, courteous response will get you through practically anything. You don't need to be witty (some people just aren't gifted that way) or tell private things about yourself or your family.

You warm this old heart the way you lavish praise on me, but I am basically just a country girl without much education who has tried to keep her dignity and make the most of the cards dealt her. As I sit at this handsome desk my son restored for me and look around me on this quiet afternoon (and yet the world is at war) in our safe house on top of this mountain, I am astonished that things have turned out for me as well as they have. And my wish for you, Flora, is that when you reach my age you will be able to say the same—and much more!

Yours truly,
Honora Anstruther

XIX.

Dear Rachel,

You cannot imagine what a horrible

Dear Rachel,

How is the pool?

Dear Rachel,

Little did I know that the week with you would be the best

Dear Rachel,

I certainly hope your summer has been better than mine

How could writing a letter be such torture? I had expected that sitting at my grandmother's desk and using her writing materials would work some kind of spell and out would flow the words I needed to mend my fences with the Huffs. But so far I had crumpled four sheets of Nonie's good stationery and I couldn't even throw them in the wastebasket because Mrs. Jones would discover them and think less of me. I knew the effect I wanted my letter to have (to soothe Rachel's hurt pride, to reestablish me in Mrs. Huff's graces so she wouldn't stand on street corners saying bad things about me), but after what seemed like hours I was no nearer my goal than these four infantile, though correctly spelled, openings.

Rachel was a horrible speller.

The trouble was . . . What was the trouble? I didn't really care about the Huffs all that much, but needed them to like and admire me. Was there something left out of my moral makeup, or did I just require more social lessons in how to act as if I cared? I could see Flora, for instance, scrawling a heartfelt letter that would redeem her with the Huffs. But, then, Flora wouldn't need to be redeemed because she would have written a thank-you note in the first place. No, wait a minute! Didn't Flora neglect to write Nonie after spending a whole week in our house after my mother's funeral? ("we have been worrying and wondering ever since you left. We never heard from you")

Oh, it was not easy when you had lost the person who had taught you how to act. I took a fifth sheet of stationery from Nonie's box and tried to hear what she would advise if she were in the room.

Think what it would be like if you *did* care about them, darling, and then write the letter. Be simple and modest and don't complain. Don't make excuses for the delay, it only reminds them of the delay. The letter doesn't have to be long. In fact, it's better if it's not long. That way they will be better able to read into it what they need.

Dear Rachel,

I hope you are having a good summer. I had a really nice time at your house. Please tell your mother hello for me and thank her for her hospitality. See you back at school. I really can't wait.

Your friend,
Helen

Oh, hell. I had used *really* twice. Which would be worse? To waste another sheet of Nonie's good paper or to have Mrs. Huff think my writing style was childish?

Flora was upstairs, working on her lesson plans for her real class in Alabama. This morning in our fifth grade she had assigned the children to be different parts of speech and get together in small groups and form sentences. It was something our English teacher had done with our class, but I let Flora think it was my idea. She said I was brilliant and then her usual thing about how she hoped she didn't have anybody as smart as me in her real class or she wouldn't know what to do. I thought it was all right to take credit for the parts of speech idea since I had run myself ragged being everyone in all the groups, from Suzanne the Noun and Brick the Verb to "Milderd" the Preposition and Jock the Interjection.

Deciding that childishness might work in my favor in this particular letter, I addressed a matching envelope to Miss Rachel Huff, put a three-cent Victory stamp on it, and headed down what Finn called our holy terror of a driveway to be in time for the postman. I pictured Rachel scuffling down her driveway, kicking up as much white gravel as she could, and finding my letter in their box. She would rip it open the brutal way she opened her presents, scan it with a shrug, and take it back to the house to show her mother. "Well, well, better late than never," Lorena Huff would say. She would read it over several times, cheered by my childish *reallys*. I wasn't *that* superior to her Rachel, after all. "You know, Rachel, maybe we've been too hard on Helen. The poor child can't be having a good summer. You can tell from all she doesn't say. You notice she doesn't mention that excitable cousin, and you can tell she misses our house and the pool."

It wasn't lunchtime yet, so I went to sit in Nonie's car and go on with my story of how it would be when Finn came to live with us. Any branch of the story could lead to satisfying little branchlets. Finn's driving lessons could turn into the first time he lets me drive to school and how everyone sees me with him in the passenger seat, or it could take us on a trip around town where I point out significant landmarks of my history. ("That house over there was my grandfather's first lodge for the Recoverers, but you have to keep in mind that this was a better part of town back then and things looked much nicer . . .")

"Guess what?" Flora greeted me when I came in for lunch. "Finn called."

"Did he ask for me?"

"Well, he seemed ready to talk to whoever answered."

"What did he want?"

"Mr. Crump had told him we were worried about him, and—"

"I wasn't worried. Maybe *you* were."

"What happened, honey? You were in such a good mood this morning."

"What happened was I spent the whole rest of the morning writing a stupid letter."

"I'm sure it wasn't stupid. You couldn't be stupid if you tried. Was it to your father?"

"I'm not writing him again until he writes me. If you must know, it was to the Huffs."

"It's none of my business. I didn't mean to pry." Then, typical of Flora, she undermined her whole argument by asking was there any special reason I was writing to the Huffs, or was it just to say hello.

"It was a thank-you letter I forgot to write sooner. But I think it's better to write a thank-you note late than not to ever write it, don't you?"

"Oh, I definitely do." I had expected her to blush or bury her face in her hands at the memory of her own rudeness, but my accusation went right over her. "Anyway, Finn said he wanted to fill us in on what's been happening to him, so I invited him to dinner."

"When?"

"Tonight. Was that okay?"

"Did he sound good or bad?"

"Good, I think. Maybe he's heard something from that military board and he can start making plans for his future. I said we were only having Juliet's wartime meat loaf recipe, which goes heavy on oatmeal for filler, but he sounded eager to come. I'm glad I still have some of Juliet's dried oregano left. Maybe I'll make some of her cheese straws for starters."

I was dying to say "Juliet who?" just to get her goat, but, looking ahead to the happy day when the Willow Fanning room would be empty and Finn would be settling into the Starling Peake room, I said, "I want to watch you make them so I can do it for my father after you're gone." She looked so pleased that I generously added, "But we will always call them Flora's cheese straws."

XX.

Finn looked more presentable, somehow. Since his last visit, his hair had grown out enough from its spiky crew cut to lie flat on either side of a part, and his beaky face had acquired a becoming layer of color. He wore a neatly ironed khaki shirt and trousers and some brown, military-looking shoes. He had brought us a bunch of fragrant roses in a variety of colors from the garden of the old lady who kept forgetting things, only he now referred to her as Miss Adelaide, and explained he had been watering her garden and feeding her cat while she recuperated in the hospital from a fall.

"Cats prefer to stay in their own home even without their owners," he said.

"So do humans," I pointed out, which struck me as a very witty comeback except that Flora sideswiped it by asking if poor Miss Adelaide had broken anything. She very luckily hadn't, Finn said, though she was bruised all over her body from head to toe. Into my overexcited brain popped the image of a naked old lady showing Finn her bruises from head to toe and out of my mouth burst a childish snort of laughter, which embarrassed all three of us.

"But we want to hear what's been happening to *you*," said Flora, taking Finn lightly by the arm and steering him into the living room. "Is there any news from that military board you met with?"

"No final decision yet," said Finn, settling into his former place on the sofa. "But if a person can guess when he's made a good impression, I'd say there's hope."

"Can you talk about it?" asked Flora breathlessly, sliding in next to him, "or is it a confidential matter?"

"Sure, I can talk about it—with friends," said Finn. "But to fill you in properly I'd need to go back a little. Ah, I was hoping you'd have that lemonade again."

"And Helen made the cheese straws."

"Not totally," I corrected her. "You were standing right over me."

"Well, you *shaped* them completely without my help," insisted Flora, which drew attention to their rather clumsily twisted bodies on the serving plate.

"Let him go on," I said.

"Well," Finn began again, "I have to go back a little for it to make sense. Maybe as far back as September of 'forty-three, coming up two years ago, when we docked at Liverpool. There were five thousand of us on this transport ship built to carry one thousand. A bit crowded, but there you are. But it made our Nissen huts in the English countryside where we ended up seem like little palaces at first. My company was training hard, building foxholes, perfecting our skills of loving the ground. Remember, Helen, on our little . . . er . . . walk that day"—his eye caught mine to signal our secret was still safe—"and I was telling you how we learned to use the ground to keep ourselves alive?"

"I remember," I said, looking meaningfully back.

"Then the weather turned cold and wet and many of the men came down with asthma or pneumonia. Pneumonia was your first choice because asthma was considered a chronic thing and they transferred you to a desk job. When I was diagnosed with pneumonia, I danced for joy because I could still be cured in time to make the big jump we'd been practicing for two years."

I could picture Finn dancing for joy the way I had seen him do it that day in the crater. Flora couldn't have such a picture because she didn't know we'd been in the crater together and she never would.

"Then my lung collapsed and this one doctor saw scar tissue on an X-ray which he thought was a sign of tubercles, and I was evacuated so as not to infect others."

"You had TB?" I asked excitedly.

"Don't be rushing me, darling."

"Sorry." But it was the first time anyone had called me darling since Nonie died, which somewhat lessened the shame of his reproof.

"As it fell out, I didn't have TB, but they weren't sure till they got me to the military hospital here. And then there was the long recovery from the collapsed lung, and I missed the big jump on D-Day."

"Well, I'm glad you missed it!" Flora cried. "So many boys were killed!" She had her arms crossed over her chest and was rubbing them up and down, the way she did during our scary programs.

"Ah," said Finn, not rebuking *her* for interrupting but giving her an appreciative nod as if she was helping him along. "Which brings us to the second part of my sorry tale, how I joined the ranks of the mentalers. By now I was all clean in the X-rays but I still had to undergo a regimen to build back my lung power.

Every day we . . . Recoverers (I love that word) were driven out to a mountain near the hospital and had to walk up and down a trail, a bit farther each day, and have our breathing monitored. The big jump had happened without me, but I was expecting to be sent back overseas soon. The D-Day casualties had been heavy and there was plenty of fighting left to do. Then, one day they told me I had a visitor and I went down and there was my mate Barney's mother. Barney and I had gone through jump school together and he was in the Nissen hut with me in England. While we were training in Georgia, he had taken me home on leave to his mother's apple orchards, which he was going to run as soon as the war was over. She was a widow and he was the only child. When I came into the reception room, she gave me a strange smile and said I looked a little fatter than when I had visited. She had ridden the bus up from Georgia, she said, to bring me some baked goods and a few keepsakes. She hadn't said Barney's name, but as soon as she said "keepsakes" I knew he hadn't made it. She said she had heard "from overseas" that I had been sent home to this place. I knew it must have been in a letter from Barney in the winter of 'forty-four. Still there was no saying of his name. It was like we were in a contest not to be the unkind one to speak it first. Then she said she'd brought a drawing I'd done in the Nissen hut, it was in the tin, along with a snapshot of me taken at her house. I knew she meant my drawing of Barney because I remembered him sending it to her. When I said she should keep it, she said she'd rather not. Still no saying of his name, and then she switched to asking about me and the state of my health and she was smiling that strange smile again."

"How was it strange?" I needed to know.

He didn't say "don't be rushing me, darling" this time, but gave it some thought. "It wasn't a friendly smile," he presently said. "It was more what you'd call a malevolent smile. Like there was something more to come that you weren't going to like. Only I didn't know yet what that something was."

Flora, still rubbing her arms up and down, hung on to his every word.

"I told her my lung was healed," continued Finn, "and that I was expecting to be sent back into combat: there was still the war to be won. 'Yes,' she said, 'well, I hope you see some action, if that's what you want. Maybe there will be more *jumping* to do.' Then she said she had a taxi waiting and a return bus to make and she was glad I had been spared. I was touched by her being able to say that just as I was extremely touched that she'd come all this way, and I must have made some move toward her, but she shoved the tin of baked goods into my hands and said, 'He didn't get to make the jump because their plane was shot down. A few of them jumped and then it was shot down. You could have been on that plane, waiting your turn to jump. Though maybe with your good luck you'd have been one of those first few who made it out.' And then came that smile again and she said, 'You know what I keep asking myself? Why couldn't he have been as clever as you, getting yourself evacuated like that?' And then she was gone."

"Oh!" cried Flora, unclasping herself. "What a dreadful thing to say!"

"If I hadn't been hugging that tin to my chest, the whole thing could have been something I'd dreamed," said Finn.

"You must have felt awful," said Flora, whose eyes were predictably brimming.

"I felt nothing, nothing at all. Instead, there were these important tasks I had to fulfill to set things right."

"What kind of tasks?" I asked.

"Oh, very logical, orderly tasks. Or they seemed so to me. They presented themselves to me in a very logical and orderly fashion, one after another, hour after hour, day after day, and within a week or so I had crossed right over the line into madness, following my logical, orderly little list. First, I had to obtain the names, ranks, and serial numbers of every man in the stick—the eighteen paratroopers carried by each C-47 make up a stick. Then I had to ascertain the fate of each man: Did he jump or did he go down with the plane? And if he made it to the ground, did he survive and accomplish his mission or— Then it got more and more complicated and more and more specific. What was his mission if he lived and where, exactly, was he buried when he died? I can tell you, I made a nuisance of myself with the hospital staff. I required all this special information and I told them they had to go through the channels and get it for me quickly because lives were at stake. 'Don't you realize much of this stuff is still under censorship?' they said. Until they started looking at me differently and saying, 'Don't worry, son, we're taking care of it. In the meantime, swallow these pills and get some rest.' But somehow I escaped back up that mountain we had to climb to strengthen our lungs. I don't remember at all how I got there, they say I must have slipped out of the hospital during the night and hitchhiked. When they found me at the top of the mountain I was wrapped around a tree, starkers, covered with leaves. Just as well we were having a warm November. Not that I thought so when they found me. It took three of them to hold me down. They had aborted my final mission, you see. I was supposed to exchange myself for Barney."

"What's 'starkers'?" I asked.

"Without any clothes," said Finn.

"What happened then?" Flora asked.

"Oh, then, I found myself in another wing of the hospital, talking to mental doctors rather than lung doctors, and then one day last spring I found myself signing papers for a medical discharge. The thing about the medical discharge is that you still receive certain benefits—for instance the Army continues to pay for my visits to a psychiatrist, but other benefits, like education, are forfeited."

"Like the GI Bill," moaned Flora. "But Mr. Crump did say your father had pulled some strings and they might upgrade the discharge so you could get it after all."

"That's the plan," said Finn, looking suddenly impatient with the whole subject. He chose one of my crippled cheese straws, bit into it, and pronounced it perfect, which I thought was going too far.

THE PHONE RANG while the three of us were having dinner.

"It could be my father," I said, jumping up to take the call in the kitchen.

It was my father, unusually talkative. He went on and on about the huge complex they were building, going into minute details about the ductwork and the roofing and how he'd gone to the local jail to spring one of his crew who'd drunk too much and reportedly had a "dangerous concealed weapon" on him. "I had to explain to the sheriff that Willie was a roofer and the 'dangerous weapon' was a roofer's tool for cutting felt." He sounded so pleased with himself and was talking to me as an equal, only why had he picked just now to call? I stood on one foot, then the other. I leaned against the kitchen counter and studied my distorted reflection on the back of a dessert spoon. I could hear a hushed, intimate exchange going on in the dining room. Finn was probably telling Flora the parts about going mad that he had judged best to leave out when "the child" was with them. How perverse life was. Nothing came at the right time.

"You and Flora getting on all right?" At last my father was winding down, or so I thought.

"Oh, yes. You want to talk to her?"

"Not specially. Unless you think I ought to."

Though it would be good to get Finn to myself in the dining room, what if Flora forgot and revealed that we were having company? My father would start off being prejudiced against Finn for violating the quarantine, which could put an end to my plans for the Starling Peake room.

"Not specially," I said back.

"Where is she now?" my father asked.

"Probably working on her lesson plans or writing a letter." I was speaking low.

"Flora's letters!" My father snorted. "Mother spared us those, didn't she? She couldn't dispose of them fast enough. Who is left for Flora to write to?"

"That colored woman who lives with them. She writes to her every week, she . . ."

But my father was now attacking the next thing. "Lesson plans! How happy I'd be never to see the inside of a schoolhouse again."

I was shocked. "But what would you do?"

"Oh, stay here at Oak Ridge. They're turning it into a little town. The pay is good and there's plenty of building left to do."

"But what would *I* do?"

"You'd go to school, just as you do now. They've built a school here. We could have a little house. I wouldn't have to live in a men's dormitory if you were here. What do you think?"

I could hardly reply. "Are you joking, or what?"

"Maybe I am, maybe I am. I'm feeling light-headed tonight."

"Where are you?"

"I drove out a little ways—can't drive far with this rationing. There's a nice lake where they'll make you a sandwich with a pickle and you can rent a boat. If you were here, we might take a boat out."

"But what about our *house*?"

"I take it you mean Old One Thousand, the old death trap. We could sell the damn thing. Start a new life with no ghoulish emcun—cum—*cum*brances."

Only when he messed up *encumbrances* did I realize they were providing him with more than a sandwich and a pickle at the nice lake.

Which would I have hated more? For him to have been sober and serious about our starting a new life and moving us off to a place in the middle of nowhere, or for him to have fallen off the wagon and be "flying high," as Nonie used to call it, when he had imbibed just the right amount to tease her with fantasies of how he was going to escape, one way or another? Fortunately, "just the right amount" always sloshed over into the darker hour where he crashed to earth and we three remained safely together on top of our mountain.

Of the two options, I preferred the sloshed safety of Old One Thousand.

"MY, YOU TWO did some talking," said Flora. "I guess your father didn't want to talk to me." She and Finn had assumed that innocent look of having said nothing of any importance while I was away.

"He asked about you, but we had a lot to talk about."

"How is he?"

"He was at some lake, having a sandwich. He said if I was there we could take a boat out. I told him we were doing fine here."

"That was nice of you, honey." Then more to Finn than me she said, "In a little over a month I'll be teaching fifth grade in Alabama. It seems hard to believe."

"I'll be starting sixth grade." I said. "And my father will be back as principal of the high school." I looked at Finn. "Where do you think you'll be?"

"I'd rather not be thinking till I know, darling. Maybe I'll still be right here. Finn, your deliverer." With a resolute laugh he improved on it: "Finn, your *Recoverer*-deliverer."

December 12, 1938

Dear Flora,

If I were you, I would put out of my mind what you overheard in your house. One person was crying hard, you say, and the other person was very angry, and words aren't necessarily heard clearly when someone is crying hard and the other person is spluttering with anger. Also, when we're angry we snatch at straws and make up things to hurt the other person. I think that is what happened. He was afraid he was going to lose his share of the house and wanted to accuse her of something that would scare her. So he snatched at something that could put her in real danger. What was especially odious was that the other person being accused had just died and couldn't defend himself. And, as you say, it was cruel for the accuser to insinuate that the long and trusting friendship between the two who raised you was something else, especially when that something else is against the laws of the land.

But I have written more than is wise and must ask you to destroy this letter.

As you say, Flora, people we trusted can be downright treacherous. I could furnish you with a few examples but I have buried them in my heart and I advise you to do the same. To end on a positive note before I take Helen off to the Recreation Park, let me assure you that we are never "completely helpless." A person always has control over *how* she meets her adversities, and the good news is that the facing of them, one after another, year after year, builds an inner strength that nobody can take away from you.

Yours truly,
Honora Anstruther

XXI.

There was a sink in the Starling Peake room, which wasn't officially called that because, though he had been charming, he had let everyone down. When I was little I asked Nonie why that room had a sink and she said it was a consolation prize because it was inferior to the other rooms.

"Why was it inferior?"

"It didn't open onto a porch."

"But the other Recoverer's room across the hall doesn't open onto a porch either."

"No, but that room gets the morning sun and is next to the bathroom."

When I was older, I asked my father the same question about the sink and he said because a man could piss in the sink without having to walk to the bathroom.

"But what if a woman was staying in there?"

"We only had one of those and she had the big front room with the private half bath."

"The Willow Fanning room," I said.

"I wish Mother would leave off her precious room naming. It's been a quarter century since this has been a halfway house for rich malingerers. We don't need their old ghosts rattling around: we have enough of our own to avoid stumbling over."

I COULDN'T IMAGINE Finn pissing in the sink, and didn't want to. Besides, there would be no need for him to. Flora would have gone back to Alabama and my father would be at school all day and if Finn were using the upstairs bathroom or taking a bath when my father was home, my father would make use of the half bath in the Willow Fanning room, or go downstairs, which he would probably prefer to do anyway so he could freshen his drink.

Finn's recent visit to us had gone downhill after dinner. When we adjourned to the living room for coffee and pound cake, Finn brought out his sketchbook and said he wanted to do a portrait of Flora. After her predictable fluttery protests, he arranged her in Nonie's wing chair because he said that had worked so well with me last time. I sat beside him on the sofa, which was nice at first, but then he became so rapt with his subject that there seemed to be a lit-up path between him and Flora that left the rest of the room in darkness. He was oblivious of me, but Flora kept darting nervous little glances to see if I was getting resentful or bored. When she asked me how the picture was coming along, I couldn't very well say, "He's making you prettier than you really are," so I borrowed Mrs. Jones's phrase and told her it was going to be suitable for framing.

"Oh, we will, we will!" exclaimed Flora.

"Please, love, don't . . . move . . . your face," Finn said.

"Sorry," said Flora, but she flushed up at his use of the love word.

When he was done and she finished uttering her little yips and saying he'd made her nicer-looking than she was, he reclaimed the sketchbook and said, "I'll take it away with me, then, and work on it some more. Give you a squinty eye and a few whiskers." Then they had a mock tussle, after which he still insisted on keeping it in the sketchbook to work on some more. And she got all emotional and said, "How I wish I could draw. Then I would have a likeness of you to take back with me to Alabama."

Only at the tail end of the evening did I manage to get him to myself by following him out to his motorcycle. "Listen," I said (I had rehearsed this): "We have some nice empty rooms upstairs, and when it starts getting cold in Crump's storage attic, you could move in here. I'll discuss it with my father. I'm pretty sure he'd welcome the company."

He looked surprised, then laughed. "Will I be one of your Recoverers, then?" He stooped and gave me a hug. "We'll have to see, darling," he said. "We'll have to see how things fall out."

But he had also given Flora a hug. And called her "love."

IN THE LAST days of July, Flora's and my fifth-grade class languished due to sudden breakdowns and interruptions at Old One Thousand. First, the garbage truck got stuck in a rut and we had to call a tow truck and the garbage man yelled at us that he wasn't coming again until we got our f——ing driveway fixed.

"Please, sir!" cried Flora. "There's a child present. Her father is off doing important war work in Oak Ridge, Tennessee, and it will be fixed as soon as he returns next month." She began to cry softly and also the driver had heard of Oak Ridge, and he and the driver of the tow truck ended up fashioning a makeshift bridge of planks over the rut and gratefully accepting coffee and hot corn bread from Flora in the kitchen before they left.

Then the downspout that had been hanging tipsily sideways from the gutter fell down across the lawn—or former lawn.

"Oh, dear," moaned Flora, "we'll have to get someone."

"Leave it till my father gets back," I said. I didn't say that I was hoping he might surprise us and show up for my birthday, which was a little over a week away.

"Well, I don't know, honey. Nobody likes to come home and see pieces of their house all over the ground. It looks like someone hasn't been taking care of things."

"It's just one piece, and you can't even see it when you drive up. You're only supposed to be taking care of me, not the house."

But Flora decided to phone Mr. Crump at Grove Market, to ask if he knew of a "reasonable" carpenter, and Finn answered and said he could do it if we had a ladder, which we did. He asked if it could wait until the weekend and Flora said it could and thanked him too profusely.

Then the toilet in the Willow Fanning half bath got clogged, and Flora cried and said now everyone would blame her for flushing something down it when she hadn't. She phoned the plumber listed in Nonie's little "Majordomo" book, but the number had been disconnected. "And I can't call Mr. Crump again," she wailed.

"Why not? He's bound to know a plumber."

"*Because*, don't you see? Finn might answer again and offer to fix it himself when he comes to do the gutter and that would be humiliating."

I saw Finn kneeling in front of Flora's toilet, pulling out something disgusting. It made me want to laugh, but not for long. It would reflect on me, too, and make him not want to live in our house.

But Flora fetched the plunger and went at the Willow Fanning toilet so violently it choked up an enormous soggy wad, which she insisted on my inspecting. "I want you to see there's nothing in it but toilet paper. But it's still my fault, I've been using too much. At home, Juliet had this rule: two squares for number one, four for number two, unless it was—"

"Okay, okay!"

I SET TO work on my refurbishment of Starling Peake's old room, which I was already secretly calling the Devlin Patrick Finn room. There wasn't any deep cleaning to do; Mrs. Jones had been faithful with that. The floor was regularly vacuumed, the windowsills scrubbed, the curtains and bedspread laundered, and the furniture polished—though there was way too much furniture. The two "lesser" Recoverers' rooms had become repositories for castoffs, like my father's Persian carpets that had tripped him once too often and twiggy-legged tables and plant stands and framed pictures and mirrors turned to the wall.

I first thought I'd tell Flora I was fixing up this room for when new friends came to stay over. But I had grown so adept at predicting her responses I could hear her ask why I didn't put them in my old room downstairs. So instead I told her I wanted to make a study upstairs for myself.

"But, honey, why that gloomy old room? If you want an upstairs study, why not take your grandfather's consulting room, with all its nice shelves?"

"That's for family trophies and things. And my father goes in there to look things up in books."

"Oh, in that case. But wouldn't the Recoverer's room across the hall be more cheerful? It gets the morning sun."

"I don't always want to be cheerful. I like gloom, too. Besides, when I get home from school it will be the afternoon."

"That's true," she conceded.

"I just have a feeling about that room. I like it."

"I wonder if—?"

"What?"

"Your mother kept her clothes in the big old wardrobe in there. I remember going in and sniffing them after her funeral. There was still her scent. Maybe rooms can— Oh, I don't know, honey. It's your house and you can pick whichever room you want. I should learn to keep my big mouth shut."

IN STARLING PEAKE'S old room was a hulking old cheval dresser with a tilting mirror. Its drawers were crammed with the saddest detritus you could imagine. Each item must once have had a purpose but now gave up its history to a meaningless mound of junk. The prospect of emptying the drawers was so depressing I decided to wait for Mrs. Jones.

"What do you want to do with all this?" she asked, after a grim survey.

"I want it not to be in there."

This prompted one of her rare closed-mouthed laughs. "Let's take it out, then, and lay it down on a cloth. You can go over it better that way."

"One drawer at a time, or all three?"

"Oh, let's get it all out." She made it sound like a daring proposal.

She found an old quilt in the wardrobe and spread it out on the bed.

"Flora said my mother used to keep her clothes in that wardrobe."

"She did. There wasn't enough room in your father's closet."

"I wonder where they went."

"Your grandmother gave them away. I helped her box them up. It was hard for her. She set great store by Miss Lisbeth."

"Do you remember my mother?"

"Well, naturally I do."

"Did you like her?"

"She was always very nice to me. I didn't see much of her because she was at the high school all day with your father. The only time I got to know her a little was the spring and summer she was expecting you. She would rest on the bed in here sometimes."

"In this room?"

"She said it was cooler and she liked being out of everybody's way. When I was going over the room we would talk."

"What about?"

"Oh, she asked what it was like when I was expecting Rosemary and if I had been as big and felt as awkward in my final months. I told her I had a much bigger frame than her and could carry the extra weight better and that I had been born awkward. This cheered her up. Usually she had a book or two on the bed with her. If she was reading we didn't talk, unless she spoke first."

"What kind of books?"

"Schoolbooks. She couldn't wait to go back to her teaching. One time she read a poem to me about a lady who had to stay in a room with her back to the window. She couldn't look out directly or she would bring down some kind of curse, but she rigged a mirror so she could see the reflection of the road below and could watch life going on through the mirror."

"What was that poem?"

"I don't rightly recall, but I do remember her saying this room was like it because you could look out the window and see the road down below, only she didn't have to use a mirror."

"But how could she see the road from the bed?"

"The bed was over by the window, then. You could lie on it and look down through the trees and see Sunset Drive. It's all blocked in now, but you could still see the road back then."

Checker pieces with no board—a perfume atomizer—a rusty harmonica with dust in the holes—a shaving brush with stiff bristles—a crudely carved wooden giraffe with its broken neck glued back on—empty gift boxes and folded Christmas wrapping paper—string and ribbons—a cloudy magnifying glass—a tarnished sugar spoon with something crusty in its bowl—a cut-glass bottle of dried-out smelling salts—an empty tin of Sears, Roebuck gunpowder tea filled with rubber bands and paper clips—pen nibs and pencil stubs—boxes of rifle cartridges—a small square porcelain dish with a scene of trees and a lake and HANDPAINTED IN NIPPON written on the bottom—a used elastic bandage—an ivory cigarette holder—a silk sleeping mask—a guide to palmistry with the cover torn off—an extension cord—two buckeyes—a silver flask (no monogram) without its top—a rubber stem syringe with a red bulb—an empty box that said: "German Liquor Cure: 24 doses"—a sealed pack of playing cards—a Standard Accident Insurance Company of Detroit date book for 1923 with "nb" faithfully recorded in pencil for every day in the month of January, followed by empty pages for the rest of the year—a small tarnished silver tray stuffed inside a wad of tissue and brown paper; on the tray was engraved the profile of a bird and ALABAMA, THE YELLOWHAMMER STATE.

"I'd go over each item with a damp cloth before you lay it out on the bed," Mrs. Jones had suggested before leaving. "If there's things you're not sure what to do with, we can look those over when I come next week."

The sorting-out part took longer than I expected. There were things I knew I shouldn't throw out, even though I wanted them out of the room. There were some puzzling objects that I wanted to look at some more before I consigned them to the trash. And there were a few things that might be of use to Finn: the extension cord and the sealed pack of cards, and the buckeyes for good luck—I could tell him about the local legends if he didn't know them. But he definitely wouldn't want someone's disgusting old shaving brush or a flask with no top, or even if it had a top because he was on the dry. Each survivor of the trash I carefully wiped down before placing it on the bed. (Would Finn like to have his bed moved back to the window?)

When at last I surveyed my final collection on the bed, I ferociously regretted the loss of Annie Rickets.

("Oh, boy, let's get to work. There are different ways we could do this, Helen. We could each take one patient at a time and pick out items for them and then deduce their secrets from their items, or we could go item by item and decide who it belonged to, and then— No, that's much too infantile for us: my first idea is better. I'll go first if you let me start with the Willing Fanny. The sleeping mask is definitely hers, and probably the cigarette holder, and she has to have the perfume atomizer, unless one of the male patients was a fairy, and also the smelling salts, and I think she should have the crusted spoon—a ladylike slurp of opium for the long, boring afternoon ahead at Shangri-la. Oh, sorry, I'm taking too many? Okay, you can have the opium spoon back. But I have to insist that syringe is hers, because it's not the kind you use for enemas, it's what women use when they need to shoot water and Lysol up inside them. My mammy has one and she says it has kept us from being a family of ten. That date book could be a man's or a woman's, so I won't be greedy. But I'll bet anything those *nb*'s stand for either 'no blood' or 'no booze.' The 'no booze' is if they were on the wagon. The other could be either someone who's missed her period or, more boringly, a former tubercular who's counting his good days. Breaking off like that could mean they fell off the wagon or got her period or didn't get it, or, in the case of the tubercular, the blood came back and he expired.")

Flora was standing in the doorway. "Supper is ready when you are, honey. Goodness! What is all that?"

"Junk from the drawers in here."

She approached the bed. "It's not all junk. That's a perfectly good extension cord, and, look, what a sweet little painted dish—"

"I *know*. I'm sorting it *out*. I just don't want it in those drawers, in a big *clump*, where it's been laying useless for years—"

"Oh! That's our calling card tray!"

"Whose calling card tray?"

"The one we sent to Lisbeth for a wedding present. Where did you find this, Helen?"

"I told you. In those drawers."

"Just . . . lying with all the junk?" She scooped it up and cradled it in her palms.

"No, it had lots of paper around it."

"What kind of paper?"

"Just the brown paper things get mailed in. And there was some tissue paper, too. It was all scrunched up together."

"Where is it? Did you throw it away?"

"Yes, but it's still in the trash basket over there."

Already she was at the basket. "Oh, God, here it is!" Now she was pulling apart the brown paper from the tissue. Such a frenzy over some old wrapping paper. "Oh, I don't believe this! The card's still in here!"

"I didn't see any card."

"Here it is. Oh, my daddy's own sweet handwriting." The tears were at the ready. "All of us signed it. See?"

She proudly showed me the signatures on the card: a younger Flora's, the bold scrawls of the men, and, familiar to me from her letters to Flora, the proper slant of Juliet Parker.

"It is sterling silver," said Flora. "Juliet picked it out, but we all contributed. But why did Lisbeth stuff it away with all that junk? Still in its paper! I wonder if she even saw the card."

"Who says it was her? It was probably someone else after she died. They saw it out on a table and said, 'Oh, what is this for?' and then put it in the drawer."

"No," said Flora, cradling the little tray like a wounded animal. "It wasn't ever out on any table. When I stayed here that week after the funeral I looked everywhere. I understand now. I was a fool not to see it before. Lisbeth hated it. She was ashamed of it. Just another piece of Alabama trash."

"That is just ridiculous," I said (though suspecting she might have a point). "You really need to have more faith in yourself, Flora. And if you don't have it, you at least have to act like you do."

"That is exactly what your grandmother would have said," marveled Flora, regarding me with fond respect.

"What *is* a yellowhammer anyway?"

"Why, it's our state bird. It's the sweetest little woodpecker with these bright yellow underwings. Juliet has three yellowhammer boxes in our backyard. My daddy made the boxes for her. They have to be made just so. When the babies fledge, our whole backyard is aflutter with yellow wings."

As we went down to supper, I had to congratulate myself for deflecting Flora from her trash talk and staving off those ready tears. There had not been a single tear shed. I felt like a proud parent who, after hard work, sees her child growing into sociability and self-control.

XXII.

It was the last Sunday in July. Then there would be next Sunday, and two days after that, August seventh, would be my birthday. My father had not written or phoned since he was having his sandwich and pickle out at that lake. I chose to interpret his silence as meaning that he planned to surprise me by simply showing up on my birthday.

Today was a sultry, overcast Sunday like the Sunday Flora and I had taken the taxi to church and heard the awful news about Brian. And then Father McFall had driven us home and we hadn't been down the mountain since.

But at least it wasn't raining, which meant that Finn would be coming to fix the gutter in the afternoon.

Lately I had been composing scenes where my father and Finn would meet, maybe as soon as my birthday. I made myself do it two ways. First I had to imagine my father finding something in Finn to scorn, and then, before I could allow myself to go on, I had to figure out what that thing would be. Finn's orange spikes had grown out into an acceptable head of hair, he looked less like a wraithlike outsider since he had gotten some sun weeding the old lady's garden; and the only time he had been really silly was when he had danced for joy at the bottom of the crater, and nobody had seen that but me. Finn was friendly, but not "familiar," which my father couldn't stand in people, and he spoke well, even with his funny *will we*'s and *a-tall, a-tall*'s. He showed no signs of having been "a mentaler," the type of person who would escape from a hospital and wrap himself naked around a tree trunk in order to exchange himself for a dead friend.

Having gone through the negatives and discounted them one by one, I could then move on to the Finn who would catch my father's interest, charm him, and eventually earn his respect. This was a much pleasanter proposition, and I approached it so well that I kept getting excited and losing my place and having to start over. The consummation point I worked toward in these scenes ended with the two of them (with myself present, of course) in animated dialogue, each at his best: my father witty and slightly world-weary but without the sarcasm and Finn sweet and caring in his masculine way, without any hints of mental problems. And then Finn would say something, maybe about me, and my father would say, "Look here, why don't you join forces with us in this crumbling old pile? We've got lots of empty rooms if you don't mind a few ghostly *encumbrances*." "Ah, if you mean the Recoverers," Finn would say, "Helen has told me about them and I wouldn't mind them a-tall, a-tall. I'd be honored, Mr. Anstruther." "Please," my father would say, "call me Harry." And then they'd toast it with cocktails that I would mix. Maybe just one for Finn, if he was still on the dry. But you needed a cocktail for a toast.

And then the whole project had collapsed in a miserable heap because I had forgotten to include Flora. Flora would still be here on my birthday. She had to be somewhere in the picture, and if she were my father couldn't be asking Finn to live with us yet. Also who could predict how she might derail things or what unwelcome bit of information she might blurt out at any time? My imaginative powers had made a serious miscalculation in timing and logistics, and I was disgusted with myself.

AT LUNCH, FLORA said, "Listen, Helen, what should we do about supper?"

"We're still eating lunch."

"You know what I mean."

"No, I don't."

"Finn is coming to fix the downspout."

"So?"

"Well, I haven't asked him to supper."

"You *haven't*?" I had just assumed she had, even though there hadn't been her usual agonizings over which Juliet-dish to prepare. "Why ever not?" (One of Nonie's pet phrases.)

"Well, I didn't want him to think we're running after him."

"Why on earth would he think that?" I was stalling for time, Nonie-like, until I figured out how to get the upper hand.

"Because . . . Oh, I don't know. You think we should ask him?"

"Oh, no. Just let him come and fix our gutters for free, and then say, 'Oh, thanks, bye now. Hope you're not hungry or anything.'"

"Oh, dear." The tears were mobilizing.

"So he'll climb on his motorcycle and ride away thinking, *I wonder what I did to make them not like me anymore.*"

"I'm going to call him right now."

"Now, that *would* look like you're running after him. Besides, the store's closed on Sunday. Just wait until he comes this afternoon and say we're having a light supper, nothing fancy, but he's welcome to stay."

"But, he'll be all sweaty and might feel he should wash." She seemed to have given this previous thought.

"Well, let him wash here. We certainly have enough bathrooms."

"In that case, what should we have?"

"You'll think of something. You always do."

But Finn already had supper plans. Miss Adelaide, the old lady who was losing her memory and had bruises from head to toe, was back from the hospital and was making him fried chicken and waffles to thank him for taking care of her cat and her garden.

"Oh, chicken and waffles, I can't compete with that," said Flora, folding her arms and looking away to hide her mortification.

"Don't be like that, love. If I had known—"

"No, it's my fault," Flora eagerly rushed on. "I didn't ask earlier because I was afraid you would get sick of seeing us, but then Helen said she wanted you."

"I did *not*."

"Ah," Finn teased me, "so you *didn't* want me."

"That is not what I meant." I could have killed Flora for getting me into this trap. Why did she have to proclaim her every self-doubt from the rooftops? Now both of them were anxiously regarding me: the child who might fly off the handle. Well, I would show them. "He *is* going to get sick of us," I scolded Flora, "if we won't let him get on with what he came to do." Toward Finn I was all business. "Come on," I said, "I'll show you where the extension ladder is."

But once the two of us were in the garage, I relented. He stopped to run a hand lovingly down a rear fender of Nonie's car. "Nineteen thirty-three Oldsmobile Tudor touring car," he said like an incantation. "We won't see its like again."

"I wish we could drive it," I said.

"Well, why can't you?"

"Because Flora never learned to drive and I'm too young to get a license."

"Are you saying you can drive then?"

"No, but if somebody would teach me I would have a head start."

"Flora never learned to drive?" he asked just as I was getting ready to add that maybe he would teach me.

"None of her people in Alabama learned. They couldn't afford a car."

"That's no cause a-tall. A lot of folks drive who don't own automobiles."

"The school she really wanted rejected her because she couldn't drive." Might as well show interest in what interested him, since I had missed out on my chance.

"Ah, was she sorely let down?"

"She cried, but that's what she always does. She said she wished she had told them she could drive and then had someone teach her before school started."

"What a shame," Finn said angrily.

"But she's real excited about the school that does want her. And some man she met at her interview wrote and said he'd be glad to teach her to drive."

"I'll bet he would," Finn said. "Has anyone been charging the battery?"

"I wasn't sure how."

"Turn the key and let the motor run is all it takes."

"I think the battery is dead," I said quickly because he was starting to look annoyed with me. "In fact, I'm sure it's dead."

"How do you know that?"

"Because a man came and tried, but it wouldn't start." I had almost said the man was Mr. Crump, but Finn might check. Let it just be a man.

"That's a shame," said Finn.

"My father will see to it when he gets back," I assured him.

"Well, it's still a bleeding shame," said Finn.

I helped him carry the long extension ladder, which he set up at the needy corner of the house with a great deal of shaking and rattling, and then when he had fastened on his tool belt and climbed to the top, Flora and I did our part by lifting up the downspout pipe and holding it steady until he had reattached it to its gutter.

"That should do it, ladies," he said.

"That's all?" said Flora, looking woefully up at him. "You mean you're finished already?"

"With that little task I am. But while we've got the ladder up, will I have a look at the other gutters all around the house? I could bail out some of the gunk while I'm about it."

"Well, I— Helen, what do you think? It's your house."

"That would be really nice of you," I said to Finn on the ladder. "If you're sure you have the time."

"Oh, I have. Miss Adelaide doesn't want me till half past six. What I'll need, though, is something to put the gunk in."

"I'll get a bucket," cried Flora, already running for the house.

"Are you going to need *two* people?" I called up to him.

"Come again?"

"Will you need two of us for the bucket part? I've got something I need to do in the house."

"You run on then, darling. Your cousin and I will manage fine."

"Will you come and say good-bye before you leave?"

"Sure I will. Where will I find you?"

"I'll be upstairs. It's easy. You turn left at the top of the stairs and it's the first room. I'll be working in there. Will you come when you've finished the gutters?"

"I will. But it might be an hour or so. Is that all right?"

"Perfect. I have something I want to show you."

AT LAST, AT last, I thought, triumphantly racing up the stairs—stairs Finn would be climbing for the first time in "an hour or so"—*I am learning how to get people to do as I want.* Flora didn't count. She was too easy, too much like someone my own age. No, not even that. She was easier than wily Annie Rickets; easier than Rachel Huff, whose sullen moods somehow insulated her like a black cloud from the demands of others; easier, even, than tranquil Brian Beale, so congenial to play with but stubbornly set in his ways when it came to what he wanted us to play.

It was almost ready, the Devlin Patrick Finn room: the room that had not been named for Starling Peake because he had let us down, the room my mother had chosen to lie and read in when she was expecting me. The drawers of the old cheval dresser had been emptied and lined with paper (the perfectly good extension cord, the sealed pack of cards, and the two buckeyes placed neatly in the top drawer for Finn); I had cleaned its tilting glass with vinegar and newspaper, the way I had seen Mrs. Jones do it, and I had shined the mirror above the sink, where Finn's pointy face would look back at him when he shaved. ("We'll need to get a desk or a table in here," I heard myself telling him, "but we waited to see which you preferred for your artwork." "One thing this old pile has plenty of," my father might add, if he was accompanying us, "is furniture. You'll trip over it and bust your head if you're not careful.")

If only I hadn't told Finn, "I've got something I need to do in the house." He probably thought I had to go to the bathroom. I should have said, "I've got some work I need to do in the house." But aside from that I felt I had developed my social arts this summer, even in all our isolation, and had to concede that Flora had contributed to my progress. Flora, however easy, had provided me with a round-the-clock living human specimen to practice on.

There was one thing left to be done before Finn came upstairs, and it turned out to be harder than I had expected. I wanted the bed to be back at the window, the way it was in my mother's time, but in my impatience and frustration in moving it I made an ugly gash in the floor. I dragged my father's oriental rug over it, but that left a big square of bare floor that was lighter than the rest because it had been under the rug for so long. There was nothing to do but drag in the other oriental rug from the other Recoverer's room to cover the naked square. The result was a success, but it had worn me out. I lay down on my mother's old bed by the window, thinking of the poor lady in the poem who had to watch life through a mirror, and felt myself sinking alarmingly toward a childish nap. But that would be all right, too. Finn would come up and wake me, like that day when I crouched like a catatonic by the side of the road. "Hello, hello," he would say, bending over the bed. "Is anyone there?"

XXIII.

Once, when I was five, I took an afternoon nap and woke up and found things had been done without me. Before the nap, Nonie and I had been sitting on the sofa coloring together. I always did the characters in the picture and allowed her to color in the background, which she did in such a way that enhanced my artwork. It was a superior coloring book, or at least I'm remembering it that way. The paper was smooth, not porous, the pages lay flat, and the pictures were from myths, fairy tales, and the Bible. The picture was on the right side and its story was on the left side. We always read the story first so we could get an idea of how the picture ought to be colored in. I don't remember the picture we had finished before Nonie said, "Someone looks sleepy," and walked me to my room, but I remember some of the pictures in the book. There was Cinderella and Snow White and the Seven Dwarfs, and Noah receiving the dove telling him the coast was clear, and Ruth and Naomi, and Joseph in his coat of many colors (but not what his brothers were going to do to him on the trip) and Aladdin and Pandora, and Psyche holding a candle over Cupid while he slept. The coloring book was called *A*

Color Book of Old Stories. I still look for it sometimes online, but have never found anything remotely like it. For a while I had this fantasy that I would suddenly hit on it, *A Color Book of Old Stories*, and order it, and when it arrived I would get some crayons and turn to the page in question and redeem my lost colors.

When I woke up from my nap and went looking for Nonie, I found her sitting on the sofa with the closed coloring book on her lap. She looked guilty when she saw me.

"What did you do while I was asleep?" I demanded.

"Well, I colored another picture," she said, an odd blush rising in her cheeks. "I don't know what came over me."

"Which one? Let me see."

She turned to the one of Pandora opening the chest full of bad things, the entire picture colored in with her choice of colors. "Is that all right?" she asked rather sheepishly.

"That's the one I was saving—to do BY MYSELF!"

"Then I have overstepped."

I looked with disgust at the pink-cheeked figure in her blue gown. Pandora's dress was supposed to be blackish purple, her face chalk white with dark shadows from what she realizes she has set loose on the world. And the sinister faces and writhing bodies of the plagues and sorrows floating out of the open chest that I had been planning to do one by one in devilish, jarring colors, Nonie had crayoned over so they all looked submerged in a watery green effluvium.

"I'm sorry, darling," Nonie said. "But you've still got Aladdin, which has a similar story."

"I wanted Pandora," I said.

* * *

WHEN I WOKE up from my nap in Finn's future room, I immediately had the feeling that something had not happened, but I did not begin to imagine all that had happened without me.

The light in the sky was too late for it to have been just an hour. I had drooled on the bedspread. It was very quiet outside. *He didn't come* was my dismal thought. Then I heard a man's voice in the living room below. Then a clink of a teacup in a saucer and Flora's eager-to-be-impressed response, then the man again. His voice was deep and harsh, at the other end of the scale from Finn's spun-glass tenor, and he spoke in blunt clumps, like someone who liked making his points more than he liked making friends.

I got up and checked my woozy self in the cheval glass, but that part of the room was in shadow, so I went across the hall to the mirror in the big bathroom. I looked for signs that Finn might have washed up in here, but the fresh hand towels were folded just as Mrs. Jones had hung them.

As I crept down the stairs it occurred to me that the man was probably Mr. Crump, returned for more of Flora's corn bread—and probably with another unwelcome offer to buy Nonie's car. But it was a much older man than Mr. Crump on the sofa beside Flora, having tea from a pot and pound cake.

"There you are!" cried Flora.

"Where is Finn?"

"Oh, honey, he had to go. He had his dinner engagement with Miss Adelaide."

"He *promised* to come upstairs before he left."

"He did, but you were sound asleep in your new office. He said he couldn't bear to wake you."

"It's a study, not an office." (It's not going to be a study, either, but you won't know that.)

"Sorry, honey, study."

Holding his teacup and saucer aloft in front of his chest, the old man impertinently danced his beetle-black eyes on my distress.

"Helen, do you know who this is?" Flora asked.

"I'm . . . not sure." He was an old man in a Sunday shirt and a stand-up tuft of wispy white hair and those rude little beetle-black eyes. I might have met him before, but I couldn't think where.

"This is your grandmother's half brother, Mr. Earl Quarles," she announced as though she were presenting royalty.

It was the Old Mongrel himself, sitting on our sofa inside our house.

"Stepbrother, not half brother," I corrected.

"The young lady's right," the Old Mongrel spoke up. "Honora and I were no relation. But I thought the world of her."

I lingered resentfully against the archway separating the living room from the hallway. How had this happened? My father would be beside himself with disgust. If people did such a thing as turn over in their graves, Nonie would be doing that right now.

"How about a slice of pound cake, Helen?"

"I'm really not hungry."

"Well, come in and keep Mr. Quarles company while I get more hot water."

"Not for me," said the Old Mongrel. "I reckon I ought to be getting along home." But Flora was off to the kitchen with the teapot and he made no move to leave.

I walked sedately across to Nonie's wing chair and sat facing him.

"I haven't had a cup of pot-brewed tea since my wife died,"

he said, with the return of the singsongy whine I recalled from the funeral home. "Now they just serve you up a bag with lukewarm water on the side and call that tea."

Unwilling to make small talk about tea bags, I sat erect on the edge of the chair and stared at him.

He put down his cup and saucer. "You favor her," he said.

"Who?" I was not going to help him.

"Honora. Your grandmother. You must miss her a heap."

I certainly wasn't going to respond to *that*, even if he started to think I was a cretin.

"She wasn't much older than you when we met. Oh, me, it was a bad day for her." He uttered a wheezy, almost soundless laugh. "Hated me on sight. Well, I don't blame her. But after a while we made friends. She ever talk about me?"

I could barely shake my head. My lips felt pasted against my teeth.

"I was nine years older. So there was a period there when she was still a child and I was already a man, but then that changed and we were more like equals. But she was always smarter than me. I knew that right from the start. Smart and high-tempered." Another wheezy chuckle. "Oh, me."

Oh, *God*, Flora, where are you?

"What grade are you in school?" Even a slow-witted child could answer that.

"I'll be going into sixth."

"Your daddy's the principal, isn't he?"

"He's principal of the *high school*."

"That's what I thought. I was looking at some acreage that's about to go on sale at the top of your hill this afternoon and thought I'd drop by and pay my respects to him. But your cousin says he's over in Oak Ridge doing some important war work. How old is your father now?"

Never ask a person's age, I had been taught practically from infancy. "My father is the age of the century," I said, which would show that I knew his age without actually saying it.

"Oh no, he couldn't be."

This was too much. "I guess I ought to know my own father's age," I said as coldly as I could.

"With all due respect, young lady, you must have got your figures wrong."

"My grandfather wrote a poem on the day my father was born. 'Midst our cloud-begirded peaks / on this December morn / a boy is born.' It's in a book upstairs in my grandfather's consulting room. The date at the bottom of the poem says December the eighth, nineteen hundred. That's my father's birthday."

This silenced the Old Mongrel. He looked gratifyingly flummoxed. And my small victory was that I still hadn't said my father's age.

Flora came back with the pot just as he was heaving himself up from the sofa. "Oh no, Mr. Quarles, you're not leaving?"

"I better be getting on home, Miss Flora. My cataracts don't operate so well when the dusk sets in."

"I hope you and Helen got a *little* acquainted."

"Oh, I would say we did." Standing up, he was taller than I expected. "She takes after Honora all right." Again the almost soundless, wheezy chuckle. "Well, you all have been very kind to me and I thank you for your hospitality. At least I got to meet the young lady and your nice friend, and I'm glad I could help with the Oldsmobile."

Looking down at me he explained, "We jumped Honora's batteries with my cables and gave Miss Flora her first driving lesson while you was having your nap. She needs to mash on the brake less, but she's going to do real well. She'll tell you all about it."

Flora and I stood outside the kitchen door and watched the Old Mongrel's big, sloping car with whitewalls cautiously bump down our driveway.

"That is the last Packard Clipper model they made before we entered the war," said Flora dreamily.

"How do you know that?"

"Finn told me. He worked on cars like that before he joined the Army. He says Mr. Quarles must have money."

"Of course he has. He got all the inheritance that was supposed to go to my grandmother. What I don't understand is how he got inside our house."

"Well, I invited him, Helen."

"If I had been awake, that would never have been allowed to happen."

"But he and your grandmother grew up together, honey."

"Oh, grew up together," I said bitterly. "People are always growing up together, according to you."

"What do you mean?"

"He was nine years older than Nonie and my mother was twelve years older than you. You can't 'grow up together' when there's that much difference in your ages."

"What on earth has gotten into you, Helen?" At last she had picked up on the fact that I was shaking with rage.

"My father would *never* have let him in the house."

Now she blanched. "Why not?"

"*Because*. He's an old mongrel. That's what my father calls him: the Old Mongrel."

"What has he done to deserve that?"

"He's a crook. He tried to bribe the funeral director to make him open Nonie's casket."

"Well, that's not exactly a crook, honey. He probably wanted to see her one last time. You heard him say how much he thought of her."

"He's ill-bred. He asks people's ages. He says 'while you was having your nap.' "

"Everyone doesn't speak the King's English, Helen. Mrs. Jones slips up on her grammar and you are very fond of her."

"You leave her out of it. She stays in control of her days and Nonie admired her. And he's a sneak and a bully and thinks nothing of taking what isn't his."

"Goodness, where did you get all that? I've never heard you even mention him before."

"I got it from Nonie and my father. I never mentioned him because the last thing I expected was to take a nap and wake up and find you'd polluted our house." I was starting to cry for the first time in front of Flora, and this made me all the more angry with her.

"Now, listen, Helen, that's enough. I think you ought to go off by yourself and cool down before supper. We're having spaghetti. I used up the last of Juliet's herbs for the sauce."

"I don't want her fucking sauce and I'm sick of eating! I'm sick of you! I can't wait till you leave!"

XXIV.

I remember feeling, after my blowup that Sunday, that I could still give myself credit for some adult restraint. I hadn't actually cried. I hadn't hit. In the past, even the recent past, I had sometimes hit Nonie in aggravation, but during this summer I had never once hit Flora. Okay, I had lashed out verbally in a childish way—and gotten a child's satisfaction from the instant response—but I knew I could still reap some longer-term benefits if I apologized. I wasn't really sorry about using my father's worst swearword. It was a thing men said, but if a female used it sparingly it had great shock value. I had shocked Flora. Then I had hurt her by saying I was sick of her and would be glad when she was gone. But though Flora was easy to hurt, she was also an easy forgiver. When I went off to cool down, as instructed by her, I used that time by myself to compose my scene of contrition.

I knew even while screaming at Flora that I was going to have to apologize later, because my goal was to get along with her *on the surface* for the rest of the summer while keeping my serious schemes to myself. First, though, I checked myself over for wounds and then laid out the pluses and minuses of the afternoon. I had first done this after Flora's one outburst—if you could call it that—when I had been snotty about refusing to send my picture to the Alabama people, and she had lost control and "told me things" about my mother's selfishness and cruelty. What I had lost that other day was my illusion that Flora adored my mother unreservedly, but what I had gained was valuable information as to what Lisbeth had really been like and the realization that I wouldn't be sorry to behave with her cold expediency under similar circumstances. It felt gratifying being allied with my mother in this way.

Today's losses and gains weren't as simply tallied. Finn hadn't come up to say good-bye; or, rather, he had come and couldn't bear to wake me. The Old Mongrel had been in our house, and I would have to tell my father; but the downspout had been reattached and the gutters cleaned, which would please my father and make him like Finn. Nonie's batteries had been charged; but Flora had been given her first driving lesson as a result. The Old Mongrel had referred to Finn as "your nice friend" when he was thanking Flora: had his 'your' meant Flora and me, or had he thought Finn was Flora's boyfriend?

The best way to apologize, according to Nonie, was to come right out and say you were sorry and get it over with. You didn't have to belabor it, but you did have to convince the other person you were sincere.

As we were spreading our napkins in our laps—Flora used old prewar paper ones from the pantry when we had spaghetti—I stayed focused on my lap and murmured, "I apologize for what I said. I didn't mean it, I was just mad."

"Oh, Helen. And I'm sorry, too. I had no idea how you felt about Mr. Quarles. And I know you didn't mean . . . all you said to me."

She went on some more, overdoing her forgiveness and her gratitude for my apology, and how she had no idea, et cetera, until I felt it was time to get her off that subject.

We twirled our spaghetti. I thought of saying something nice about Juliet Parker's herbs in the sauce, but couldn't trust it to come out sounding a hundred percent sincere. "You know what I really want to know?" I asked.

"What, honey?"

"How did it feel to drive?"

"I can hardly claim I *drove*, honey, with Finn right next to me, ready to grab the wheel if I messed up and Mr. Quarles shouting his advice into my open window."

"But where did you go?"

"What do you mean where did I go?"

"Did you go down our driveway and onto the road?"

"Goodness, no, honey. We just went around and around the house on that old circular driveway."

"But that thing's so overgrown you can barely walk on it!"

"Well, we flattened it down some with our big car," said Flora with more satisfaction than I cared for. "And Finn is going to ask Miss Adelaide if he can borrow her scythe and work on it some more."

"For more . . . driving lessons?" I asked, knowing the answer.

"Finn says I will be driving before I go back to Alabama. Who would have ever thought! If only I had kept my mouth shut during that interview."

"Spoken word is slave," I said. "Unspoken is master."

"That's just what *she* would have said! But it would still have been a lie, wouldn't it? Not speaking up can be a lie, too."

"I guess."

I couldn't wait to go to bed. Shut the door to my room, climb between Nonie's sheets, and let this day drain out of me. When I woke up it would be the next day, and that day would be one day closer to my birthday. I had decided my father was going to come. He had to come, because I needed him to. If I could just get to my birthday and have some support, I could make it through the remaining weeks until he was home for good and we put Flora on the train to Alabama.

"You want to listen to anything on the radio later?"

"No, I'm too tired."

"Oh dear, I hope you're not coming down with something. Your father would never forgive me. But where could you have gotten anything?"

If I hadn't been so depleted, I could have tormented her a little. From the strangers you keep inviting into the house for hot corn bread and milk. And pound cake and "brewed tea."

"No, I'm just really tired. I moved some furniture around upstairs."

"Oh, right, for your study. You go on, then, honey. I'll clean up. And then would you like me to bring you anything in bed? Some milk? One of your Clark bars?"

"No, I'll already have brushed my teeth. I just want to sleep."

After I got into my pajamas, I took down the hatbox from the closet shelf and removed Nonie's hatpin from the new hat. I replaced the hatbox. I fingered around in her purse until I found the hatpin's sheath and stuck the pin back in its sheath. I held it in my closed right hand and put my left hand on top. "You have got to help me get through these next days," I told the hatpin. "And *make* my father come for my birthday." Then I placed it under my pillow, arranged myself between the crisp sheets marked MASTER, squinched my eyes shut, and willed myself into oblivion. But I went on being awake. I heard Flora's clatter as she finished putting away the dishes, then her footsteps on the stairs and going down the hall, then the Willow Fanning door opening and closing, then the toilet flushing in the Willow Fanning half bath. I reminded myself that a month from now I would be lying here listening to more agreeable sounds coming from other people in the house as they finished up their day and settled down for their night.

"I KNOW YOU didn't like Mr. Quarles, Helen, but I did enjoy hearing him talk about her when she was a young girl."

"What did he say?"

"Oh, that she was a grand cook, even with their old wood-burning stove, and she could wring a chicken's neck without making a face, and milk a cow and ride a horse bareback. He also said she was high-tempered."

"What did he mean by that?"

"Well, I think he meant it as praise. After all, he didn't say hot-tempered, or bad-tempered." Flora giggled. "Though he did say she could hold grudges like an elephant."

"From what *I* heard, there was plenty to hold grudges about."

"You said something about that, uh, yesterday." Flora was curious, but I could see she was also nervous about starting things up again.

"He had so many bad traits it was hard to single one out. He was a bully and sneaky and thought nothing of taking what wasn't his. And he had his eye on the farm and was willing to tell lies about her to get it."

"She told you all that?"

I nodded.

"I wonder what he took."

"What wasn't his."

"Oh, well, it was a long time ago, and it worked out all right for them both, didn't it?"

"How do you mean?"

"Well, your grandmother married the wonderful doctor and had your father, and you, and Mr. Quarles thought the world of his wife."

"He says that about everybody," I reminded her.

"No, from what he said they were real happy. They didn't have children, but she was a big help to him in his business. He wasn't much of a farmer, he told me, but he knew how to buy and sell land. He kept a few acres for corn and a couple of cows and his wife kept these pet chickens—for eggs, not for eating—but what he really likes is discovering land that loggers have ruined. He clears it and then sells it to people who want to build houses on it. That's why he happened to be up here. He—"

"I know, he told me. He was looking at some acreage about to go on sale at the top of our hill."

"So you two did get to talk some. He told us when the men come home from the war they'll want starter houses to raise their families in. Finn thinks he's going to make a bundle without so much as lifting an eyebrow."

"You can't make a bundle unless you have something to start with," I explained world-wearily. "And what he had to start with was Nonie's property."

* * *

FLORA WAS GETTING ready to leave in her mind. She had begun saying nostalgic things like "I'll never forget the time we . . ." and "I'll always remember when we . . ." She was already bundling her memories of this summer into little packages, like Juliet's herbs, to take back to Alabama. I could hear her telling other teachers at her school about our fifth-grade game: "My little cousin was just so *smart.* She made up this whole class full of children for me to practice on and played all the parts herself." We had discontinued playing Fifth Grade when things around the house started breaking down, and then somehow the time was past for that game. I had my "study" (a.k.a. the Devlin Patrick Finn room) to work on, and Flora, with her driving lessons to look forward to in the late afternoon, had to fit in her meal preparations earlier in the day. Finn had cleared the old circular driveway with Miss Adelaide's scythe and I had helped him neaten it some with a rake. My father was going to be so pleased with all our improvements. Finn still had not been given a decision about his discharge status.

"They're taking their time," he told us. "They're waiting to see whether I'm truly recovered or whether I'll go balmy again."

"Oh, don't say that," cried Flora. "Not even as a joke." We were sitting around the dining table. Finn often stayed for dinner with us now, after the driving lesson. Flora had promised him not to go to any special trouble.

The latest letter from Alabama had given Flora something else to think about. "Uncle Sam has offered to buy Juliet's share of the house so he and Aunt Garnet can live there when they get remarried."

"But where will Juliet live?"

"She could come to Dothan and live with me."

"Did she ask if she could?"

"Oh, Juliet would never do that. But I've been thinking how nice it would be."

"But—"

"But, what?"

"Would she be like your maid?"

"I've told you, honey. Juliet is not a maid. We would keep house together. She would have her own money." Flora laughed. "With the money from her share of the house, she would have a lot more than me."

"But what about when you get married?"

"Who said anything about my getting married?"

"All these people keep asking you."

"Who?" she demanded, flushing.

"The farmer with the truck you didn't ride in to the interview, and the lawyer with hairs in his ears."

"Oh, those," she said. "Well, there will always be a place in my home for Juliet, whether I marry or not. And I will always have a guest room for you, Helen. Maybe you'll miss me and want to visit. You could ride down on the train and I'll take you to all the places your mother knew as a girl. I'll have my license by then. Who knows? Maybe I'll even have a car."

She was obviously looking ahead.

THOUGH WE WEREN'T playing Fifth Grade any longer, I was often upstairs in "my study," daydreaming about when Finn would live in this room. From here it would have been easy to slip next door into the Willow Fanning room and take away more of Nonie's letters to read. But here, too, Flora had been looking ahead. The letters were all bound together again and tied tightly with the ribbon, in a hard-to-imitate bow, ready to go back into Flora's suitcase. Next to them was the smaller pile of Juliet Parker's weekly missives. Without any ribbon, they would be easy to steal away and read if I wanted to. But I didn't, not in the least. It was while pondering this one morning, while looking down at the two piles, that I realized I didn't really need to take the risk of reading more of Nonie's, either. I had found out some things, been disappointed at not finding other things, and hadn't been caught. What more was to be found out, and would it be worth getting caught for?

It was sad, in a way. Like our Fifth Grade, the time now felt past for the letters as well. It was like the summer light, which was changing into autumn light around the house. If the Recoverers were still here, they would be leaving the south porch earlier now and carrying their books and blankets and cards over to the west porch to take advantage of the last sun. I was moving over into something else, too. Rather than wanting to dig into old things that had already happened, I was pouring all my time and imagination into preparing a place for the new things that were going to happen after Flora was gone.

Mrs. Jones said the two oriental rugs made the room look more lavish.

"And the bed looks nice by the window. Did you have trouble moving it by yourself?"

"A little. I may have scratched the floor some."

"Where?"

I lifted up the second rug and prepared to be lectured.

Mrs. Jones knelt down so her nose was practically level with the floor and ran her finger back and forth over the wood. "Well, you did a job, didn't you?"

"I'm sorry. I was just rushing, and that bed was heavier than I thought."

"Doesn't pay to rush." Now she had laid down her cheek on the floor and was inspecting the damage sideways.

"Is it bad?" Would she feel obliged to tell my father?

"Not too bad. As long as it stays under the rug. I've seen worse. But we ought to doctor it a little so it can get better while it's under the rug. Go downstairs to the pantry."

"Downstairs to the pantry," I repeated.

"On the lowest left-hand shelf, toward the back, you'll find a little brown bottle with a handwritten label that says 'linseed oil.' "

"Who wrote it?"

"Your father. It's one of those stick-on labels with a red edge. Linseed oil."

"Linseed oil," I repeated. "Will that fix it?"

"We'll make a start," said Mrs. Jones, rising cumbersomely to her feet. "In future, though, try not to be in such a rush." She was breathless and had to steady herself against the wall for a minute, and I felt bad.

I had changed my mind about showing Finn his room. I wanted the circumstances to be as perfect as possible. More important, I had realized I ought to talk it over with my father first. What an awful thing it would have been to have shown Finn the room and invited him to live there and then have to go back and tell him my father had said no. Just the thought of having brought on such a near disaster made me cringe.

So for now I kept the room for myself. I liked lying on the bed Finn might soon be sleeping in, if I could only manage everything in a mature and diplomatic way. I liked reading the new book Mrs. Jones had brought from the library. This one, a book of fairy tales from around the world, she had chosen herself, and had read some of the stories herself before bringing it to me. Her favorite was one from Denmark, "The Princess in the Coffin," and I had read that one first so we could talk about it when she came next Tuesday, which was my birthday. And I also liked lying there and thinking of my mother, soon to give birth to me, lying in this same spot and wondering what I would be like.

The whole experience of being in Finn's room was like lying in a hammock with my past, present, and future all tucked around me.

XXV.

Monday morning, the day before my birthday, Flora knocked on my door earlier than usual.

"I thought we'd wash your hair before you get dressed." She had brought along the saucepan we used for rinsing.

"Why are you up so early?"

"I was lying in bed thinking of all the things I wanted to get done today, and when I couldn't go back to sleep I decided to just get up and start doing them."

"We always have breakfast first, then order the groceries *before* we wash my hair on Monday."

"And you always have to get undressed again. I don't know why I didn't think of this sooner. I'm such a numbskull."

"Well, wait a minute," I said irritably. "I have to pee first."

"Don't you want to take off your pajama top?" she asked, when I was getting ready to kneel on the stack of towels beside the tub.

"I always leave on my undershirt."

"Well, goodness, Helen, we're both girls. Oh, what does it matter? I'm in a good mood today."

"I bet I know why."

"Why?" She looked guilty.

"Because you'll be leaving in two weeks and four days."

"Look who's counted up the actual days. Don't be silly, honey. I'll miss you and I hope you'll miss me a little. I'll never forget this summer. I've learned so much I feel I ought to pay your father tuition."

I bowed forward over the tub and thought, as I always did, about the guillotine. Flora ran the water to just the right temperature and poured panfuls over my hair until it hung down in one heavy mass. I groaned with pleasure at her deep, diligent lathering and was always a little sorry when the rinsing was over and every strand squeaked.

"Your hair is the color of wheat," Flora mused, as she always did when toweling it. "And such a lot of it."

"I wish I knew what I looked like," I said.

"Well, have a look." She turned me around so I could see myself in the full-length mirror: a pink, cranky girl in pajamas wet around the collar. "Finn says all your features are the right distance from each other. You notice things like that when you're drawing someone, he says."

"But that doesn't mean pretty."

"It's better than pretty. It means you'll look good even when you're old."

"I don't care about when I'm old, I care about right now."

"Well, there is one thing you can do for right now."

"What?"

"Stop frowning. And when people come into a room, look happier to see them."

After breakfast, we made our list and Flora called in the order. It was Mr. Crump on the other end, and, Flora being Flora, she sounded just as happy to be speaking to him as to Finn.

Neither Flora nor I worried now if Finn didn't answer, because we knew we'd be seeing him for the driving lesson at the end of his deliveries.

Flora's big project for the day was the pantry. "I want to take everything out, scrub down the shelves, and then organize things better for you and your father."

"Mrs. Jones can do that."

"Yes, but if Mrs. Jones does it, you won't think of me every time you go into the pantry to look for something." She was indomitably cheerful today. Nothing new had happened that I was aware of. She had received no mail on Saturday. She had washed her own hair yesterday and sat on the west porch drying it. Finn hadn't come because Miss Adelaide invited him to Sunday supper again. We had listened to the radio some and then gone our separate ways to bed. Maybe she had had a nice dream. What would a nice dream be for Flora? Which brought me back to my first reason: she was looking forward to leaving. She had done a good job "caring" for me and now she wanted to go back to her life. Was I hurt by this? A little.

"What did you do this summer, Flora?"

"Oh, I took care of my little cousin Helen up in North Carolina. Her mother and I grew up together. Her father was off doing important war work in Oak Ridge, Tennessee, and he asked me to stay with her. Did you ever hear of the Manhattan Project?"

"How old was she?"

"Ten, going on eleven. Very smart. Helen certainly kept me on my toes."

"But?" If Flora had a friend like Annie Rickets, she would poke at Flora until the negative things started trickling out.

Flora would be cheerfully loyal at first. Then she would say,

"Oh, I don't know. It was just the two of us alone up there on the mountain. This big old house. And at the start of the summer there was a polio scare. It never did turn into an epidemic, but her father quarantined us. We couldn't go anywhere or have any company. But as he'd had polio himself it was understandable."

"Nobody? For the entire summer?"

"Well, there was this person who delivered our groceries." (I couldn't decide whether Flora would call Finn a boy or a man.) "And the family's minister dropped by to bring news of this little friend of Helen's who came down with polio."

"It's a wonder you didn't go crazy. I mean, what did the two of you *do*?"

"Oh, we had our schedule. I made the meals. Wait, I forgot the cleaning woman. She came once a week, on Tuesdays. And Helen and I played school, so I would be prepared for my fifth grade, and we listened to the radio in the evenings if there was something good on. In many ways, Helen was an easy child. She liked to go off by herself and read, and sometimes mope."

"Mope?"

"Well, she missed her grandmother, Mrs. Anstruther, who, I've told you, was just the most—"

"Yes, yes, the most wonderful woman who wrote you all those wise letters you read over and over. I've heard all about her. Get back to Helen's moping."

"I don't think she liked me very much at the start. She found fault with me a lot. Of course there are a lot of things about me to find fault *with*."

"Okay, okay. We all know your low opinion of yourself. What did *she* find fault with?"

"Just my general way of being, I think. Her mother was the

same. Even when she was being sweet to me, Lisbeth always thought I wasn't good enough."

"It's sounding more and more like you had a perfectly awful summer, Flora."

"I admit it had its tense moments. But there were also joys."

"Oh? Let's hear about those."

"Well, as you know, I finally learned to drive."

FLORA WAS SO caught up in her pantry reorganization that she could hardly keep still at lunch. I, on the other hand, felt so bad over the things I had imagined she would say about me to her Annie Rickets friend, that I made an extra effort to linger at the table and create some good memories of myself for her to take home. I complimented her on her thoroughness. (She had taken every single thing out of the pantry and set it out on the floor and washed down all the shelves.) I entertained her with the story of "The Princess in the Coffin," which she didn't know.

"Goodness, that was in a *children's*—I mean, a book for young people?"

"Which part do you find so awful?"

"All those young soldiers she killed. I mean, the soldier who finally gets her out of her coffin and wins her love still has to look at all those bodies she tore apart and buried under the church floor."

"It's stories from all different countries. This one's from Denmark."

"Well, I'll certainly be careful if I ever go to Denmark."

"You're a girl, you wouldn't have to worry. It's the men who—"

"Did you just hear a car, Helen?"

It was Father McFall. The minute I saw his somber countenance looking down on us from the other side of the screen door, I was sure he had come to tell me Brian Beale had died. He entered, took in the pantry items spread all over the floor, and raised his eyebrows at the silent radio on the kitchen counter.

"You two haven't been listening to the radio?" he asked.

"We just finished lunch," said Flora. "Has something happened? Won't you come in?"

"Yes, thank you, I will, and yes, something has happened."

Stalking ahead of us into the living room, he gestured for us to be seated while he continued to pace back and forth in his black clericals. "I take it you haven't heard, then, about the bombing over in Japan. That's good, I was hoping to get up here first. With all the reports coming in about Oak Ridge, I wanted to assure Helen there's absolutely no danger. Everyone is fine in Oak Ridge. I've just been on the telephone with Chaplain Dudley, who's working there for the summer in much the same capacity as your father, Helen, though on another site, and he assures me that no one there is in any danger."

"Why?" I asked. "Are the Japs planning a bombing raid back?" Nonie and I had gone to see *Mrs. Miniver* twice and I was not unfamiliar with bombing raids.

"I don't think the Japanese will have much stomach for any more bombing raids, Helen. The thing we dropped on Hiroshima is something new in warfare. It's—" He searched for words, then threw up his hands like someone releasing a flock of birds. "They're saying it means the end of the war. But you'll also be hearing unfounded rumors that the people at Oak Ridge, where the materials for the bomb were made, might be in some radioactive danger. That's why I hurried up here. To dispel any of those speculations. Because they just ain't so."

("Poor Father McFall," Nonie used to say. "Whenever he tries to talk like plain folk, all he does is sound condescending.")

"You mean," Flora gasped, rubbing her arms like she did during our scary programs, "Helen's *father* was making the bomb? *That* was the secret work?"

"Helping to make, along with thousands of others. Yes, that was the secret work, although they didn't know. Only the scientists and some highly placed government and Army people were in on the whole picture. The best kept secret in the history of the world, they're saying. But they're speculating all kinds of wild things on the radio and calling it news. I wanted to assure you that nobody at Oak Ridge has been harmed by what was being made there and that nobody is in any danger." He permitted himself a wintry laugh. "Chaplain Dudley said when the news first came through that they had made the biggest bomb in the history of the world, some workers packed up and hightailed it out of there because they were afraid the place might explode any minute."

"Does this mean my father might be on his way home now?"

"He wouldn't be one of those, Helen. He'd go right on with his job for the rest of the day. That's what Chaplain Dudley is going to do. After all, it's Monday, a workday. They'll clock in and clock out, maybe celebrate some among themselves after work." Father McFall shot up a black sleeve and consulted his wristwatch. "Actually, though it's my day off, I have opened the church and put a sign on the door that we'll have Evening Prayer at five. Parishioners will want to thank God that this long war is finally going to end. And they may want to pray we won't misuse this frightening new power we have just unleashed on the world."

As Flora and I were walking him to his car, we heard the phone. "I'll get it," I said. "It's probably my father."

"Well, be sure and tell him I was here," said Father McFall.

But it was Finn. "Have you girls heard the news?"

"About the bomb? Yes, my father helped make it."

A bump of silence. "Is it a joke with me you're having?"

"No, it's true. Father McFall was just here to tell us. He's been on the phone with someone he knows at Oak Ridge."

"Holy Mother of God."

"Of course, my father didn't *know* what he was making," I felt I should add. "Only the scientists and a few top government people knew. It was the best kept secret in the history of the world, Father McFall says."

"Have you talked to your father?"

"Not yet. He might—he just *might*—be coming home for my birthday tomorrow, but that's a secret, too. Not even Flora knows."

"Where is Flora?"

Flora rushed into the kitchen. "Is that your father? I want to speak to him."

"No, it's Finn. But I think he wants to talk to you."

WE KEPT THE radio on while Flora finished her pantry rearrangement. I was given the job of wiping down each item with a damp dish towel before it was allowed back in, which unfortunately recalled to me the night I had wiped my father's bloody brow after he had passed out on the kitchen floor. As Father

McFall had warned us, there was all kinds of news. Between the national bulletins, some with gory details of what had been done to Hiroshima and its people, local citizens were interviewed and encouraged to express their reactions to the bomb, which was now being called the atomic bomb. Some of these reactions were pretty vindictive about how the Japs had it coming to them, but when some man, or woman, on the street went too far for good taste, the radio person quickly intervened, saying the loss of life was of course deplorable but think of the American lives saved because the war would end quickly now. Flora listened carefully to everything, occasionally uttering yips of pity and horror, whereas I was mainly interested in the mentions of Oak Ridge. I kept expecting to hear my father's name.

After we had finished the pantry and admired it, Flora turned off the radio and said we needed to go for a walk.

"If I had these weeks to do over," she said, as we skidded arm in arm down our driveway, "I would do some things differently."

"What?" I was really curious.

"I would have got you out more."

"But we couldn't go anywhere."

"We could have walked."

"We have walked."

"Oh, I don't mean to the mailbox and back. Real walks. We could have gone on little hikes through the woods. Taken picnics."

In the mailbox, along with the flighty black ant that seemed to have taken up residence there, was a single pink envelope addressed to me by an adult. Inside a birthday card with a picture of two rabbits hopping off together, Rachel Huff had written in her tortured script: "See you back at school!" My belated thank-you note had achieved its purpose: at least they weren't my enemies anymore.

"Isn't that nice of them," said Flora.

"Mrs. Huff keeps a drawer full of cards for all occasions," I informed her. "And she has this book with everybody's address and their birthdays and anniversaries. All she had to do was pick a card, write my address, put on a stamp, and make Rachel write something."

"Well, it was still thoughtful of them."

I conceded it was. "Even though my birthday's not till tomorrow."

"You have to tell me what kind of cake you want. Did . . . your grandmother make you some special cake?"

"Please don't say any more until tomorrow. It might be bad luck."

"Oh, okay," said Flora, as though she understood, which she didn't. She had no idea about the hatpin under the pillow.

"Let's walk up to the top of Sunset Drive," she said. "I've never been that way."

"There's nothing up there but logging roads, but be my guest."

"I blame myself for not getting you out more," said Flora. "It's my own lack of imagination. I didn't grow up with all this land around me. And yet we walked more in a day in Alabama than you and I have done all summer. We walked to the grocery. Then if we needed something else, we walked there again. And then Daddy started what he called his regime."

"What's a regime?"

"He made himself walk a mile every day. The doctor said he was too sedentary, sitting around playing cards so much, and also he was getting fat. So Daddy started walking all the way around the roundhouse between fixing the engines. He worked out it would equal a mile if he walked it twice a day. He got so used to his walk that he went to the roundhouse on his days off and I would go with him. Though we only went around once, which was just half a mile."

"Are you saying I'm getting fat?"

"Oh no, honey, I wasn't. I'm talking about him. Oh, poor Daddy. I still catch myself thinking that when I get home he's going to come out the door and hug me." A brief spate of tears followed, but by now they were the expected thing, a part of Flora, like her childish feet with the too-friendly toenails. "Today I thought we'd look at that land Mr. Quarles was talking about. Where they cut down all the good trees and left a mess and he wants to build the houses for the GIs. What was it your father called him?"

"The Old Mongrel."

"What had he done to deserve that?"

"You don't have to *do* anything to be a mongrel. You just are one, like a dog without a pedigree."

"My goodness," said Flora, with an uneasy laugh, "I guess that must make me one."

XXVI.

I was glad Finn no longer dressed up before he came to us. He had wet-combed his hair and he must have washed his body after his other deliveries because he didn't have that smell like the day I rode behind him on the motorcycle. He wore his paratrooper boots, shined, with the pants tucked inside, and he had on that shirt with the eagle patch on the sleeve. He said people had waved to him on the street as though he had been part of what happened today.

"Well, you are part of it," said Flora. "Just as Helen's father is part of it." That was going a bit too far, I thought. My father had been at Oak Ridge making the bomb, whereas Finn, as much as we liked him, had spent the last year in the hospital.

We all three carried in the groceries and Flora put everything where it went.

"I got your baking powder and the vanilla," Finn told her, "but there wasn't a block of baking chocolate to be found—"

"Never mind, we'll think of something tomorrow," said Flora, hurrying him past that subject. "Helen, why don't you show Finn our beautiful pantry?"

Flora had her driving lesson. Finn was teaching her to back

the Oldsmobile out of the garage, but she kept sideswiping the garbage can until he said, "That's enough for today, love, we'll try again tomorrow," and backed out for her. Then they proceeded with their usual lesson, stopping and starting and reversing and changing gears, round and round the circular drive Finn and I had restored together.

Then Flora put her casserole in the oven and excused herself for a quick bath because she said she was all sweaty. Finn and I were left by ourselves, which was nice, except I was nervous. Not expecting Flora's bath, I hadn't prepared anything to say.

"You must be so proud of your father," said Finn, following me into the living room. "I hope I can meet him someday."

"You will. He's coming home in two weeks and four days. Maybe sooner. But I don't want to think about it till tomorrow."

"Which is your birthday." Finn sat down next to me on the sofa and placed a parcel tied with string on the coffee table. "The wartime wrapping you'll have to excuse. But I hope you like what's inside."

It was a handsome wooden box of colored pencils, accompanied by an artist's drawing pad. "They're the kind I use, when I can get them," said Finn, running his fingers lovingly across the pencils in their separate velvet trenches. "Made in Holland. After supper, we'll try them out."

I was taken aback when the freshly bathed Flora reappeared in the blue dress I hadn't seen her wear since Nonie's funeral. Its cut and drapery suited her better than any of her other clothes, and she had put on her high heels and some makeup. I felt not only upstaged but put at a disadvantage. I was in my same clothes from the morning and hadn't been given a chance to wash off our day's activities.

We ate after the six o'clock news with Lowell Thomas. The big-name evening newscasters themselves had been upstaged because by now everyone had heard the shocking highlights earlier in the day. Blast equal to thousand tons of TNT. Most destructive force ever devised by man. Sixty thousand dead and still counting. The entire Japanese Second Army wiped out on their parade ground while doing morning calisthenics.

"I know it's unpatriotic," said Flora, "but I can't stop feeling horrible about all those dead and burned people."

"It's not unpatriotic," Finn corrected her, "it's human."

"How will this affect your chances with that Army board?"

"I've been wondering myself. It scotches my chances of getting shipped off to fight the Japs and redeeming my war record. But maybe they'll find a place for me in demobilization. I can sit behind a desk for a year or two and help send others home."

"What is scotches?" I asked.

"You scotch a wheel with a wedge," explained Finn, "to keep it from rolling."

"Oh," I said, understanding.

"Well, I'm sorry," said Flora, blushing through her makeup. "But I'm *glad* your getting shipped off to fight the Japs is scotched."

"Well, and I'm not sorry that you're glad," Finn softly responded.

AFTER SUPPER WE returned to the living room to try out my pencils. There was still plenty of light coming through the west windows. Finn sat next to me and demonstrated how to alter the shade of a color by applying various degrees of pressure. Then he showed how you could blend a red with a yellow to make orange, a blue with a red to make purple, a blue and a yellow to make green, and a red, yellow, and blue to make brown. For these exercises, he used a page from his own sketchbook, which he always carried with him, so I wouldn't have to mess up my new one.

Flora kept up a steady murmur of accolades as she paced back and forth behind us or perched on the sofa arm on Finn's side. "This is just so impressive . . . I can use this with my class at school. Will it work the same with Crayolas?"

"Not exactly," said Finn. "These are very soft leads. Crayons are mostly wax. But your kids will get the idea."

Then he said it was time we tried an actual portrait, if Flora would be so good as to sit in the chair and serve as our model.

"Oh no, please," she protested.

"How will I teach her to draw a portrait, then? Do you see someone else I could ask? Of course, Helen and I could *imagine* some person besides yourself sitting in the chair, but what if we don't imagine the same person?"

I thought this was hilarious and it shut Flora up. She took her position obediently in the wing chair and let Finn tell her how he wanted her to arrange herself.

"The first thing I want you to do," Finn instructed me, "is to fix your eyes on Flora. Then I want you to squint until she gets all blurry and you can see only the shape she makes in the chair."

"Just her head?"

"No, the whole body. The shape it makes against the chair, but not the chair. Get that shape firmly in your head. The angle of it, where it bears its weight. Now, we'll take a pencil, this yellow will do, and laying the point sideways on the paper we lightly *rub in* the shape." He demonstrated on his own pad, making Flora in her blue dress no more than a yellow bag leaning sideways. "Now you have a go." He handed over the pencil.

I sat paralyzed over my new drawing pad. "What if I make a mistake and ruin my first page?"

"Will we switch, then?" He handed over his pad with the yellow blob. "But will you care to have my drawing on your first page?"

"I wouldn't mind." People would think it was my drawing.

"Well, in that case—" He took back the yellow pencil and duplicated the blob in my pad. "There. Now we each have our shape to work with. And inside this shape is a person. Unlike any other person in the world."

"Oh, I don't know about that," said Flora with a nervous titter.

Finn gave Flora one of his sweet, accepting looks. He probably looked at Miss Adelaide that way when she remembered one more thing she'd forgotten. "Now," he said, handing me a blue pencil and taking a darker blue for himself, "we'll start at the top with the hair on the head, but here, again, we're after a shape, not a hairstyle. How the cloud of dark sits on the face below . . . I know, I know, we haven't done the face yet, but the whole thing's a package, don't you see, you've got to keep this whole package of a person in your mind, seeing how one thing flows out of another, an arm out of a shoulder, the curve of the body that allows the hand to rest so naturally on the thigh of the crossed leg. The mistake most beginners make is they draw each thing separate and then nothing connects. But we've put down our yellow shape to guide us, so we won't make that mistake."

"This isn't working," I said, after a minute. "Yours already looks like her hair but mine doesn't."

"Yours looks fine. Leave it for now and find the curve of the neck in your shape and sketch it in. Great, that's great. Now we come round the shoulder and round out the arm, and then, er, there's this fullness" (he was doing Flora's breast—or bust she would call it) "and notice the shadows it makes against the inside of the arm . . ."

We continued on like this until a likeness of Flora, the real essence of her presence in the chair, emerged under Finn's hand.

"I don't understand," I said. "I make the same marks you do, but mine look different."

"It's looking at the model you're meant to be doing, not at my 'marks,'" Finn scolded with an affectionate nudge of his arm against mine. "Yours is coming along, wait and see. You must have faith in yourself."

"That's exactly what Mrs. Anstruther would have said!" exclaimed Flora from Nonie's chair.

"Shush," I said. "You're the model."

My body shape, or rather Flora's as I had drawn it, wasn't hopeless. Finn's instructions had protected it from beginner's anatomical naïveté. But when he finally let us fill in the face, I got something wrong and spoiled the whole picture. What made it worse was that I couldn't locate what I had done wrong. I was furious with myself. I had suppressed a childish giggle while we had been working on Flora's "bust," but what if I failed to suppress my childish tears of frustration?

"Honey, I think you're getting tired," said Flora.

"You shut up."

"Ah, now," Finn sorrowfully chided. "What is it that's made you cross?"

"I ruined the face." Now a tear escaped. To keep from doing a complete Flora, I silently strung together the filthiest words I knew.

Finn lifted up a layer of the pencil box and extracted something. "Do you see this? It's called an eraser."

"Erasers *smudge.*"

"Not this eraser. It's made to go with these pencils. There's also a wee sharpener under here, for when you'll be needing it for the pencils. Now, how did you ruin the face?"

"I don't know."

"Well, start at the top. Is it the forehead? The eyes?"

"The eyes, I think."

"What about them? Don't be looking at my marks, look at the model."

"Hers are further apart."

"Right! Those far-apart eyes are one of her most beguiling features. So, let's fix them."

Flora had turned on the lamps before it was time for the 7:45 news we sometimes listened to. I was not sorry to see the summer light fading earlier. It meant school would be starting and my father would be home and Flora would be back in Alabama. H. V. Kaltenborn, or Hans von Kaltenborn, as Nonie liked to call him, had no new horror stories from Japan to offer, but he pointed out in his ominous, rat-a-tat diction that, for all we knew, we had created a Frankenstein's monster, and with the passage of a little time an enemy might improve it and use it against us.

"If it's all right with everybody, I'm going to switch to some music," said Flora.

"That is a lovely dress," Finn said as she swished past him to the console radio in her high heels. "Doing your portrait, I was thinking there ought to be a special name for its color. Darker than cobalt and purpler than Prussian:'twilight blue,' perhaps."

If it had been just the two of us she would be barefooted by now. And of course would not be in the "twilight blue" dress.

"Juliet Parker made it for me," Flora said, finding a dance music station. "She bought the material for herself, but then when Mrs. Anstruther died she wanted me to have something nice for the funeral."

"I'd like to meet your Juliet Parker," Finn said.

"Well, who knows? Maybe you will," said Flora gaily, tapping him on the head as she passed behind the sofa. "I'm going to make us some coffee."

"Major Glenn Miller," said Finn, nodding at the radio. "Another irreplaceable mortal whose plane went down." He shook his head sadly, then sprang to his feet and held out his arms. "Let's dance, Helen."

"I don't dance very well yet."

"Well, here's a chance to shorten that 'yet.' "

"Really, I *can't*—"

"Ah, I know what you're capable of when you say really you can't. I've seen it, remember? I've seen you jump into the unknown."

"Shush," I said, frowning toward the kitchen as I let him pull me up, like that day he pulled me out of my stupor from the side of the road.

"I know, I know. It's our secret."

Annie Rickets and I had devised our own frantic version of jitterbugging, and last summer Mrs. Beale had found some hard-up old couple who had once run an Arthur Murray studio to teach Brian and me (poor Brian) the basic ballroom steps. But with Finn's palm warm and solid at your back and him guiding you with your joined hands, your movements were in his custody. It was a world apart from two separate bodies striving to "dance."

"You see?" he crooned as we spun around the threadbare carpet.

"If I was taller I could reach you better."

"Don't be in such a rush, darling. I didn't get my full height till I was seventeen."

"Don't stop on account of me," cried Flora, returning with the tray. "You two look great." In typical Flora flutter she set everything out on the coffee table. On a plate covered with one of my prewar birthday napkins (sailboats, age six) she had interlaced Fig Newtons with the leftover pound cake, which wouldn't have been enough by itself. Then with a stagy sigh of contentment, she tucked herself neatly into a corner of the sofa, and made a big show of studying the two portraits of herself in the drawing pads. "Never in my life have I been made such a fuss over. And, you know, I love them both. Each of them shows me a new side of myself."

As in his earlier drawing, Finn had made her prettier than she was; but what new side of herself had mine revealed to her?

Then Finn commented, as he had once before, that you got to know a person by drawing them. "And sometimes while drawing someone"—he addressed Flora, speaking above the music—"you discover things about yourself in relation to that person."

"Like what?" Flora was all eagerness.

"Like feelings." He spoke over my head as he maneuvered me about on the carpet. "Feelings you didn't know you had about that person."

Each new time Finn spun me around while continuing to talk to Flora above the music, a certain object began to annoy me. I became vexed, then indignant, then enraged, by the eight-ounce glass of milk set down so emphatically among the cozy coffee things.

The music stopped for a commercial break. "You are going to be a fine dancer," Finn said, releasing me. "Helen doesn't know her own powers," he remarked to Flora.

"You don't have to tell me that," said Flora, now busily pouring coffee into the two cups. "I was saying to her only the other day 'I feel I should pay your father tuition for all the things I've learned from you this summer.' "

"It wasn't the other day, it was this morning," I corrected. "And you didn't say you learned them from me, you just said *learned*." It suddenly occurred to me that both of them were patronizing me, making me feel important so they could say things to each other over my head.

"You're right, honey, it was this morning," Flora instantly capitulated. "My, what a full day it's been. So many things happening in one day." She tucked her twilight blue skirt closer to her body, indicating Finn should sit next to her. "Come have your coffee while it's hot."

"Did anyone hear me say I wanted milk?" I asked, still standing in the middle of the carpet where Finn had left me.

"Well, no, but you always have a glass at"—she swerved wildly, just avoiding the bedtime word—"the end of the day."

"Yes, but tonight I want to celebrate my father." I walked over to the sideboard, and opened the center cabinet, which smelled musty from staying closed all summer. Out came the cognac bottle and the fluted crystal aperitif glass Nonie always used for her nightcaps. I sloshed the glass full, raised it to the orange sky outside the western window, and before Flora could react I drank it down.

"Oh, honey, no—" she said with an intake of a breath, like someone begging a person not to jump off a high building. Except that I had already jumped.

I poured a second glass and raised it to the pair on the sofa. "I'd like to drink to my father for helping make the bomb," I said.

Finn was the first to collect himself. "Hear, hear," he said, raising his coffee cup before he'd even put in the cream. "To Helen's father."

"To Helen's father," Flora barely whispered, raising her cup.

We all three drank. I would have liked to drain the second glass, but my nose and chest were still on fire from the first. I managed a respectable gulp, and then said, in a somewhat shaky voice, "I think I'll sip the rest of my nightcap in my room."

"Don't you think that's enough, honey?" Flora half-rose to take the glass away from me, but I cut her short.

"Good night, Finn. Thank you very much for the pencils and the art lesson. No, please, don't get up. Good night, Flora. Thank you for dinner and all the things you did for me today."

"Would you like for us to come and tell you good night after a while?" Flora asked, sounding defeated.

"No, thank you. I'm really very tired."

HERE I WAS again on the upholstered bench that fitted into the alcove of Nonie's dressing table. Hardly past infancy, I had begun clambering up this bench and flailing my little legs until I achieved a sitting position in front of the three-way mirror. In the long mirror was myself as a whole child, from curly top to socks and shoes. The mirrors on either side were shorter because they only started above the drawers where Nonie kept her grooming items. They gave you what was called your profile. You could never see your own profile except in mirrors like these. People had preferences about their profiles. A movie star would tell the cameraman, "Shoot my left profile, it's better." And if you adjusted the side mirrors, pulled them closer around you like a wrap, you could see more reflections from more angles, even the way you looked from the back. But who would want to see any more Helens? Certainly not the pair I had left behind in the living room. Not Brian, not the Huffs (despite the birthday card), certainly not Annie Rickets ("You've got a few more months of people feeling sorry for you. But after that, you'd better take a good, long look at yourself in the mirror."). Not Father McFall, not my father, and sometimes not Nonie ("I'm going to pick up Helen from school and take her to the movies so my son can have a quiet house."). Even for Mrs. Jones, one of me was probably sufficient.

Okay, Annie, I'm here, taking that good, long look you recommended. I'm not going to ask you what you would see if you were standing behind me—the way I was not standing behind Nonie that day she was trying on the Easter hat. In fact, I'm not going to think your thoughts, at all. I can imagine only too well the kinds of things you would say about what just happened in our living room. No, shut up, I said I wasn't going to think about it. This is just between me and me. Helen in the looking glass assessing Helen on the bench.

Now she's picking up the glass, which is dusty, and swallowing more cognac and making a face. How could Nonie enjoy this stuff? Wine I could see: like all sophisticated children, I had been allowed wine mixed with water on special occasions. But this was like swallowing pepper. It made you shudder all the way down. Nonie said it stimulated your heart more than wine.

Maybe I would grow up to have a faulty heart. I might have one already. ("Her little heart just stopped. Barely four months after her grandmother died, she was found dead. Found dead on her birthday in the grandmother's bed. It was the cleaning woman who discovered her. The person who had been staying with her for the summer thought she was just sleeping late. 'There was too much excitement the day before. I mean, with her father and the bomb and all. She'd had a long day and was a little cross by the end of it, but I never suspected there was anything wrong. I ought to have checked on her, but she said she was very tired and didn't want to say good night and closed her door. Now I will never forgive myself. I just wasn't up to the task. I failed her father and I failed her.' ")

Beyond my closed door, the dance music went on. They could be dancing now. The firm palm of Finn bracing her back, the twilight blue dress swishing all over his legs. ("You are so good to her, Finn. You will make a wonderful father someday. But, did you see the way she tossed back that brandy? Her father would kill me if he knew. Of course, he doesn't set a very good example himself. She's such a moody child. Smart, but so moody. There have been times when I thought we were doing real well, and then there have been other times when I'm counting the days and the hours and the minutes until I can say good-bye forever to this strange old house.")

I stood up and pushed away the bench and pondered my full length in the long mirror. A girl in a shapeless blouse and skirt and socks and loafers because her nice dress no longer fit. I would need new clothes for school and who would be there to say, "Now *that's* smart"? I was not tall enough to drape a hand over my dancing partner's shoulder, but Finn said he hadn't gotten his full height until seventeen. "Hair the color of wheat" sounded just like Flora: "And over here Juliet Parker has planted us a little field of wheat." I preferred "tawny," or "dark blond." According to Finn, all my features were the right distance from each other, which Flora said meant better than pretty. But Finn had also praised Flora's far-apart eyes. Flora said my looks would improve if I would look happier to see people when they came into a room. I smiled at myself in the mirror and the image responded with a simpering grimace. If you were really happy to see someone come into a room, you wouldn't necessarily smile. I had seen people not smile who were glad to see me. Brian didn't smile, he just looked as though something that belonged to him had reappeared. Nonie wasn't a natural smiler, either. When she was really appreciating something I'd said or done, she looked like someone looks when they have been proved right.

("She's a little girl who's had a lousy summer," Finn might be saying as he danced Flora round the threadbare carpet. "Seeing nobody but us, one friend getting polio, the other moving away, and the third one you say she doesn't like so well. And it's her first summer without her grandmother. She's entitled to a few moods. And didn't she thank me sweetly for the pencils, and you for all the things you did for her today?")

I gulped another swig from the aperitif glass and kept my mirror face from registering the cognac's ravaging passage down my gullet. I practiced looking like a person happy to see someone without needing to force a simpery smile. There. You did have some control over how you appeared to others.

A welcome new feeling of invulnerability lit up my insides and I decided to be generous on the eve of my eleventh birthday and go back and say good night like the kind of person people would want to see more of.

* * *

They were not dancing to the music as I had permitted them to do in my thoughts, and they were not on the sofa where I had left them. The tray and the coffee things were gone from the coffee table, but the glass of milk remained. The plate underneath had been removed, but two Fig Newtons and a shard of pound cake huddled together on the sailboat napkin from my sixth birthday. Flora was obviously planning to pay a bedtime visit against my wishes. Our two sketch pads, Finn's and mine, lay at one end of the sofa, both opened to the Flora portraits. Maybe Finn had gone already, but why had I not heard the motorcycle?

I crossed the carpeted dining room and was about to enter the kitchen when a muffled sound made me stealthy. Flora and Finn were locked in an embrace by the sink. This was no movie kiss. Their mouths mashed together as though each was trying desperately to disappear down the other's throat. I fled, stopping briefly by the coffee table long enough to pour the glass of milk over the two portraits of Flora and the unguilty sofa cushion that happened to be lying beneath.

XXVII.

How was it that I was magically skimming our treacherous driveway in the almost-dark without a single stumble? And in my leather-soled loafers, not my rubber-gripping Keds. (Was I doomed for the rest of my life to think of Mrs. Huff every time I thought of Keds?)

I felt weightless and glowing with the power of revenge. Was it the cognac or was it the hilarious replay of myself dumping the milk—or was it both? Just beneath the hilarious replay crept a curdling flow of loss and shame. I needed to outrun this flow until it had hardened solid and could no longer suck me into it.

Sunset Drive was already in darkness, but the tops of the trees, raucous with insect life, made black cutout designs against a greenish metallic sky. What color would Finn give it, or did his "special names" apply only to dresses?

The last time I had walked down Sunset Drive by myself had been at midday in early summer. Flora's clothes had just arrived and I was fleeing her Alabama talk and her insulting notion that I had undergone "a strange childhood." On this midday walk I had hoped to get some of myself back only to find it slipping away with every step I took. At this first bend in the road,

I had looked through a veil and seen Sunset Drive going on just the same without me. And then had come the awful draining away and the loss of words to account for what was happening to me. That's when Nonie's voice had told me to sit down on the ground in the shade and let everything go.

"Don't children have little imaginary friends?" Flora had wanted to know, ironing her Alabama clothes and telling that story I would rather not have heard about a certain skirt. When I said I was going for a walk, she asked should she come, and I said no, I was going out to look for an imaginary friend.

And then someone's boots creaked and someone's armpits smelled and I was brought back from nothingness by someone saying, "Hello, hello? Is anyone there?"

Together we scuffed downhill so I could show him my grandfather's shortcut. I pointed out the streetlight at the hairpin curve that "ruffians came all the way across town to shoot out," and he delighted me by falling into the same trap I had fallen in when Nonie explained about the ruffians. "Why didn't they shoot out the streetlights on their own side of town?" he wanted to know. "Because," I crowed triumphantly, "they already *have*."

The ruffians had been here again—no streetlight illuminated the hairpin curve tonight. But my eyes had grown used to the darkness, and I could make out the entrance to my grandfather's overgrown path that followed the broken-down railing until it dipped out of sight into the crater. ("Ah, I know what you're capable of . . . I've seen you jump into the unknown. . . . I know, I know. It's our secret.")

Branches slapped and brambles clawed as I felt my way through the indistinct undergrowth, no yipping Flora following close behind at noontime, no fast-moving paratrooper crashing ahead in daylight. I hoped, vaguely, to be hurt. Not killed, or crippled like Brian, or even to have my face scarred for life with slashes, but just damaged in some way that would make people sorry I'd had to go through this night and equally amazed that I had come out of it as well as I had.

I tripped and went down. Reaching out with my hands, I groped emptiness just ahead of where I had fallen. I was at the edge of the crater! I had almost gone over! But no, it was just a deep rut, like the bad one on our driveway the garbageman and the towing man had covered with a piece of board. Nevertheless, I decided to crawl the rest of the way to the crater on my hands and knees. My plan was to let myself carefully down its side, holding on to the sassafras tree the way I had been taught. And then what? To be found curled at the bottom, exposed to the night? But it would be harder to freeze to death in August than in November, when he had done it, and I had no intention of taking off my clothes and being found naked.

I scraped my knee badly while edging backward down the slope, and paused to reassess my strategy when I finally gained hold of the sassafras tree. Crouching at its base, I indulgently dabbled in the blood running down my leg. When it kept coming, I wiped some of it on my face and licked its metallic flavor off my fingertips.

Had they discovered the damage back at the house yet? (Flora: "Oh! What happened here?" "Well, I think some milk was spilled," Finn would say matter-of-factly, noting the empty glass. "But—oh dear, the sketch pads! Both of them ruined. Maybe we can save them. Not my portraits, what do *those* matter, but maybe the pads aren't completely soaked through. What do you think happened?" "I think someone was angry." "But why would she—? Oh, no! You don't think she *saw*— Oh dear, look at the sofa! Her father is going to kill me." "Leave it, love. Why don't you go and check on her?")

How long would it take for them to figure out what to do? ("She's not in her room, and the door is wide open." "Where would she most likely go?" "Well, maybe the garage. She often sits in the Oldsmobile when she's moping.")

Not in the garage. Not in the Oldsmobile, "moping." What next? Search the rooms of the house? ("Would she have run away?" "She never has before. Oh, dear, I'm sure she must have seen us in the kitchen, but how? She had gone to her *room*, she had said *good night*."

"People," Finn would reason patiently, "have been known to come out of their rooms after they have said good night and gone into them.")

If she wasn't in the car and wasn't in the house, where would she have gone? The gift of tears would surely have kicked in by now, and Finn would have to perform some manly comforting while organizing what to do next. "I want you to stay here at the house, in case she shows up. I'll do a bit of reconnaissance work outside." "Will you take the motorcycle? Or since it's an emergency I'm sure her father wouldn't mind if you took the car—" "No, reconnaissance is best done on foot. Now, I want you to stay here, is that agreed?")

I slouched down at the base of the sassafras tree and rested my feet on the bumpy root below. If someone were to come after me soon, they wouldn't have to descend all the way into the crater. Or, if I thought it best, I could always scramble down at the last minute, though it wouldn't be so easy in the dark and with no one to catch me. But for now I would wait here and count how many nature noises I could identify. Cicadas, tree frogs, rustlings of larger bodies on the ground that I didn't want to think about right now. Mrs. Jones said when you heard your first cicadas it was just six weeks till the first frost, and they had been going strong for days now. Starling Peake had kept a tree frog in his room for a whole winter; it lived in a fern pot and liked to come out in the daytime and cling to the top of an upholstered chair with its little sucker feet. ("There was something adorably boyish about Starling, even though he let us down badly.") I had been planning to tell this anecdote to the next inhabitant of Starling's room, after I had finished with the more important stories of the house.

Distant gunfire exploded from below. Then I realized they were shooting off fireworks in town. To celebrate the bomb, of course. Would my father be a local hero? "There goes Harry Anstruther, he helped make the secret bomb that finally ended the war." I wasn't clear whether Oak Ridge would be someplace people would keep working at, now that its purpose had been accomplished. Just as well if it closed down. I loved my father, but he had sounded tempted by the prospect of staying on there, and I knew without ever seeing it that I would hate living there in a little house and going to school like a child on a reservation. Maybe they would send him home with a bonus: big enough so we could fix up Old One Thousand. If he came tomorrow for my birthday he would be surprised by the repaired gutters and our reopening of the circular driveway around the house. If only things hadn't turned out the way they had tonight. But whose fault was that? I was the one who had been ambushed by the unimaginable. How could people be so double-dealing?

Officially, my birthday wasn't until late tomorrow. I had "finally decided to make my entrance" at six fifteen in the evening, according to Nonie. The time was recorded by her in blue ink in my baby book.

"Was she very tired when I finally came out?" I always wanted to know.

"You are always tired when you finish having a baby," Nonie said, "but I would say she was more relieved than anything else."

"Why?"

"She had been working hard to make you come out for eighteen hours. That's a long time. But between her contractions she could be quite droll. 'Honora, I've just had an awful thought,' she said. 'What if he decides he'd rather not come out?' 'Then,' I said, 'we'll have to think of something really special to bribe him with.' This made her laugh."

"But where was my father?"

"He was waiting at a proper distance to be informed. I was the one who saw her through. Early on, the nurse came in and said, 'Mrs. Anstruther, what, pray tell, are you doing in the bed with Mrs. Anstruther?' 'Isn't it obvious?' I said. 'I am lying beside her, sharing her labor pains.'"

I liked this story except for one thing. "Why did she have to call me a he?"

"Oh, darling, that's nothing. It's just gender shorthand for babies who haven't been born yet. It's the same as when people refer to 'the history of man,' or 'mankind.' She knew you were *you*, all along."

The fireworks had stopped. Had they run out or gone to get some more? I thought of Mrs. Jones waiting for the pretty fireworks Rosemary liked best and then saying "Stella Reeve, you are not forgotten," even though people looked at her funny.

What if nobody came after me? Would I have to stay here until my father started searching tomorrow? And if nobody was going to come, what was the point in spending the night with my bottom getting damp from the ground and goose bumps on my arms and tree bark digging into my shoulders? Maybe I should drag myself back through the undergrowth and walk down Sunset Drive to the village. I would be just as hard to find if I spent the night in the church, which Father McFall was leaving open for people who wanted to thank God or be sorry about the bomb.

Something horrible with a huge wingspan passed directly over my head and I was back in the nightmare where Nonie flew through the air and shrieked before breaking apart at the bottom of the crater, one dismembered leg twisted sideways in its old-lady shoe. Only this time I was the one who shrieked. Why was life so treacherous and unfair? It was enough to make you want to stop being in it.

A circle of light jittered back and forth across the treetops. "Helen? Is that you?"

Don't answer. Give the false-hearted more time to imagine the world without you in it.

Louder: *"Helen!"*

The tree frogs abruptly ceased their night chorus. The bouncing circles of light grew larger. "Are ye in there? I'm sure I heard you."

Now my own mind was double-dealing me: Had I known all along he was going to come, like the soldier who finally wins the princess out of the coffin before she can destroy any more men? Or had he come too late for it to count?

The light played back and forth over the floor of the crater. "Will I find you down there?" he called. "Or are you wanting me to jump so you'll have time to hide somewhere else?"

"I'm not hiding, stupid," I said in my normal voice. "I hurt my leg climbing down."

"Ah, the Sphinx speaks. Is it bad, the leg?"

"It's stopped bleeding, but I'm resting it awhile."

"Good idea. *Where* are you resting?"

"At that sassafras tree."

The light skittered about until it found my face. "Ah." The voice could not conceal its relief. "Will I come down?"

"Suit yourself."

The light shut off. There were no footsteps, just the rustling dark, and then he swung down and was sitting beside me.

"How did you do that?" I said. "I didn't hear you coming."

"Didn't I spend two years training to outsmart my enemy in the dark?"

"Am I your enemy now?"

"Let's have a look at the injury." He played the flashlight, which I recognized from our hardware drawer, on my legs. "Which one is it?"

"The one with the blood on it." I stopped myself from adding "silly."

"Hmm. Can you walk on it, or will I have to carry you home?" I caught something less than playful in his tone.

"It's more of a *cut* than anything else. I'd prefer to walk."

"Up you go, then. And no, you're not my enemy, but just imagine yourself handcuffed to me as my prisoner of war till I get you home."

He lugged me up the side of the crater and then towed me ungallantly along behind him. What a disaster this place was after dark. It was hardly possible to imagine my father and Willow Fanning running away at night, even though it hadn't been such an obstacle course back then. How naïve of Flora to have thought we could "repair" such a jungle as a "surprise" for my father at the end of the summer.

"Do you have to go so fast?" I cried. "You're hurting my wrist."

"Sorry," he said, stopping to let me catch my breath but not letting go of my wrist. "It's only that I want to get you home. The poor girl is beside herself with worry. She takes it mortally seriously, you know, being left in charge of you, and now she's terrified she's let your father down. I had a feeling you might come here, but she thought you could have gone back to that place you walked to. That land on top of the hill that old Mr. Quarles wants to buy."

"Why on earth would I want to go back there? The loggers have ruined it. That's why he wants to buy it, he loves making a profit on other people's losses."

"Well, you weren't there to tell us that, were you? She said you seemed to have enjoyed the walk, so we tried that first."

"Enjoyed! How stupid can you get?"

"A pity, isn't it, how stupid we all are."

"I didn't mean you. But Flora's simpleminded, you must have realized that by now."

"I must be simpleminded myself because no, I hadn't. I think you are confusing simpleminded with simple-hearted."

"I'm not sure I know what 'simple-hearted' means," I said haughtily.

"When there's no deceit or malice in your heart. Most of us have some; it protects us. People without it are rare. My friend Barney came close, but he'd built up a layer of sludge to protect his heart against his mother. That's why Flora is so rare, it's just her heart she offers, with none of the sludge to wade through."

"You sound like you love her," I remarked scornfully, but his answer, if he gave one, was drowned out by a shriek of braking tires, headlamps dancing crazily toward us, as though someone thought it might be fun to drive into the woods and run us down, then veering off wildly at the last minute to hit something else up ahead with a crack and crush of metal.

"God in Heaven," said Finn, letting go of my hand.

"It's because they shot out the streetlight again," I said, feeling a surge of excitement accompanied by shameful relief. An accident would surely wipe my misconduct from Finn's memory of this night. "Will we go and help out?" I was starting to talk like him.

"From the sound of things, we need to get an ambulance. You're going to run up that hill as fast as you can and tell Flora to phone. She's waiting at the house in case you come back. Tell them exactly where, on Sunset Drive."

"But I want to help you."

"Who'll go and call for the ambulance, then? Who is being simpleminded now?"

"But shouldn't we go and look first? We don't even know how badly—"

"Christ almighty, Helen, is it your morbid curiosity we must satisfy before we get help?"

"I need to see!" I screamed. "It might be my father. He's coming for my birthday! What if he decided to come tonight? You can't keep me from my father."

I was already running ahead of him toward the trees broken by the crash. Finn had hurt and insulted me, and I had screamed what I did in order to punish him and win my point, but when I got closer to the wreck it seemed that I had wreaked a hideous magic. The crumpled, steaming car, whose innocent headlights still beamed reliably ahead into the woods, was my father's Chevy coupe and the numbers on the license plate were the ones I knew by heart.

XXVIII.

Annie Rickets's claim that her parents were privy to secret information because they worked for the telephone company was not a total fabrication.

My grandfather had installed one of the earliest phone lines in town for Anstruther's Lodge, and our three-digit number had remained the same, though most people had five-digit numbers by this time. In 1945, you still took the receiver off the hook and an operator, often one whose voice you'd heard before, said, "Number, please." You said the number—Annie's was 34598—and the operator said, "Thank you" or "I'll connect you" (and sometimes both) and she would plug you into the right hole on her switchboard and the number you wanted would ring. If someone didn't pick up after a certain number of rings, the operator would say, "I'm sorry, but your party doesn't answer, will you try again later?" Annie's family was on a party line, and sometimes when we were talking a petulant woman's voice would break in with "Are you little chatterboxes *ever* going to get off?" "Oh, dry up, you old bag," Annie once shot back, and the party complained to the operator, who told Annie's parents. They made her phone the old bag and apologize. Until the dial system came in, the voice of the operator was an integral part of all telephone intercourse. Talking to callers, the operator could learn about things that were happening and make further calls on her own and thus contribute to the outcome of events.

In an emergency, it was enough to tell the operator what it was and she would plug you into the proper service, or you could just tell her what was the matter and she would contact the service and relay your message.

I had been preparing my message as I ran uphill, a stitch in my side: Operator, you've got to help me, my father's had a bad wreck on Sunset Drive and we need an ambulance quick. She connected me and stayed on the line while the hospital took down the information. Hairpin curve, near the top. Thrown through the windshield. The person with him said a severed artery in the neck.

The ambulance was on its way, but the operator kept talking to me until I told her I really had to go. How old was I? Was there anyone with me? I told her I was eleven and that my father had been one of the people at Oak Ridge helping make the bomb, only we hadn't known what he was doing, he himself hadn't known, it was so secret. He had been driving home to be with me on my birthday tomorrow.

Where was Flora? I had yelled for her as I ran into the house. She must have gone out looking for me some more. I was glad she hadn't been there to make the phone call. She would have included who knew what unnecessary digressions.

("For God's sake—run!" croaked a bare-chested Finn, spotlit by the faithful headlights that hadn't seemed to register that the rest of the car was smashed. I had left him kneeling over my father's crumpled form, stuffing his own shirt, already blood-soaked, against the side of my father's neck. "And stay in the house with Flora. You're under orders!")

Quickly I circled the downstairs—no Flora, though at some point she had found time to work on the milk damage. Wet kitchen towels had been carefully laid across the sofa cushion, and the assaulted sketch pads placed facedown on a dry towel. I stopped by my room long enough to change into my Keds, which were better for running up and down hills, and then galloped upstairs to check out all the rooms so I could truthfully say I'd looked everywhere. If someone wasn't in the house, you could hardly be under orders to stay in it with them.

There were two hospitals in town, St. Benedict's on the south side, and Mission on our side. Mission was only twelve blocks from the entrance to Sunset Drive, and as I skidded down our driveway—this descent less effortless than the one when the cognac was fresher—I could already hear the approaching ambulance.

My father could not die because Finn had been on the spot to save him. And why had he been on the spot? Because he had been out looking for me. My mind raced ahead, binding up the wounds and preparing a desirable outcome. I had worried that my father would find fault with Finn, but how could you find fault with the person who had saved your life? They would become fast friends, the Starling Peake room would be the Devlin Patrick Finn room, Finn would help repair Old One Thousand and drive me to school and attend the local junior college. Even if he didn't get his status revised and be eligible for the GI Bill, my father would pay the tuition. If only there was more money! But we would manage somehow. In five years, when I turned sixteen, I'd have my driver's license and could get an afterschool job.

When I rounded the first curve I saw the parked ambulance below with its front spotlight trained on the woods. There was a police car, as well, and a fire truck was just arriving. Men tumbled out of vehicles and shouted back and forth and carried handheld searchlights toward the spot where my father lay. From my invisible vantage point above the activity, I seemed to split in half. One half could not suppress the thrill of elation rising in my throat at the enthralling spectacle of human beings organizing themselves to save a life, while the other recoiled from the possibility that my father might die, or indeed was already dead, and that my life would be completely changed.

Now they were carrying him out of the woods. Bare-chested Finn, holding one of the searchlights, followed, directing the high-powered beam on them loading the stretcher into the back of the ambulance. Unable to make out whether they had covered up my father's face (which I knew from the movies was a bad sign), I edged closer. Still invisible in the dark on the other side of the road, I risked another couple of yards until I could make sure that I really did see the oxygen mask over the face and white wrappings around the neck.

Now that they were getting ready to close the doors, I felt it would be all right to declare myself. Finn couldn't begrudge me speaking to the men who were carrying away my own father.

I stepped forward to cross to their side of the road, tripped over something substantial, and fell down with a cry. Now the light was on me as I picked myself up from the pavement.

"Another one!" a man cried as the light moved away from my face and shone on the crumpled body of a woman in a blue dress.

XXIX.

"I let you sleep as long as you could," Mrs. Jones said, opening the blinds in Nonie's room to let in the bright, sunny day.

"What time is it?"

"Almost ten."

"Where is Finn?"

"He left last night. After I came. Don't you remember?"

"Yes, but tell me again."

"Well, he phoned and said for me to come—you'd said where to find my number—and I got here as quick as I could. You were here on the bed, with the blanket over you. He said you had refused to get undressed in case you were needed. Do you remember me helping you get into your pajamas and washing your face?"

"Why did it need washing?"

"There was dried blood on it. He said something about you hurting your knee, and I cleaned it off, too. How are you feeling?"

"My head hurts. I want you to tell me where everyone is."

Mrs. Jones pulled over Nonie's dressing table bench and sat down close to me. She was not the sort of person to plop down on your bed. The stoic slabs of her cheeks lay calm and flat against her bones. Her gray gaze was direct without being probing or judging. "Your father is in the hospital. The preacher from your church is with him and will be coming to tell you how he is. Mr. Finn has seen your father, too."

"Where is Finn now?"

"There's arrangements have to be made. Mr. Finn is tending to those."

"What kind of arrangements?"

"Well, he had to get in touch with her people. And fix up things with the railroad to get her home. Oh dear, I never did know what to call her."

"You mean get her body home."

"That's what I mean. Would you like me to bring you something or would you rather go to the kitchen?"

"Thank you, I'm not hungry."

"I squeezed lemon juice all around those spill marks on the sofa cushion and put it out in the sun. What was spilled on it?"

"I spilled some milk."

"Well, it ought to dry up fine, then. The drawing books didn't fare as well, but you can still see the pictures. One of them of her is real good, it's a pity it got spoiled."

"What time is Father McFall coming?"

"Right after the hospital, he said."

"I better get dressed."

"I'll be in the kitchen," said Mrs. Jones.

Beryl Jones, Nonie said, was one to answer your questions or carry out instructions "and stop right there. She doesn't elaborate, argue, or say what she would do. Would there were more like her!"

You could trust Mrs. Jones to give you her candid responses

and respectfully desist from opinions, whereas Father McFall was not one to hold back when he thought you were in error, which is why I thought it safest to be fully dressed and on my guard to receive whatever he deemed me ready for.

But when he arrived, he didn't treat me as sternly as I had anticipated. Taking my hands in his, he asked almost humbly, "Helen, how can I serve you? Tell me what I can do." For the first time I noticed how the dry, wrinkled folds of his neck hung down like an old dog's over his clerical collar. Though it was the kind of thing you expected to hear from waiters or gas station attendants, his choice of words for the occasion completely disarmed me.

"I n-need," I began. Then harsh, barking sobs burst out of me and I had to wait for them to run their course. "Nobody will tell me anything," I began again, "and I need to *know*."

"What do you need to know, Helen?"

"Is my father going to die?"

"He's pretty banged up and there are some problems, but thanks to that young soldier's quick thinking, he's not going to die."

"What did Finn do?"

"He packed his shirt against the ruptured artery and then he stood on top of it with his heavy boot till the ambulance came."

"Can I go and see my father?"

"Not just yet, but I'll come and see you every day, maybe twice a day, and bring you reports. Why don't we go in the living room and sit down?"

"Not the living room!"

"Here in the kitchen, then."

"No, not here, either."

"Well, where would you like to go?"

"Let's go out of the house."

But when we got outside I couldn't think where we should go. My mind had lost its power of decision. Father McFall seemed to understand this and started walking slowly around the circular drive that Finn and I had cleared. I followed along beside him. It was going to be a warm day. I had not forgotten it was my birthday, but thought it would sound crass to bring it up.

Presently he asked, "Is there anything else you want to know, Helen?"

"Where is she now?"

"At the funeral home."

"Was she dead when I fell over her, or did she die at the hospital? Finn made me go back home when the second ambulance was coming."

"It appears to have been instant. She was hit by a car."

"Was it my father's car?"

"We think so, but he's in no condition to be asked yet."

"What was she doing out in the middle of the dark road?"

"Finn said that, as far as he could tell, she had walked down to see if he had found you yet."

Finn did not come that day. In the middle of the afternoon, Mrs. Jones said she had to drive into town for a few things. She returned with some groceries and a bakery cake with HELEN written on it in pink and eleven candles waiting to be lit. We had beef stew for dinner and then afterward the cake. The icing wasn't chocolate, but of course I didn't say anything. "Rosemary always loved a bakery cake," Mrs. Jones said, apologetically adding, "though maybe it was because I was no great shakes at baking." The stew was filling, though without the benefit of Juliet Parker's famous herbs.

"Will you be spending the night again?" I asked her.

"I'll be staying with you until we get things figured out. For now, I'm in your old room, I hope that's all right. When your father comes home, he'll have to be down here for a while."

She had a present for me. Its plain brown wrappings reminded me of Finn's present the evening before, when Flora had gone to take her bath and change into the blue dress.

"I bought it off the librarian," said Mrs. Jones. "She had ordered it for the young people's library, but someone on the board said it was too pessimistic and not Christian. But the librarian assured me it was a wonderful book, she had read it as a teenager, and thought you were old enough for it. And the pictures in this one are real beauties."

It was the *Rubáiyát of Omar Khayyám*, the Fitzgerald translation, with color illustrations by Dulac. I still have it on my shelves, with "All best wishes on yr. 11th birthday, from Beryl M. Jones" inscribed on the flyleaf. If I balance it by the spine in the palm of my hand and joggle it lightly back and forth, it falls open to a familiar page.

> The Moving Finger writes; and, having writ,
> Moves on: nor all thy Piety nor Wit
> Shall lure it back to cancel half a Line,
> Nor all thy Tears wash out a Word of it.

Finn did come the next day, but Father McFall came earlier and brought the morning newspaper. PARATROOPER SAVES LIFE OF A-BOMB WORKER. It wasn't as flashy as the story about the lady in a nearby town whose son was a bombardier on the plane that dropped the bomb, but both stories were on the front page, grouped beneath the caption LOCAL HEROES. There was a head shot of my father, with his acerbic smile, taken when he was promoted from assistant principal to principal of the high school, which made the picture the same age as myself. Next to it was an Army photo of Pvt. D. P. Finn with a frowning blur of a face, in full paratrooper gear, cradling his helmet next to his chest. You could see that his image had been lifted out of a group picture, which reminded me of the story of my mother cutting herself out of the Alabama photo. Though I prided myself on my rapid reading skills, Father McFall standing over me made me nervous and I had to keep doubling back over lines before they made sense.

They referred to my father as "the esteemed principal of Mountain City High," which would make him snort when he got well enough to read this, and went so far as to name the building (K-25) his crew had been working on at Oak Ridge. Then came a quote from an Oak Ridge barber describing how everyone in the government town of 75,000, built in 1942, was bound to secrecy: "My customers and I talked about everything under the sun except the project." The story said my father had been on his way home for his daughter's (no name) birthday the next day. Could this information have come from the telephone operator who had kept me on the phone asking more questions? She probably had a sideline of calling in things like this to some contact at the newspaper. Annie would have known for sure. Finn had been quoted as saying, "I only did what I could. In combat training they taught us to use what we had in an emergency, and I had a shirt and a boot." It said that until recently he had been a convalescent at the local military hospital, and that was all.

"But there's nothing about *her*," I said to Father McFall.

"There's a separate item in 'Deaths and Funerals.'" Father McFall found the page for me, folded the paper in half, and handed it back. ALABAMA WOMAN FOUND DEAD. Flora Waring, of Birmingham, Alabama, presumably hit by a vehicle, found dead on upper Sunset Drive. Body at funeral home awaiting burial arrangements. Authorities say accident is still under investigation.

"But we *know* what happened!" I said. "Why isn't it in here?"

"We think we know, Helen, but nobody saw it. Until your father is able to tell us what he remembers, authorities can't speculate, at least not on the record. There are legal deterrents."

"You saw my father this morning?"

"I did."

"You said there were 'some problems,' but you didn't say what."

"Why don't we wait till we see which ones go away before we make a list?"

"Take it a day at a time," I said.

"Exactly, Helen." He looked pleased, not seeming to realize I was only quoting back his own hedging answer when I had asked whether Brian was going to be a cripple.

FINN DROVE UP later that morning in a strange car. I had been more or less watching out the window since Father McFall left.

"You're in a car," I said stupidly. He was wearing his dress-up clothes from the first time he came to dinner.

"I am," he said, not appearing to note this infantile greeting. "Kindly lent by Mr. Crump, but it has to be returned to him within the hour. Ah, Mrs. Jones." He stepped over to the sink, where she was washing up, and offered his hand. "Devlin Finn. I didn't introduce myself very well last time."

"Oh, Mr. Finn," she said. "My hands are all wet."

He waited while she dried them to her standards on her apron and then clasped them firmly between his, which I could see flustered her a little. "How is everyone doing up here?" he asked in a confidential voice, as though he and she were by themselves.

"It was a shock, Mr. Finn, but we're managing. Is there anything I could get you? A glass of water?"

"Thank you, Mrs. Jones, but all I need is Helen here. I've come to pack up Flora's belongings to take with me on the train to Birmingham. It leaves in a little over an hour and I'm going to need her help."

It was the first time anyone had said her name.

I LED THE way upstairs, past Starling Peake without saying anything about whose room I hoped it would be, and on down the hall to the Willow Fanning room. There were important questions I was aching to ask, but something about Finn's countenance held me back. If this had been in a fairy tale, a magician might had encased Finn in a lifelike mask and said, "You are safe behind this mask unless someone says something that can crack it. You need to guard against this happening or you'll be destroyed." I must have wanted Finn not to be destroyed more than I craved to have the answers to things only he could tell me because I held back, though it was very hard.

There was the old carpetbag in which she had carried the filled mason jars, Uncle Sam's apple-cured ham, and her special flour ("I never go anywhere anymore without my self-rising flour . . ."), and there was the suitcase that, aside from underwear and some sanitary napkins discreetly concealed in hand-sewn wrappers, had contained the sack of cornmeal, tea bags, a cake in a tin box, and the wax paper parcels of Juliet Parker's herbs.

Without the food, all the clothes that had arrived later in the box fitted easily into the suitcase. We did the closet first, and Finn showed me how to fold blouses in three parts, Army-style.

"You remember, Helen, that day on the walk, when we were telling our family histories, and I said I had a brother?"

"Yes."

"And you asked me whether he was jealous when I got to go to America, and I cut you short."

"You said, 'That's another story,' and that it was enough about you."

"What a memory you have! Well, now I want to tell you about Conan. When he was fourteen, Bill and Grace, my adoptive parents, invited him to come to Albany for a long visit. I was sixteen by then and had been with them for six years. Things weren't good back in Ireland, my father was ill and unlikely to work again, and it was sort of assumed by all in an unsaid way that if Conan wanted to stay on with us in America he could. Well, he was over the moon with joy. Now I'll get to the sad part quickly because there's no use drawing it out. A week before he was to sail, he went into town to buy presents for us, and he was gunned down on the street."

"You mean he was killed?"

"Shot right through the heart."

"But why?"

"Because Ireland's just that way now. It's like your Civil War, only the two sides don't wear uniforms and fight out in the open. They mistook him for another man's red-haired son. All of us were heartbroken, but then as time went on I became sure I was the one responsible for his death."

"How could you be?"

"Ah, because I had written letters praising everything, bragging about my good fortune, making him want my life."

"But that doesn't make you responsible—"

"Don't rush me, darling. It doesn't, but I *felt* that it did. Then the war started and I joined up and things got better until I lost my friend Barney, or until his mother came to see me and said she wished her son had been clever enough to get out when I had. After that, the two sorrows linked up—or, no, a better way to put it is that the weight of Barney's death piled on top of Conan's death made me feel so unworthy I didn't want to live. Of course I didn't understand the mechanics of all this going on inside me until the mind doctors explained it after my little failed attempt to extinguish myself. Now you're wondering why I'm telling you this story, I can see it all over your face, Helen."

"Why are you?"

"Because it may be useful to you if ever you start feeling that something bad that happened is all your fault. Fate is far more complicated than that, and thinking you're in charge of it is egotistical and will only make you sick and waste your life. Are you hearing me?"

"Yes."

"Now, where are the rest of her things?"

"There's just what's in those drawers."

I had been dreading the drawers because I hadn't decided what to do about the top one. I wanted to keep Nonie's letters, but I also wanted Finn to respect me and I hadn't figured a way to achieve both things. So I started with the bottom two drawers, leaving the top for last. Her stockings and lingerie and the hand-sewn wrappers in which she stored her sanitary pads. She hadn't used up the second supply, which had come with her box of clothes. I was pleased with my tactfulness as I took charge of these very personal items, tucking them away in the suitcase with my own hands so he wouldn't have to touch them and be embarrassed.

Finn glanced at his watch. It could no longer be postponed, the top drawer. But it was not as I had last seen it. On the left was Juliet Parker's faithful stack of summer letters, but on the other side, where Nonie's letters had been, was a package done up in gift paper I recognized from the stash of old wrappings from Nonie's deep desk drawer. My first thought was that if Flora had gone snooping in our drawers, even in the interest of wrapping a present for me, then it sort of equaled out my intrusions into hers.

"These are letters from Juliet Parker." I handed over the stack to Finn. "She wrote every single week." I still couldn't say Flora's name aloud. "This other . . . I don't know." For me to say *there used to be another pile of letters in here* would be to admit I'd been snooping.

"It looks like a present," Finn said.

"I know, but—"

"It might be for you. For your birthday."

"But there's no card."

"Well, maybe there was no time for a card. Why don't you open it?"

"I don't— If you think it's all right."

"I know it's all right," he said, making a noble effort not to be caught looking at his watch again.

Inside were Nonie's letters, all done up neat and tight in their ribbon. The folded note inside said,

> Dear Helen, I hand these over to you, on your eleventh birthday. May they sustain and guide you as they have me. There are some personal parts, but I didn't want to black things out like in those censored letters from soldiers overseas. It would seem an insult to her. I will miss these precious letters but you have taught me so many things I'm grateful for, which I will try to incorporate into my life and my teaching.
>
> Love from your admiring cousin, Flora Waring.

"Oh," I said. I couldn't look at him. It seemed I also was encased in a mask that one wrong word or move could crack. "Did you know about this?"

"I did. We talked it over. She said you had asked to read them, but she was worried some parts were too old for you. Then she thought about it some more and decided you would grow into them. She said she wanted to give you something you'd treasure and the letters were the best thing she had."

XXX.

I think of Mrs. Jones, who was seventy that summer, driving after dark by herself to stand among the crowd gathered at the lake and say aloud, "Stella Reeve, you are not forgotten," every time a pretty firework went up in the sky. Beryl Jones didn't even know Stella Reeve, the little girl who had caught polio at the lake and died a few days later. She had only read about her in the newspaper, but she did it because her dear dead Rosemary, who in life had loved to make little memorial ceremonies, had suggested it.

I spent all those days and nights with Flora the summer I was ten and she was twenty-two: three weeks of June, all of July, and the first six days of August. I thought I knew all there was to know about her, but she has since become one of my profoundest teachers, though she never got to stand in front of a real class and teach.

These pages are for her. They are my attempt to stand among the crowd and say aloud for all to hear, "Flora Waring, you are not forgotten."

"I came across this sentence I wanted to run by you," my father said. This was back in the seventies. We were talking on the phone. There had been years when we didn't talk, but now we had started again. "Here it is. I wrote it down for the next time you took it into your head to honor me with a call: 'Suppose love were to evolve as rapidly in our brains as technical skill has done.' What do you make of that?"

"Where is it from?"

"*A Burnt-Out Case.* Dr. Colin, the leprosy doctor, is talking to Querry, the burnt-out architect. The doctor is still opting for evolutionary progress in spite of all the terrible things men have done to one another in the first half of our century."

"You were reading that *again*?" I was playing for time while I tried to work out what I thought about the sentence.

"Greene satisfies my perennial cynicism. But that little nugget of hope stuck out like a thorn this time around. What do you make of it? Is such a supposition likely?"

"Not in my lifetime," I said, sensing his relief and approval through the receiver. "Certainly not in yours," I generously added.

"Nope. I consider myself lucky to have gotten off with just an eye for eighty thousand and one lives. Well, just thought I'd run it past you."

We both knew who was meant by the one life added to the final Hiroshima death count.

("I had planned to leave Oak Ridge the next morning, the morning of your birthday, but then we got the news of the bomb. I went back to my room to leave Harker a note, since he might not have heard due to his deafness, but he had cleared out and left *me* a note. It said, 'Fucking hell, Harry, this went too far, there will be retribution.' When I got back to the site, half my crew had left and those who had remained were exhibiting the usual unsavory aspects of human nature. One announced that

God had informed him about the bomb a week ago, but he had been under divine orders not to tell. Several of them petitioned for immediate jeopardy bonuses in case the whole place blew sky-high. One enterprising rogue was collecting bets on how many Japs had been killed and when the war would be over. And then there was the usual quota of worthy fellows cutting their eyes at you for approval: well, here I am, sir, ready to get on with the job, some of us have to be responsible around here. I realized I was more than a little unhinged and decided to leave at once, drive over the mountain before nightfall, and get out of this madness. I hadn't touched a drop on the premises, but I was looking forward to driving up to the house and surprising you and Flora and then pouring myself a well-earned glass, or maybe more than one. I was *thinking* about that drink, in fact it was the last thing I can remember thinking about before I rounded the curve. It was dark as hell and then something flew out at me like a ghost. I turned the wheel as hard as I could to miss it, but I obviously didn't succeed.")

My father took a long time to recover from the accident. He "sustained," as the jargon goes, a punctured lung, five cracked ribs, a broken femur (the polio leg), and the loss of his left eye. He referred to the eye almost cavalierly, especially in the old Hammurabi sense of an eye for an eye, and wore a black patch over it, but rarely mentioned the tragicomic dragging lurch, increasingly compounded by arthritis, that became his normal gait. He took even longer to emerge from a severe darkness of spirit in which he seemed to turn his unsparing disgust for human foibles completely against himself. ("Didn't I tell you they'd find themselves a prince of an assistant principal, a young war hero and social scion with a good word for everybody and willing to coach the track team free of charge while one-eyed, gimpy, bad-assed old Harry takes his perpetual leave of absence?")

His unlikely redeemer was the Old Mongrel himself, who took him out for long drives, settled his hospital bills, paid for us to have the Huffs' cook (Lorena and Rachel had vanished into thin air the day after the bombing of Nagasaki, leaving a house that turned out to be rented and furniture that was leased, and without paying anyone except the manly riding teacher, who wisely got her fees in advance. They left behind a swath of delectable rumors, the prevalent one being that they were German spies. I think Annie Rickets's speculations may have been closer to home: there was no Mr. Huff. Tall stories told by a woman of imagination and some ready cash who moves to town with her child are more easily swallowed in wartime.)

My father went into business with Earl Quarles, much to my amazement and disgust, and the two of them prospered in the postwar housing boom. When I was twelve I was sent to boarding school and became a little snob who vacationed with new friends and went home as seldom as possible—then on to college, followed by a breakdown and lengthy stay in an expensive institution, where I began writing, for therapy, but also out of disdain and boredom, a sort of elegiac tale about the Recoverers and the house my father and the Old Mongrel had torn down to build more of their mountain-view "estates." Many reconstructions later, it was published as my first novel, *House of Clouds*.

When the Old Mongrel died in his upper nineties, my father demanded that I get on a plane and show myself at the funeral. Driving me back to the airport afterward, he dropped his bomb.

"Well, dammit, Helen, it was your doing."

"*My* doing!"

"You were the one who told him I was the age of the century. And quoted the old doctor's poem about the 'cloud-begirded' December day I was born. All he had to do was go look up the birth records at city hall and count back to his stepsister running away in May. It was there in front of our eyes, but none of us saw it—or wanted to see it. You might as well get used to having his genes. I have. It's made sense of a lot of things for me. He was a crude, wily old rascal, a raw slice of genuine Americana, and that's not the end of the world. For me, it was the beginning in many ways."

These days it is easy to locate most people without leaving your desk. The question becomes what do you want to do with them after you've found them? Dr. Brian Beale has a private clinic in the Tidewater. He found me first, in the eighties, and has since critiqued all my books and told me why I wrote them, what I left out, and who everybody was. He's a much honored member of the psychiatric establishment, one of his sons is in Congress, and he still gets about on metal crutches. He flies to London twice a year to see all the new plays and speaks with a distinct Carolina mountain twang.

Then there are those others you put off tracking down because you'd rather keep them as they were, or keep making them up, recycling them into new incarnations. Finally, when I was nearing the age of Mrs. Jones when she came to live with us for a year, I was just about to go to the Army's website and do some serious searching, but instead on a hunch I looked up auto parts suppliers in the upstate New York area and found a chain of Finns. It was almost too easy to make the phone call.

"What a shame! You just missed him," a woman told me.

"Do you happen to know when he'll be back?"

"Ah, no, what I mean is, we buried him day before yesterday."

"Oh, dear. I did just miss him, didn't I?"

"Did you know Grandpop?"

"It was a long time ago. He delivered our groceries one summer at the end of World War Two. He'd just come out of our local military hospital, where he'd been recuperating."

"Wow, that *is* a long time ago."

"Listen, do you mind my asking something? Did he—did he have a good life?"

"Well, I'm probably not the most objective person to ask. I loved him to pieces. We all did. If you mean did he make a big splash in the world, his obituary ran almost an entire page in the Albany *Times Union*. He was the great benefactor, Grandpop. He was a *huge* supporter of the arts."

"That sounds like him," I said. "Well, I'm sorry I missed him, but it's been nice talking to you."

"Wait a minute!" she cried. "I think I know who you are, now. You're that haunted little girl, aren't you?"

"I'd never thought of it that way," I told her, "but I suppose I am."

Acknowledgements

Moses Cardona at John Hawkins & Associates for his astute first reading of *Flora.*

Nancy Miller and the house of Bloomsbury for reconnecting me with the passion of publishing.

Rob Neufeld, editor of *The Making of a Writer* and of our forthcoming volumes *Working on the Ending,* for his historical research on Asheville during World War II.

The late Gale D. Webbe for the invaluable chapter on his two summers spent working in construction at Oak Ridge in *Sawdust and Incense:Worlds that Shape a Priest* (St. Hilda's Press, 1989).

A Note on the Author

GAIL GODWIN is a three-time National Book Award finalist and the bestselling author of twelve critically acclaimed novels, including *Violet Clay, Father Melancholy's Daughter, Evensong, The Good Husband* and *Evenings at Five.* She is also the author of *The Making of a Writer,* her journal in two volumes (ed. Rob Neufeld). She has received a Guggenheim Fellowship, National Endowment for the Arts grants for both fiction and libretto writing, and the Award in Literature from the American Academy of Arts and Letters. Gail Godwin lives in Woodstock, New York.

Visit her website at www.gailgodwin.com